A SHAMAN'S POWER

A SHAMAN'S POWER

CHRONICLES OF AN URBAN DRUID™ BOOK 8

AUBURN TEMPEST

MICHAEL ANDERLE

DISRUPTIVE IMAGINATION

Version 1.02, January 2022
eBook ISBN: 978-1-64971-807-5
Print ISBN: 978-1-64971-808-2

THE A SHAMAN'S POWER TEAM

Thanks to our JIT Team:

Dave Hicks
Dorothy Lloyd
Rachel Beckford
James Caplan
Jeff Goode
John Ashmore
Deb Mader
Paul Westman
Debi Sateren
Micky Cocker
Kelly O'Donnell
Diane L. Smith
Larry Omans

Editor
SkyHunter Editing Team

CHAPTER ONE

"Yer gettin' slow, oul man." I duck the end of Da's staff as it whizzes past my ear and roll across the training mats with Birga in my hand. Rising back to my feet, I anticipate the leg sweep and jump over my father's thigh as he makes his play to take me to the floor.

Landing with the grace of *Feline Finesse*, I scan my surroundings to keep from getting surprised. Sweat drips from my brow and stings my eyes. It's also trickling down the cracks and crevices of my body.

I wipe my face with my wrist and continue to anticipate the next attack.

The timer sounds, and we relax.

Sloan stops the buzzer and resets things. "Fi, switch to offense. Niall, on yer guard. She's comin' fer ye."

I chuckle, straighten, and stretch out the tension in my shoulders. After a little fancy spear spinning, I settle into starting position and waggle my brows. "You ready for the heat?"

Da pauses for a breather as well and chuckles. "All right, yer the shit, baby girl. Now come tan my hide, if yer able."

"Challenge accepted."

Lunging forward, I go in hard from the top, swinging Birga with two hands in a downward strike. Da won't allow us to practice at anything less than an authentic level of commitment. He believes we need to test our limits in a controlled environment to understand them in the heat of a real battle.

The two of us keep the pressure on for the four minutes of my offense and call it quits at the sound of the next buzzer.

"Dillan and Sloan, yer up, boys." Da grabs a fresh towel from the pile, and we step out of the practice arena. "I'm done."

"You're whipped, you mean." I laugh, ducking the towel as it flies at my head.

"Och, *mo chroi.* I'm more than happy to have ye teach me who's boss. I want ye to best me every chance ye get. I worry a little less each time ye do."

I send my enchanted spear back to her resting place in the tattoo on my forearm and pick up the towel from the floor to pat myself dry.

Da worries. It doesn't matter that I'm almost twenty-four and the chosen druid to represent the Fianna in the modern world. I'll never stop being his little girl.

Which is fine by me. I'm truly blessed.

With that thought in mind, I plunk down on the upholstered bench along the wall and watch my brother and Sloan spar. Sloan is by far the more skilled fighter, but Dillan and the other boys are honing their skills faster than most druids in training.

Clan Cumhaill is coming on strong.

Yep. Life is good. My guy is amazing. My family loves him. He loves them, *annnd* most importantly, we love each other.

"Da? At the risk of sounding utterly sappy, can I ask you something?"

Da has his shirt off and is leaning back on the bench sucking great gulps of water from his water bottle. He's fit for his fifties—being a cop, that's important—and even more so since I embraced our druid heritage last summer and he had to up his game.

His hair is dark, slicked back with sweat, but normally it's the same russet red as mine…only with a few silver highlights near his temples. "Sappy, ye say. All right, consider me warned. Go ahead."

I feel the flush on my cheeks, but thankfully, with the workout we just finished, he won't notice. "When you and Mam fell for one another and started planning your future, did you feel like you might explode and spray love shrapnel all over everyone around you?"

He chuckles, his smile as warm and easy as I've seen since Brendan's shooting last summer. "Och, I remember that feeling. Yer Mam and I may not have had much in the way of pennies at the start, but we were blessedly rich in the ways that mattered."

"I remember. She'd be all ours during the day or after school and would light up and change her focus after you'd call to say you were on your way home."

"She worried—as most spouses of cops do—so I made sure to let her know all was well before I left the station."

"That's when she'd start singing." My memories drift back to a life I don't think about nearly enough. "When she knew you were coming home, she'd start humming or singing as she puttered around getting dinner set."

He nods. "I used to walk into the house after a double-shift, my body exhausted and my mind filled with the troubles and violence of my day and the moment I saw her or heard her singin' or even scoldin' one of yer brothers, I was free of it all."

I breathe deep, picturing our family back then. My heart still aches for Mam and Brenny, but I believe in the magic of the universe and know they live on in us.

"Did your love stay like that for all the years?"

He shakes his head. "It was always there, but love changes over time. It deepens and matures. It goes from filling yer heart and lungs and stealin' yer breath to settlin' in yer bones and flowin' in yer blood. It becomes a strength within, a tangible part of yer foundation that alters who ye are—both as a couple and as individuals."

I smile, watching Sloan take Dillan to the mats. The two of them are laughing and tussling, and I press my hand against my chest. "I'm still in the full heart and stealing my breath phase."

"I couldn't be happier about it. Ye wear it well...the both of ye." Da sits forward and follows my gaze to the weapons training that has now devolved into a wrestling match. "He's a rare sort of man, our Mr. Mackenzie. Ye picked a good one."

I chuckle. "We both know he picked me, but I like to think he has good taste."

"The best. It's a wise man indeed who sets his sights on a treasure and goes after it."

"Maybe it's the Shrine-Keeper in him. We all know he has a good eye for priceless treasure."

The buzzer goes off, and I jog over to reset their time. "I'm not sure who was on offense or defense there but switch it up."

Sloan rolls off Dillan, both of them red in the face and laughing. "That went a little more freestyle than usual."

"Freestyle?" I start the timer for them again and retreat to the bench. "Is that what the kids are calling it these days?"

Dillan rolls to his feet and extends a hand, helping Sloan up. "Okay, one serious round and we hit the showers. Liam's expecting us in top form for tonight."

I check the time on my Fitbit. "Yeah, good call, D. St. Patty's is a madhouse at the pub. It's an all-hands-on-deck scenario."

Sloan nods. "I've never worked in a pub, but I've tipped enough pints to be of some help, I'm sure."

Da stands, grabs his duffle, and heads into the back room. "I'll have my shower here and speed things up at home. You boys finish yer round."

. . .

Sloan *poofs* the four of us from the eighth floor of our new Acropolis hangout to my childhood home fifteen minutes later. Dillan strikes off straight away to hit the shower, and I take a minute to check in with Aiden, Kinu, and the monkeys.

"Helloooo…where is everyone?"

Kinu's voice calls from the kitchen at the back of the house. "Aiden's in the grove with Jackson, and I'm in here with Megs."

I follow her call and flop down in the kitchen chair next to Meggie's highchair. After stealing a wedge of apple, I point at the procreation in progress. "How are Kerry and Ireland growing?"

"Quickly." She frowns at the round of her belly. "The calendar says I have eight weeks until full-term for twins. I don't know how that's possible. I swear these two have used up all available space and are about to burst out my navel at any moment."

I chuckle. "I've never heard of babies pulling a Sigourney Weaver and making an *Aliens* escape. I think you're probably fine."

Kinu rolls her eyes. "Says the beautiful young thing that isn't two hundred pounds and prone to peeing every time she sneezes. Babies are the death of a rocking bod. I used to be able to crack walnuts with my hoo-haw. Now, look at me."

Sloan has the spectacular timing to walk in at that moment and freeze. Kinu and I burst out laughing as he turns on his heel and makes a hasty exit. "I'll be in the shower gettin' ready for the pub."

"Okay, right behind you, hotness." I stand and kiss Meggie's forehead. "Are you coming to Shenanigans?"

"No. I'm putting the kids to bed and having a long, hot bath. Aiden's going for a couple of hours though."

"Cool. Enjoy your tub time."

"Will do…oh, and will you take the bag of sweet and salty popcorn to the grove on your way out? Jackson took his treat out, and I was supposed to bring the popcorn out with Meg, but she's falling asleep in her chair. I'm putting her down for a nap instead."

"Yep. I'm on it." I grab the bag of popcorn and exit the back door, heading to the enchanted grove of trees in our backyard. The downfall to Sloan *poofing* us everywhere is that when unexpected excursions come up, I don't have a proper jacket for mid-March in Toronto—especially after sweating the past couple of hours.

Thankfully, with global warming, it hasn't been as cold for as long the past couple of years. The worst of winter is usually in January and February.

I catch my thought and wince.

Sorry, Mother Nature. I send an apologetic glance toward the gray, cloudless sky. *There's no 'thankfully' anything with global warming. My bad.*

Druids are protectors of nature. Global warming is a natural occurrence but not at the rate it's currently happening. Humanity needs to kick its own ass and realize nature supports our lives and everything we do.

We *all* need to protect the balance.

"Hello, the grove. Anyone want a tasty treat?"

"Auntie Fi," Jackson whispers, waving from where he's sitting in Sloan's wicker hanging swing. "Mopsy and Nilm wants some, don't yous?"

Aiden is sitting in my swing and moves to get up.

I wave him back down. "No. Stay and enjoy. I'm dropping off the popcorn and heading straight inside to get cleaned up for the pub. Meggie is too tired for an outing right now and is getting a nap instead."

"That's cuz Meggie's a baby," Jackson says.

"Yeah, but soon she'll be big like you, buddy."

"I'll always be her big brother. Daddy says."

"He should know. Daddy is my big brother, and he took good care of me like you do with Megs." Jackson isn't paying attention, so I abandon that convo and turn my attention to Aiden. "Kinu says you're dropping by later for a few rounds?"

"Who can say no to green beer?"

"Green beer?" Jackson wrinkles his nose. "That sounds yucky, Daddy."

Aiden chuckles. "If you tried it, you'd definitely say it's yucky. When you grow up, you might change your mind, though."

"When I grow up, I wants to be a cow." Jackson's nonchalance as he declares things like this never ceases to amaze me.

"A cow might be a tough one, buddy." I blink at Aiden's grin.

"Mommy says I can be anything I wants, and I wants to be a cow."

Aiden nods and pulls open the foil bag of the popcorn. "Well, Mommy is always right, so a cow it is."

I snort, steal a couple of kernels of popcorn, share a couple with Mopsy and Nilm, and leave them to their picnic in the grove.

Brittle brown grass crunches under the rubber soles of my shoes as I cross the back yards and head next door to our place.

When the hair on my nape rises, I lift my gaze to the old woman on the master bedroom balcony next door. As usual, she's bundled up with a crocheted afghan and rocking away in her chair as if it isn't twenty-five degrees outside. I've never gotten the chance to speak with her, but now is as good a time as any.

Raising a hand, I smile. "Happy St. Patty's Day! *Slainte Mhath.*"

"*Ní neart go cur le chéile.*"

My footing jolts to a stop as my brain catches up. It's been a lot of years since Irish classes, and I wasn't expecting it. I run through the saying in my head and look back up to clarify, but she's gone, and the balcony is now empty.

Goosebumps bristle across my skin, and I take another look. Did she go inside?

I only looked away for a second.

If she rushed inside, where's the rocking chair?

I stand transfixed for a moment as my cognitive hamster gives things a shake and climbs back into her wheel. First Janine and now the rocking chair lady.

Why do the women next door always lean toward the cray-cray side of things?

The warm air inside our home hits me as I toe off my shoes. A shiver racks me, but I don't think the icy shard running the length of my spine has anything to do with coming out of the cold.

Rounding the banister, I take the stairs two at a time, trying to leave the creepy feeling behind me. Doesn't work. It follows me upstairs, and I rush to close the bedroom door behind me and lock it.

Sloan exits our ensuite fresh from the shower, and a gust of humid steam puffs out around him. He's like a rock star busting through a wall of fog at a concert. He pauses in the doorway and his gaze narrows. "Are ye all right, *a ghra*? Ye look spooked."

"The rocking chair lady spoke to me just now...in a formal, Irish tongue."

"Oh? What did she say?"

"I wished her a happy St. Patty's and said *slainte mhath*, and she responded with *ní neart go cur le chéile.*"

The space between Sloan's eyebrows creases. "There is strength in unity."

"Yeah. Weird, eh?"

He tilts his head and shrugs. "It's an odd response to yer wish of good health, but maybe her Irish is limited. People pick up odd phrases out of tourist books and the like. Maybe it's all she knew to say."

I pull the elastic out of my hair and set the lengths of auburn waves free. "I don't think so. She didn't stumble on the words, and her thick pronunciation made me think of the way Fionn speaks—as if it's her first language. It didn't sound like something she learned on a tour bus or to keep the traditions of her heritage alive."

Pulling my shirt off over my head as I cross the room, I toss it into the basket by the bathroom door. "Anyway, it was weird."

"Did yer shield weigh in? Do ye think she might be fae or other?"

Shucking my workout pants down my thighs, I step out of them and add them to the laundry. "No. I didn't feel threatened by her, only creeped out."

He shrugs. "We have the resources in the Batcave to look up the owner of the property. Maybe we should figure out who our neighbor is."

I reach into the shower and spin the handle for the faucet. Holding my hand under the water, I adjust it to my preferred temperature. "That's a good idea. First, I need to prepare myself for a night of drunken Irishmen out to party."

Sloan chuckles. "That differs from every other night of yer life how?"

My laughter echoes off the hard surfaces of the shower. "Good point."

Lifting my face to the spray, I let the warmth of the water wash away the unsettling feeling I got from the rocking chair lady.

There is strength in unity.

Sure there is, but why tell me?

CHAPTER TWO

"Three draught specials, two Guinness, a Kilkenny, and a Wild Gose." Kady sets her tray on the end of the bar and grabs a fresh stack of coasters off the pile.

"Got you covered." I start pulling the first two draughts and laugh at Kady. The blonde waitress was one of my favorite people long before she dated Dillan and now Liam. She's fun and sweet and is currently bouncing from foot to foot.

"You all right there, girlfriend?"

"I've had to pee for an hour, but it's crazy in here."

It is…and it's exactly the kind of night I love most in the pub. "Go pee. What table are these for? I'll deliver them."

"You're an angel, Fi. Table nineteen."

As Kady runs through the swinging door to the kitchen, I set the first two draughts down in front of Sloan and grab a glass to pull the third. "You're up, hotness."

Sloan laughs, reaching over with the green dye and a long swizzle stick. "I know I said I wouldn't be much of an asset workin' in the pub, but I can manage more than stirrin' dye into beer."

"You gotta earn your stripes, Irish." Liam races behind me to grab a bottle off the top shelf. "Tonight, the entire party depends on you. Being the Man o' Green is a very important job."

He laughs. "Tell that to Patty. He's the real Man o' Green, and this is his night. Well, of course, not really, but much more him than me."

I grab a can of Wild Irish Gose from the cooler, pop the tab, and pour it into a pint glass. "You're right. I bet he'd have a ball."

When I finish pouring, I set the Gose down and let Sloan do his thing.

"That's the end of it, *a ghra*."

"Thank you, babe." I give him a quick kiss as I set the drinks on the tray. Rounding the end of the long bar, I get my block arm up to make my way through the sea of rocking bodies.

The music is blaring, the Celtic rhythm setting the tone for the night's celebration. I sway my hips, cutting my way through the mass of bodies like I've been doing this for years—which, of course, I have.

Most nights I know the faces if not the names of almost everyone. On nights like these, we get an influx of new customers wanting to raise a glass for a holiday, and that's not the case.

"*Slainte mhath*," I shout.

The toast for good health comes back to me in a riotous chorus of the same.

Table nineteen has four guys in bad leprechaun hats with straggly orange yarn for hair. Whatever floats their Irish boat, I guess. "Here you go, lads." I set down seven coasters for their multiple drinks. "Who's got what?"

They call out their drinks, and I get them sorted and ready for their next rounds of fun. "Enjoy. *Slainte mhath*."

I'm about to turn away when the guy closest to me grabs my wrist and yanks me toward his lap. Even before my druid training, that wouldn't have worked. Da taught me how to protect my personal space from the time I was a little girl.

Gripping his arm, I twist my wrist free and give him a solid but friendly smile. "Hands to yourselves, boys, or you're out the door. No exceptions."

"Ah, come on, Red," Mr. Grabby Grip says. "You can't blame a guy for trying."

I peg him with a look. "When that trying comes with unwanted contact, I sure can. Now, feel free to order food and drink, but that's all that's on the menu. Have fun. Behave. And we'll all get along."

With that, I slip the serving tray under my arm and head back to the bar. Kady passes me, going the other way. I hand her back her tray and smile. "If the guy at nineteen lays a hand on you, whistle and we'll put him out. You don't put up with that shit."

Both Liam and Sloan stiffen, looking murderous. "Did someone lay hands on you, *a ghra?*"

"Briefly, but I set him straight. I don't want him to think he can pull the same shit on Kady."

Kady catches the fire in Liam's gaze and holds up her palms. "I'll raise the alarm if anything happens. Honestly. I'm good."

Without waiting for either of the men to weigh in on that, she turns and dissolves into the crowd.

"Are you sure he got the message, Fi?" Liam cranes his head toward table nineteen.

"I'm sure. With Dillan bussing, Calum on set up, and the regulars in attendance, if Kady needs help, someone will step in to back her up."

Liam seems to agree with that, and though he still doesn't look happy, he stands down.

Getting back behind the bar, I send a text.

Happy day, Patty. Wish you were here raising a pint with us at the pub. Miss you big.

"Hey, before you dig in again, switch over the keg for Guinness, would you, Fi? I'm getting foam here."

"Yep." I slide my phone into the back pocket of my jeans and jog downstairs. After switching the Guinness line to a full keg, I grab the empty one and move it to the wall with the others for pickup.

Jogging back upstairs, I wash my hands and get back to it. Someone settles onto one of the barstools, and the movement draws my attention.

"What can I get—Patty! You're here!"

"Well, ye invited me, did ye no?" Patty's blue eyes twinkle behind rimless, spectacle glasses. His snowy white hair is tucked neatly beneath a green, velvet hat and he's wearing the suede vest he saves for special occasions.

Sloan reaches over the bar to shake his hand. "Come to show the city folk what they're gettin' wrong, have ye, mate?"

Patty looks at some of the ridiculous leprechaun costumes and rolls his eyes. "It gets worse every year, I swear. No matter. To be celebrated at all is a compliment, I suppose."

"It is." I grab a pilsner glass for his small hands and angle it beneath the tap. Pulling the nozzle, I serve him up a Guinness and slide it over to Sloan. "Are you taking it green tonight?"

"In honor of the occasion, I will, aye."

Sloan does his thing and serves it up.

Patty sips and I smile, drinking in the sight of him. I've missed him terribly over the past six weeks. "Am I ungrounded? Am I allowed to see you and the dragons again?"

Patty dips his chin and swallows. "Her Stubbornness has seen it in her oversized heart to forgive Dartamont's rebellious behavior. She's still angry he went behind the faery glass with ye, but she realizes it wasn't yer doin' and told me to tell ye so. Yer welcome to visit the next time yer in town."

"Oh, thank goodness." I twitch my nose to fight off the sting of tears. "I've missed you guys."

"We've missed our Mother of Dragons." He holds up his drink.

"Patty!" Emmet shouts, jogging up from the family table against the back wall. "I thought it was you. Welcome. Happy day, my friend. When you finish here, come sit with us. Everyone will be jazzed to see you."

He winks at me and hands Emmet his drink. "Yer sister's supposed to be workin' anyway. Carry my drink, boyo. I tend to get trampled in crowds like this if I don't have my hands free."

Emmet takes Patty's beer and leads the way. "On my six, wee man of might. I'll part the drunken sea."

After they strike off, I look at Sloan and tear up a bit. "Can we go soon? I miss my dragon boy."

He nods. "We'll call Lugh and Lara tomorrow. I was feelin' bad already. I always help yer granda prepare for the Alban Eiler ritual. He hasn't said anything about me not bein' there this year to help, but I'm sure he'll be happy to have us come and celebrate the Spring Equinox with the Order."

"That's soon, right?"

"Aye, it is. In four days."

Yikes, that *is* soon. "Okay, I'll talk to Garnet tomorrow afternoon at the Guild Governors meeting and see if he can do without us for a couple of days."

I wake the next morning, shower, and dress by ten. Then, I head downstairs to see if Sloan is around or if he's gone off to putter and fuss in his happy place.

STOA—the Shrine of Toronto's Objects and Antiquities has quickly become his passion for a future here with me. Even though it occupies most of his time and attention right now, I couldn't be prouder.

He'll rock as the Toronto Keeper of the Shrine.

When I get downstairs, there's no sign of Sloan, but his

washed coffee mug is upside down in the drying rack, and he's left me a note.

A couple of hours, luv.

I'll bring lunch.

S

Nice. Grabbing my World's Greatest Auntie mug from the cupboard, I break off a square of dark chocolate and pour a cup of java on top. My spoon *tinks* and *chinks* against the ceramic rim as I mix things up, then add a splash of milk and head down to the mancave to check on the troops.

When the boys first surprised me with the finished design of the basement, I was in awe. A month and a half later, I'm still impressed with both their vision and the result of their labors.

I'm at the bottom of the basement steps when the melodic signal for the washer goes off and sings its tune. Sloan never ceases to amaze me. That he thought to start the laundry before he left to do his own thing is only one of the fifty things he'll do today that makes me smile.

I stop at the laundry machines, transfer the contents of the washer to the dryer, hang what doesn't go into the machine, and continue to the man cave.

The rec room is still and quiet. Is everyone down here passed out? Scanning the rock wall and lush greenery, I search for our family animals.

Doc is curled up and snoring in his cushioned nook. Manx is unconscious on his climbing branch, all four paws hanging loose beneath him. Bruin blinks at me from where his massive form fills the stone dome in the corner that mimics a cave.

"How was your night, Bear?" I keep my voice low because my mythical battle beast looks a little more grizzled than a grizzly should. "Too much celebrating, maybe?"

"Maybe."

Ha! For once it's not me who's hungover.

One of the only benefits of working a drinking holiday

instead of celebrating it is that the only aftereffect I suffer the next day is being tired and a little sore.

"You realize that even though you and the companions can open the keg tap on the bar fridge, it doesn't mean you have to empty the keg, right?"

"Point taken."

I glance at the others and chuckle. "And *too* good a time was had by all."

Bruin grunts. "Och, not all. Daisy is as bright-eyed and bushy-tailed as always. Manx and Doc are doin' about the same as me."

Calum's skunk companion waddles by with her fluffy black tail waving in the air and a smile on her sweet little face.

"Looking good, Daisy. Did you have fun with the boys last night, baby girl?"

"I did. They are so funny when they drink."

I follow her to the stairs and leave the boys to suffer in silence. Scooping Daisy up, I snuggle her as I carry her to the main floor. "Boys *are* funny when they drink. Speaking of drunk boys, how are Calum and Kevin this morning?"

"Alive and well, thank you." Kevin is descending the stairs looking half-asleep. My brother's fiancé is a blond, all-American, athletic type with an artistic soul and a big heart.

He holds his arms out, and I hand him Daisy.

He snuggles her in, stroking her head and bending to kiss her nose. "Calum's showering for some volunteer time at the soup kitchen with Dora. He sent me down to make him a greasy breakfast to settle his stomach."

"Awesome. Queasy and standing in a food line for the next few hours. What could possibly go wrong?"

"I heard that's yer new motto, Red."

I *yip* and jump as Patty rises to sit on the edge of the couch. "Crappers. You scared me, Patty."

My leprechaun friend runs his stubby fingers over his hair but fails to tame the puffy white fluff. The first time Jackson saw him, he said he looked like a dandelion in seed, and it's too close to the truth not to think of it every time I see his hair out of control like this.

I didn't realize he stayed over, but he's always welcome. I sip my coffee and let the chocolatey flavor wash down to my empty belly. "Hey, I am more than the chaos I attract."

He crosses the living room and climbs up onto a stool to sit at the breakfast bar. "Ye are at that. Now, pour me a cup and catch me up on what I missed over the past weeks."

"Happy to." I get Patty set up and lean my elbows on the counter, facing him while Kevin starts cooking. "Our best news is that Kevin and Calum got engaged."

"Och, *comhghairdeachas*, lad." Patty holds up his mug. "May love and laughter light your days and warm your heart and home."

Kevin extends his juice glass and meets Patty's mug. "Cheers to that, mate. Thanks."

I hold my mug up to salute the toast and smile. "What else? Emmet and Sarah fizzled out."

"That's a shame."

"Yeah, but it's nice that he's no longer twisting himself up trying to be the perfect guy. He is who he is, and with Sarah, he suppressed his Emmetness."

"Then she wasn't the one."

"Right you are. He seems happier now, too."

"Well, that's good."

I nod and down another swallow. "Oh...Calum, Kevin, Nikon, and I got sucked back to ancient Greece and took on Hecate. That was a wild time."

Kevin chuffs. "Wild is one word for it."

Patty frowns. "What happened?"

"Long story short, Calum and I got roped into a Greek Challenge of Trials, and Dionysus helped us navigate our way to victory. He's a good guy and has become an invaluable friend."

"Dionysus? Ye mean *the* Dionysus, a.k.a. Bacchus?"

"That's him. Brunette cutie with a lust for life and usually naked and slightly intoxicated."

Patty chuckles and scrubs a hand over his chinstrap beard. "Yer a wonder, lass…an absolute wonder."

I shrug and keep thinking. "Oh, and to thank us for our help with the Hecate situation, Nikon bought a ten-story building here in town, and we've set ourselves up with a new workout center, antiquities shrine, art studio, and fae task force office. That's been fun and very useful. Ummm, what else?"

Kevin snorts, flipping strips of bacon. "Isn't that enough?"

"I'd say." Patty blinks at me. "It's been barely more than a week fer me. It slips my mind sometimes how quickly the world moves outside the lair."

I remember that feeling well.

What I thought was ten days of captivity while the dragon eggs incubated was seven weeks of me missing and my family losing their minds. "Well, I'm glad we're catching up because it's been longer for me and I missed you and my dragon brood like crazy."

"So, ye'll come fer a visit then?"

I nod. "The equinox celebration for the Elders of the Order is in three nights' time. Sloan and I plan to help. I'll be sure to stop in and visit."

Patty finishes and sets down his mug. "Good then. I'll let yer wee blue boy and the others know to expect ye. That should stir some excitement in the lair."

When he hops off the stool and heads back to the couch to gather his belongings, my breath catches. "You don't have to rush off. Spend the day. I'll give you a tour of the house and my city."

After slipping on his shoes, he shrugs into his vest and dons his velvet hat. "Not today, I'm afraid. It's feeding day fer the beasts, and no one will appreciate me dawdlin' on that duty. Leavin' the kids hungry is a dangerous thing these days."

"I suppose it is." I bend, hug him and give him an extra squeeze. "Safe home, Patty. Love you."

"Och, Red. Ye do an oul man's heart good. Now, pack yer bags and come see us soon."

I nod. "Count on it."

———

Emmet and Calum come down the stairs together, both of them looking a little like someone dragged them through a knothole. As rough as they look, they're still a far cry from some of the morning-after horror shows I've seen.

"Did Patty leave?" Emmet points at the blanket folded on the couch.

"Not long ago." Kev dishes up runny eggs and bacon for Calum. "Can I make you something while the skillet's hot, Em?"

"A couple of scrambled would be great." Emmet grabs the almond milk from the fridge and pours himself a glass.

"There's some cut ham and onion in the fridge if you want an add-in," Kev says.

"Awesome, yeah. Good call." Emmet puts back the carton of milk and hands Kev the sealed container. "Thanks, man."

Da lets himself in the back door a moment later looking as done-in as the rest of the guys. I chuckle to myself. I'm usually as bad as them, but this morning I feel pretty good.

Look at me adulting.

"Aren't those the clothes you wore last night, oul man?" Calum eyes him up and down, chuckling.

"Why yes." Emmet makes a shocked face. "Is this a walk of shame moment, Da?"

Kevin whistles. "Noice, Niall. It's about time you let your wild side loose. Good on you."

Da rolls his eyes and heads for the coffee pot. "Yer all daft.

Shannon and I are grown adults. There's no wild side to let loose nor any walk of shame."

"You're saying you kissed her on the cheek and slept on the couch? Is that the story?"

"I'll take bullshit for five hundred, Alex." I smile, sipping from the edge of my mug. "We know where our Cumhaill magic mojo comes from. You still got it, don't you, Da?"

Calum chuckles, wiping his mouth with a napkin. "Or maybe you pulled an Emmet and ended the night staying up late doing puzzles."

"Harsh!" Emmet snaps, pulling an imaginary dagger from his heart. "I tried something new. Sarah is a special girl and is careful with life. It didn't stick, but I'll have you know I rock the jigsaws."

I grab a bowl and the box of cereal from on top of the fridge. "She *is* a special girl. She just wasn't your forever girl. You need a love that will ride your wild and not try to break you in."

Emmet winks at me and smiles. "This isn't about me. We're losing focus on Da's walk of shame."

Da holds up his middle finger and flashes it around for each of us. "Yer all a bunch of eejits. I wish upon you all a wild bunch of mouthy children so you know what I go through on the daily."

I burst out laughing. "Well played, Da."

"Thanks, *mo chroi*. Ye've always been my favorite."

"Rude!" Calum shouts, laughing. "She's not the angel you like to pretend she is, Da."

I lay my hand on my chest and look innocent. *"Moi?* I'm the epitome of sweet serenity and virtue."

That sends Calum, Emmet, and Kevin into fits of belly laughter. I laugh too. I may have oversold that one.

Da's phone rings and he waves his hand. "Shut yer gobs, it's yer Gran. Fer some reason, she still thinks the sun rises and sets on the lot of ye."

We all sober up as Da hits the speaker button and answers the call. "Mam, I've got ye on—"

"Niall, Help! They've taken Lugh."

Da's on his feet as the rest of us straighten and close in. "Who? What's happened?"

"Three men in masks. They smashed the back door, and hit us with immobilization. They dragged him off."

Da looks at us, and we scatter.

I'm running to get my shoes at the same time I'm hitting Sloan's contact info on my phone. While it rings, I hang over the rail to the basement stairs. "Bruin, there's trouble. We need to leave, now!"

Sloan picks up, but before he can say anything, I break in. "Granda's been kidnapped. I need you home!"

He *poofs* into the back hall, and I end the call.

"In the kitchen." I point for him to join the others as Manx and Doc race up the stairs. Bruin circles in a rushing breeze of his mythical spirit form and bonds with me.

The flutter in my chest is a comfort as I grab my coat and race back to the kitchen.

"Sloan's back," Da says, his expression grim. "We're comin' right now, Mam."

He hangs up the phone as Calum and Emmet run downstairs with our go-bags. I take my duffle and sling it over my shoulder.

"Ready." Calum pulls on a hoodie.

Sloan frowns at the group. "I can't take all of ye."

Kevin kisses Calum and steps back. "You go. I'll handle things here and round everyone up for the second wave."

Sloan nods. "Thanks, Kev. I'm sorry."

"Don't be. Just go."

Sloan holds out his hand and Da, Calum, Emmet, and I pile ours on. Manx stands on his hind legs against my side, and I wrap my arm around him.

Sloan waits for his wayfarer power to build for long-distance travel. Then *poof* we're standing in the front entrance of my grandparent's home.

CHAPTER THREE

"**M**am!" Da shouts as we break apart. "Mam, where are ye?"

Gran rounds the broad trunk of the tree that grows up through the center of the house and runs to greet us. My gran is a classic beauty and even rolls out of bed looking ready for a *Vogue* photoshoot.

I've never seen her look so out of sorts.

Before Da can speak, she pushes a piece of paper at me. "This is the license plate and the hood emblem from the car. Perhaps yer bear can catch up with them."

I release Bruin and read him the information. "12-G-1788 is the plate, and it's a black..." I show the boys the picture Gran drew of a circular crest around a half-gold and half-silver T.

"Coupe," Sloan adds. "A black Hyundai coupe."

"On it," Bear says.

As Bruin whisks away, I look at Sloan. "Do you think it's about the shrine again? Could someone want access to the Order's collection before the equinox?"

"It's possible." He looks at my brothers. "Calum, stay with yer

Da and evaluate the scene. Emmet, come with us, and we'll check the security of—"

Sloan's phone rings and he frowns at the caller ID flashing up on the screen. "It's my mother."

"Bad timing, Janet." I press my fingers over my lips. "Oops, did I say that out loud?"

Sloan rolls his eyes and accepts the call. The woman hadn't reached out once since our family blowout back when Sloan almost died—not to check on him, not to ask about his new home, nothing. However, Sloan's a softie, and where there's life there's hope, amirite? "Mam. I'm sorry. It's not a good—"

"They've taken him," Janet screeches on the other end loud enough for all of us to hear. "Men came in and took yer father."

The hair on the nape of my neck stands on end. "Seriously? Him too?"

"Who took him, Mam?"

"I don't know. They wore masks."

Sloan's rich, mocha complexion drains pale. "All right. I'm coming. Give me ten minutes. I'll get there as soon as I can." He hangs up and curses. "I can't portal that far immediately after I came all this way."

"On it!" I pull out my phone and call up the number for Tad McNiff. After hitting send, I wait...when he doesn't pick up, I hang up and call again.

This time he answers on the second ring. "Not a good time, Fi. I'll have to call ye back."

"Tad, wait. Why isn't it a good time? Where's your dad? Has something happened to Riordan?"

"Why would ye ask me that?"

"Because masked people kidnapped Granda and Wallace."

"Fuck me. My da, too. What's going on?"

I look at the baffled faces, and my racing mind comes up blank. "I have no idea. We're at Gran's now. Any chance you can portal us quickly to Stonecrest Castle to see what happened there?

"Yeah. There's not much I can do here. Step-monster called the guard, but they haven't shown up yet. Helping you is better than standin' here while she loses her shit on me."

When the call ends, I head to the front door. Tad doesn't usually let himself in unless it's an emergency—which this sorta is, but I'm not surprised to find him about to knock.

"Hey, stranger." I step in to hug him. Tad's a tall, good-looking guy with a rich-boy arrogance to him. Thankfully, he's not so bad once you get to know him. "I'm sorry about your dad."

"Right back at ye. Lugh's a great man. I respect the hell outta him."

"Thanks. Come in."

Sloan meets Tad with an extended hand and pulls him into a man hug. The two clap each other once on the back and break apart. "Thanks fer comin', *sham*."

"Not a problem." Tad lifts his chin in greeting to Da, Calum, and Emmet. "I'm sorry to see ye here fer such an occasion, but I am glad ye've come."

Calum bumps knuckles with him and heads off toward the back door with Da.

Emmet looks up from reading something on his phone and frowns. "I sent a message on the Heirs WhatsApp group and heard back from Ciara, Jarrod, and Eric. It looks like coordinated attacks took the nine Elders of the Order all at once. Everyone's in the same boat."

"They're *all* taken?" Gran says, her tone pitchy.

"At least six of the nine. I don't know the others."

"Ye know all the grown heirs." Sloan frowns. "The others are children yet. There's Reagan and Brian Dempsey, Lia O'Malley, and Seamus Scott."

"Seamus Scott," I say, frowning. "You mean my arch-rival from the junior druid trials?"

Sloan's mouth quirks up in an uneven smile. "I mean the twelve-year-old that kicked yer ass. Yes, him."

"Hey, I'd only been a druid for two weeks before you put me in that head-to-head competition. *And*, I got a medal."

"Everyone got a medal."

Da comes back from looking at the back door with Calum and is ready to boil over. "We'll go from house to house, but I don't think we'll learn much from the scenes. This was a well-planned and highly-manned effort to hit nine elder druids at once."

"The question is, why?" Tad says. "My father is a haughty windbag at best. He isn't the keeper of magical relics like Lugh or the man savin' lives like Wallace. What use is it to take all of them?"

"Fi wondered if it might be about the ritual of the Alban Eiler," Sloan says.

Da shrugs. "I haven't the foggiest. That's an elders-only event. I have no idea what they even do."

"I do." Sloan makes a face and shrugs. "Well, at least I have a fairly good idea. I've helped Lugh prepare for every holiday every year since he took me on as an apprentice. I was never allowed to attend, but I know the setup. Maybe we can reverse engineer that to figure out what the ritual is."

"Is an equinox ritual something worth kidnapping nine people over?" I ask. "If so, will they release them after the equinox has passed?"

Da shakes his head. "We're addin' more questions to the pile and gettin' no answers. Let's look into the other families, then circle back to unravel the mysteries of why it might've happened."

I nod. "You guys go. I'll stay with Gran until Bruin gets back, then join you."

"Yer sure?" Sloan looks torn.

"Yeah. You're heading to visit your mom. There's no reason to rile her up more than she is by me being there. This isn't about me. It's about your father and getting him home quickly and safely."

Sloan gives me a quick kiss. "Be safe, *a ghra*. If yer bear turns up anything, yer to call us back and not go off on yer own. Understood?"

Normally I'd make a wisecrack about not making any promises, but my guy looks thoroughly stressed. "Understood. Now, off you go. Good luck."

When the boys *poof* out, I follow the swishing of water and find Gran in the kitchen scrubbing the floral print off one of her everyday dishes. I reach around and take it from her hand. "I think that one is clean, Gran. How about we pour a cup of tea and sit?"

My stomach growls, and she looks at me. "Yer hungry, luv. Let me make ye a quick bite."

"Oh, no. Don't let me be a bother. I'm fine." That's a total lie. I'm starving, but it's customary to refuse the first offering of Irish hospitality for the sake of politeness, and it's so ingrained in me, I can't stop myself.

Besides, Gran has more important things to worry about than feeding me.

"No, I insist." When she points at the table, I take my cue and sit.

"I can get it, Gran."

I see it then. Gran is a woman who needs to keep busy. Nurturing those around her gives her purpose and a sense of peace and accomplishment.

So, letting her fuss and feed me is actually me being selfless in her time of turmoil.

"Beef pie and potatoes?" She looks back at me from the open refrigerator.

"Perfect, thanks."

Gran busies herself heating me a plateful of homemade bliss and my heart aches for her. I know the panic of having your love kidnapped by dangerous people.

Back in October when the witches took Sloan, I almost lost my mind and we'd only been together a couple of months. Gran and Granda have been together for nearly sixty years.

Da's words about love come back to me and ring in my ears. *It becomes a strength within, a tangible part of yer foundation that alters who ye are—both as a couple and as individuals.*

Poor Gran.

"We'll get him back," I say, as much to her as to reassure myself. "Granda is not only the Keeper of the Shrine. He's a talented druid and the smartest man I know. He'll figure out a way to hang on until we figure this out."

Gran nods. "Agreed. He's upped his game since last summer. When he realized Fionn marked ye to stand as the Fianna leader, he started to polish his skills to be relevant and ready to aid ye."

It's not a surprise, but it's heartwarming to hear. "You two have taught me so much already. I'm blessed to have you in my corner."

"Well, since we're the ones who forced ye into that corner, it's the least we can do."

I wave that away. "To save Granda's life, I'd do it again in a hot minute. I might miss the simplicity of life before it all began, but I don't regret a moment of the past nine months. This has given me much more than I could've dreamed. The druid stuff is amazing, but I'm even luckier to have you two and Sloan and all my empowered friends as part of my life. It's been life-changing."

"Hello the house," Dillan shouts from the front room.

"In here, D." I gather two cups off the tea tray on the table and pour.

Dillan, Aiden, and Kevin jog into the kitchen to hug Gran, followed by Nikon, who gets swept up in the Cumhaill love-in and gets a Gran hug too.

When she eases back from the Greek, she cups his face in both her hands and leans close. "I appreciate ye bringing them, young man. Yer a good friend."

I think it's cute that she calls Nikon a "young man" when he's thousands of years older than her.

Nikon doesn't look like he minds.

If anything, he gazes as fondly upon my Gran as he did at his own while we were back in ancient Greece last month. "It's my sincere pleasure, Mrs. Cumhaill. I owe Fi and all of you more than I can ever repay."

I snort. "You gotta stop that, Greek. We're even. You've done as much for us as we've done for you."

"All right, argue that later." Dillan frowns. "What the hell is going on?"

"We don't know. Bruin went out to see if he could track down the vehicle Gran saw but hasn't come back yet. We do know the target wasn't only Granda. The Heads of the Nine Families were all taken. Each of the Elders of the Order was immobilized and snatched up in a coordinated sweep."

"What?" Aiden leans back against the counter. "That puts a whole different spin on things."

"Aye, it does," Gran says. "I'd like to think it means Lugh isn't the target of hostility but maybe of purpose. Someone wants the Elders of the Order out of the way."

"Why?" Dillan asks.

"We think it might have to do with the Spring Equinox ritual the elders perform every year. It's three days from now."

When the timer rings on my plate of beef pie leftovers, Gran takes it out of the warming oven and brings it to the table. I thank her and cut through the pastry to set the steam free.

There's no waiting to fork some to my mouth because not only am I impatient for Gran's cooking, anxiety makes me stress eat.

"What ritual could be so important that they'd kidnap nine druids to keep from having it performed?" Aiden asks.

"That's the million-dollar question." I blow on the first bite, and even though it hasn't been that long since the honey-garlic wings I ate at Shenanigans around midnight, I feel like I'm food-deprived. The beef pie is hot, and the spices and flavors explode across my tongue.

Gran's cooking has quickly become home to me. We really do need to get to Ireland more often.

Not only when the world goes to shit.

As I plow into my breakfast, I text Sloan that the others have arrived and he responds almost immediately. I read his message and relay it to the room. "He says to sit tight. They only have one more house but aren't finding anything of interest. It's the same thing at every location. Two or three men with masks busted in and took the elder they came for."

Gran clucks her tongue, dishing up food for everyone. "That's as many as twenty-seven men to kidnap them all. That's an awfully big group to come after us without us having any idea who they are or what they want."

Gran's right. That's a lot of people lining up to sucker punch the Order.

"What about Granda's portal band?" I ask. "If he's able, he should be able to access the Dragon Queen's magic and transport himself to the shrine in the old lair, then here."

Gran brightens. "I hadn't thought of that, Fi, but yer right. That's a wonderful thought."

Aiden frowns. "Will he leave the others? Let's face it, some of the elders are a complacent and whiney bunch. If I were Granda, even if I knew *I* had an out, I wouldn't leave the others there to fend for themselves while I took my freedom."

Gran sinks heavily into her chair and sighs. "No. Yer right, luv. He certainly wouldn't do that."

"Unless he can figure out where they're being held and by whom," I amend. "If he knows where and why the kidnappers took them, he might flash himself home knowing we're here to charge in for the rescue."

The timer goes off on the next round of heated beef pie and potatoes and Dillan gestures for Gran to remain seated as he handles things at the counter. "All right, so assuming Granda realizes this too, our focus should be on who and why?"

Aiden nods. "Gran, do you mind if we invade Granda's library and look for information on the equinox ritual and what it might mean?"

"I don't mind, luv, but Sloan would know best where to find things. He's been Lugh's right hand for almost two decades and works to prepare the rituals with him."

Dillan rolls his eyes. "It's crazy how far behind we are on all things druid."

Gran shakes her head. "In the time spent, perhaps, but there's no one who could look at yer family fightin' the fight and say yer any less skilled. Ye may not possess the same breadth of knowledge yet, but the late start hasn't hurt yer power any."

"That's likely thanks to Fionn and our power-up session at the Hill of Allen," Aiden says.

Dillan looks at me and frowns. "Speaking of Fionn...Fi, put out some chosen one feelers and see if you can ping him. He might know the importance of what's happening."

I swallow the last of my beefy pastry and reach for my glass of water. "Fionn always comes to me. I've never tried to reverse the polarity."

Dillan shrugs. "It can't hurt to try."

"No. I suppose not."

I take a drink and read the expectant gazes of my brothers. "Oh, now? You want me to try to reach Fionn this minute?"

"Why not? Are you busy doing something else?"

Before I think much more about how I'd do that, the others return. Da leads the pack into the kitchen, followed by Emmet, Calum, Sloan, and Tad.

"Glad you're back." Aiden lifts his knuckles to bump Tad in greeting. "Sloan, would you mind helping us navigate Granda's library and the shrine? We're hoping to learn a bit more about the equinox and what this mass hostage-taking might be about."

"All due respect," Tad frowns. "We don't know this has anything to do with the equinox."

Da nods. "Yer right, lad, but until we have a better idea, it's a place to start."

Sloan glances over to me and frowns. "Has Bruin not come back yet?"

"No. Not yet." Which, now that he mentions it, is a bit worrying. "Are ye all right, *a ghra*? Ye look odd."

"Dillan thought I should try to speak with or call Fionn, and I'm not sure how to do that. Since your primary discipline is Healing and Spiritual, maybe you could help me?"

Sloan holds his hand up for me to take. "It's certainly worth a try. Come. I'll pull some texts in the library, and we'll get you set up."

Sloan gets Da and my brothers squared away in the office library and takes me into the spare room. We sit on the floor opposite one another and settle in. He has perfect posture with his ankles crossed and his hands resting on his knees. I cheat and wriggle against the bed to sit up straight.

"Meditation for most mortals isn't about being whisked away to some spiritual plane of communication as yer accustomed to doing, so I'm not sure what ye'll need to do to take it to that level. However, ye seem to have a natural affinity fer most things, and I expect this is no different. Close yer eyes and focus on yer breath."

I stretch my neck from side to side and shake out my arms before settling in the lotus position like him. "I love you, Mackenzie."

His smile is soft and sweet. "Ye'll do fine. I'll be right here with ye the entire time...and ye already know I love ye right back, so relax and don't be afraid."

I love that even without telling him, he knows me well enough to say what I need to hear. Closing my eyes, I do as he says and relax.

"Don't force yer breath to be anything but what it is. Ye don't need big or long breaths. Let it come naturally. Nice and natural. In and out. In and out."

"And not the good kind."

Sloan chuckles. "Focus, *a ghra*. Clear yer mind of distraction and focus on yer breath. Feel the weight of yer legs and the connection of yer seat to the floor. Let the tension drain from yer arms."

I pull a deep breath into my lungs and release it.

"Relax yer face and let the last of yer anxieties go. There is nothing but this moment and yer intention. Fionn is a magical male and ever-present in yer life."

I breathe in and out, my cells pinging to life with little tingles. He is. I feel him in my powers and when I call Birga and when I activate my body armor.

"Let yer mind drift and seek him. His energy has a feel to it...a signature. Ye've felt it enough to recognize it, now drift freely among the ether and call that energy forward."

I picture the ruddy-faced, weathered warrior, Fionn mac Cumhaill. I can see his blond braid swinging against his scarred cheek and smell the musk of a male who lives rough and often hasn't bathed in weeks.

Fionn is part of me.

The energy around me builds to a slow surge and my equilibrium shifts a little off-balance. I press my hands to the floor. Only it's not the floor of the spare room beneath my palms—it's moss.

I open my eyes.

The mossy ground springing against my hands is warm. I tilt my gaze skyward, and sunlight bathes me from above. It takes a moment for my gray matter to fire back up to full power, but I get there.

"Fionn? Are you here? It's me—your faithful protégé, Fiona."

Scanning the natural setting, I take in the meadow and freeze as a chill races down the vertebrae of my spine. The bright, amber eyes staring me down don't belong to my ancient ancestor.

They don't belong to a man at all.

Prowling closer, head down, haunches bristled, is a massive ebony wolf, and he has me in his sights.

Holy crapamoly.

CHAPTER FOUR

With my mind racing, I crab-scramble to the side and reclaim my footing. Crouched on all fours, I meet the gaze of the majestic beast in front of me and reach out with my gifts. *Animal Friendship*...nothing.

Beast Bond...still nothing.

I'm not even getting resistance...it's just nothing.

"Who are you? What do you want?"

I wait, half-expecting the beast to answer and half-hoping this is a dream. So much for my first attempt at astral projection meditation. This is a giant failure. Instead of finding Fionn, I found the big bad wolf.

Who's afraid of the big bad wolf?

Um, yeah, that would be me.

"Despite my appearance, I am not your Little Red."

The wolf raises its maw and sniffs the air, its bright eyes filled with intelligence. I don't like feeling like I'm at the mercy of a powerful animal. Especially one that can block my druid abilities with such success.

Sure, I could call Birga forward and spear the thing if it comes to that, but my instincts tell me that would be a mistake.

My shield isn't weighing in. That means I'm not in any immediate mortal danger. Besides, I brought myself here. Surely I can send myself back if I need to, right?

My gaze skitters across the grassy surroundings. There are trees in the distance, but the massive wolf will overtake me long before I make it there.

The promise of hostility seems certain.

When I expect the wolf to lunge, it cants its head to one side, turns, and trots off through the long grass. He goes about ten feet and looks back at me as if to see if I'm going to follow.

Uh...no, it's fine. You go ahead.

Why would I follow? I screwed up my meditation and dropped myself at the mercy of a super intimidating wolf. I need to accept his exit as a stroke of luck and snap home while I still have all my little piggies.

Except, everything in me feels like I should follow.

Maybe I'm supposed to learn something from him.

Maybe he's not a real wolf at all, and he's some kind of spirit guide of my own making.

I doubt that. If I were deciding my spirit guide, I'd pick something less fang and growl and more lick and purr. A roly-poly panda bear would be good.

Still, after scanning the natural wonder of the wild, sunbaked meadow, I come up with nothing better.

"Okay, so if this is the dumbest thing I've ever done, you'd tell me, right?"

The wolf's gaze narrows on me. Then he turns his attention and continues in the opposite direction.

"Why do I get the feeling I'm going to regret this?"

The wild grasses of the meadow are tall and brush my hips as I plod through. Lifting my feet knee-high with each step makes the travel slow, and with the sun at full strength above, I'm sweating in no time.

The sea of pale green and gold soon swallows the massive wolf, but his ebony head stands above the growth in stark relief. He looks back every thirty or forty feet to ensure I'm stupid enough to follow him.

"Yep. Still here." Doubt stabs me like a double-edged sword every time I meet that golden gaze.

Is following good because I'll learn why I'm here or does me following him play into someone's evil big bad wolfie plan, and I'm too daft in the ways of astral plane-ing to realize it?

Not that it changes anything.

Either way, I'm still following.

When my four-legged guide stops at the edge of a riverbank, I straighten, staring at the blond man fishing on the opposite shore. Right. There he is.

Huh. Maybe I didn't blow my first astral projection after all. I only had my trajectory wrong and didn't stick the landing.

"Fionn," I call, waving. He makes no indication that he hears me, so I jog farther up the bank. "Fionn, it's me. I need your help."

When he doesn't react or make any indication he hears me, I sink to sit on the edge of the bank. It's not a total fail but successful astral projection and vision questing seem to take more skill than I currently possess.

Still, he's here, and I'm here, so there's that.

I stretch out on the bank and watch him with loving fascination. He's young here, and when he looks up, I'm shocked at the unguarded happiness in his expression.

This Fionn is not yet the hardened warrior hunted by violent enemies and angry rulers the better part of his life. In this snapshot in time, he's a teenaged boy bursting with cunning and promise.

I glance around to see where the ebony wolf went but don't

see him. I can't say I'm disappointed. I didn't feel like having my astral arms gnawed off anyway.

Fionn looks up, and I wave again.

He doesn't see me. He smiles at the sun shining at full strength above and goes back to his fishing. What do I do? I can't loiter while everyone is wondering if anything here can help Granda.

I need to get back to them. I need to help.

Still, having done this vision questing stuff more than once, I know there is often a reward for patience. Things reveal themselves in their own sweet time.

Everything happens as it's supposed to.

I smile up at the warmth of the sun and think about the Fates. It's nice knowing Clotho, Lachesis, and Atropos are out there somewhere weaving the lives of man.

It's also nice to know they consider me a friend and likely won't cut my thread before my time.

Fionn whoops, and I turn my attention back to him fishing on the other side of the river. He's grinning and pulling his line from the water. With both hands, he tightens up on his makeshift rod and smiles at the huge salmon flipping and flapping wildly in the air as it breaches the water's surface.

My heart lurches and my pulse pounds in my temples. Of course. I understand.

On my first encounter with Fionn, when he took me to the stone circle to tell me of my destiny, he said,

"If ye ever find yerself at a loss fer answers, go fishin' in the River Slate. It flows through Ballyteague and is home to a fish of knowledge that only a druid can catch. There's a secret to catchin' the Salmon of Wisdom, though, and I never whispered it to another soul. Always cast yer line from the Ballyteague side of the river. Once ye eat of its meat, the answers ye seek will come to you."

As his words rush back to me, I watch him hold his catch

against the backdrop of the blue sky. The salmon stills and its shimmering body gives off a radiant champagne aura.

Fionn's grin widens. "Aye, yer the one."

The message is clear. Catch a Salmon of Wisdom.

Gotcha. Thanks, Fionn.

Closing my eyes, I lay back on the bank and focus on my breathing and returning to the thatch-roofed home in the green countryside of Kerry, Ireland. I know what I need to know and have seen what I need to do. The swirl of magic signals the end of this quest for answers.

The vision recedes, as they have in the past, with me rising to awareness in a slow surfacing of consciousness. My family is close by looking worried.

"Here she comes." Sloan is still sitting on the bedroom floor next to me, holding my hand. "Ye managed to take a little trip, did ye? First attempt and ye make it look easy."

I chuckle. "Hardly. It didn't go exactly as planned, but I faked it until it seemed to turn around in the end."

He kisses my knuckles and helps me up to sit on the edge of the bed. "As long as ye come back, all is well."

"Are ye all right, *mo chroi?*" Da asks.

"Yeah. Fine."

"Did you meet up with Fionn?" Dillan asks.

"Sort of. I manifested into a meadow with a massive black wolf with bright gold eyes. I thought he would chomp me, but he didn't. Fionn was nowhere in sight. Then the wolf led me to the river where I sat in the sun and watched a teenaged Fionn fishing."

"Were ye able to ask him about the significance of kidnapping the elders?" Da asks.

"No. He couldn't see me or hear me. I'm not sure if that was my fault for not connecting properly or if I wasn't supposed to, but in the end, I clued in to what I was supposed to know."

"Which is what?" Dillan asks.

"He was fishing for a Salmon of Wisdom. When he caught one, he held it up against the light of the sun, and it glowed with magic. That's when his words from our first *airneal* came back to me. He said, 'Once ye eat of its meat, the answers ye seek will come to you.'"

"Well, all right, Fionn!" Emmet holds up his palm to high-five Calum. "Well done, Fi."

I hold Sloan's hands as he helps me to my feet and checks that I'm steady. "It was less me and more dumb luck. I don't think I deserve praise."

"It doesn't change the fact that the leader of our sect conveyed an answer to you," Tad says. "So, who's doing what from here?"

Sloan frowns. "As much as I'd like to go fishin', I think my skills are put to better use goin' through the library and checkin' on the shrine. Lugh's always been a planner. If there was something special about this year's ritual, he'd have made notes in one of his journals."

"Agreed," Da says. "The rest of ye, go to the River Slate and drop yer lines as Fionn showed Fi. Bring us back a Salmon of Wisdom. I'll stay with Sloan and help research the problem old-school."

"Gran?" Aiden asks. "Do you and Granda have any fishing equipment?"

"No, luv. I've never been a fan of the practice of hookin' a wild creature even if it is fer sustenance."

"I've got that covered," Tad says. "The family of a buddy of mine from private school owns a marina. They rent out fishing gear. I'll message him and set it up."

With that settled. I kiss my guy, grab my jacket, and hug my Gran. "Don't worry. We'll figure this out, and when we do, we'll bring Granda home."

"From yer lips to the goddess's ears, luv."

Tad's buddy, Bay, gets us set up without much fuss. He's a water nymph, so it doesn't throw his family off when half a dozen druids pour out of the marina's backroom and appear seemingly out of nowhere.

"Ye'll need yer fishing permits and a salmon license too," Bay says. "If ye have them, likely no one will come, but guaranteed if ye don't someone will come by and ye'll be in a hape of trouble then."

"How much is that?" Nikon asks.

"It's only fer one day and one spot, aye?"

Tad nods. "Yeah, that's right. The Canadians just came over and fancy a day on the shore."

Bay nods. "It's thirty a day for a permit to be on a river and twenty a day fer one district to fish salmon and sea trout."

"Fifty euros for us to catch one fish is pricy," I say.

"No, Red. Fifty fer each one of ye."

"Fifty euros per person?" I count our party and do the mental math. "We only want one fish. We don't need to pay four hundred euros for it."

"Just get two permits," Dillan says. "Fi should have one and the rest of us can share and take turns."

Bay frowns. "That's not how the licenses work."

Dillan flashes him the stink eye. "Then you didn't hear me say that because that's how they work today."

Nikon frowns. "Let me get it."

Aiden waves that away. "Nah, we'll get our own, Greek. You're too generous as it is."

Nikon has his wallet out frowning. "You're about to have four mouths to feed, and I have no one to spend my money on. Besides, the more lines we have in the water, the better."

I think about that, and it's not actually true. "Except you and Kevin won't need one. This catch is druids only."

Nikon pushes his bank card at Tad's buddy. "Four hundred. Ring it up. No man left behind."

Nikon refuses to hear any more about it, so we give up the fight. We'll pay it forward to him another way.

Once Bay fits us with what we need, we look up the River Slate on Google Earth and find a remote spot on the Ballyteague side of the bank.

Since Tad's never been there and hasn't locked in his wayfarer GPS, it's up to Nikon to snap us there.

Which he does without issue.

"You rock, boys," I say as we spread out and take in the natural landscape. "Is fishing in March even a thing in Ireland? It's cold out here."

Tad laughs. "Says the Canadian. I thought yer made of stronger stuff, Cumhaill."

I laugh. "It's not 'winter cold,' but I'm thinking about the fish. The water has to be freezing. If I were them, I'd be swishing around in the Mediterranean Sea for a few more months."

Tad laughs. "Bay said fishing opens in January, so we're in the thick of it. We should be fine."

Well, good. I don't want to spend four hundred euros to stand out here for two hours simply to freeze worms in the icy depths. "All right. Someone hook me up so we can get this party started."

Nikon laughs. "What? You need one of your brothers to set your hook?"

"Uh, yeah. Skewering worms is sad and gross."

"But you can skewer people?"

I frown. "I never meant to stab you, Greek. I'll be forever sorry about that."

He sobers and waves that away. "Sorry. That's not what I was saying. You cut people down with Birga and swords and whatever you have at your disposal, but you draw the line at worms?"

"I cut down *bad* people. Those worms have done me no wrong." I point at the heaving mass of aubergine bodies wriggling around in what looks like a dirty Chinese food carton. "See, they're innocent."

Nikon chuckles. "Well, I come from an island of fishermen and was practically raised on the sea. I'll take good care of you."

"My hero."

With that settled, we spread out along the bank. It's almost four o'clock and this late in the afternoon, the warmth of the day is seeping away fast. "Do you think we could communicate with the salmon and ask one to please come swim into our net?"

Emmet frowns. "I don't think so. If that were possible, Fionn would've done it. You watched him fishing and catching a salmon."

"Yeah, good point." I swing my line out and let the weight of my worm carry it toward the center of the river. The current tugs it a little downstream and I settle in. "What about our connection to Boann? Surely having a cousin who's an Irish river goddess will help."

"No offense, baby girl," Aiden says, "but what will help most is for you to stop talking."

"Oh, right. Sorry." I make a show of closing my lips and locking them shut. Silence isn't my strongest skill. In truth, it's not even in my top twenty.

Still, sometimes you must sacrifice for the reward.

Sighing, I look over at Calum and Kev and smile. Those two could be doing anything, and as long as they were together, they'd be content. Laundry...in love. Helping Dora at the soup kitchen...in love. Raising money for the Toronto PD college fund...in love.

So sweet.

In the silence that follows, I think about what's on the horizon for them. What will their wedding be like? Calum mentioned they were talking about fostering and adopting kids from the empowered community.

When will they start working toward that?

That makes me wonder if Kinu talked to Garnet about setting up a better social system for displaced children in the fae and other magical communities.

That makes me think about Imari and how amazing it is to watch her, Myra, and Garnet become a family.

That makes me think about the Guild Governor's meeting I was supposed to be at today...oops.

Pulling my phone out of my back pocket, I shift my fishing pole under one arm and send Garnet a quick apology text.

Sorry. Granda was kidnapped. All Elders of the Order missing. Rushed to Ireland. The meeting slipped my mind.

Understandably. Let me know if I can help.

Will do. Hugs to you and your girls.

"Fi, your line." Dillan points at my fishing pole. I jerk to grab it quickly and lose my grip on my phone.

Bloop.

Fuckety-fuck.

While D drops to his knees and races to rescue my poor phone, I regain control of my rod and get into position to start reeling in.

"Slowly." Aiden holds up his palms. "Nice and easy."

"Give it a yank to set your hook," Nikon adds.

"No. Reel in quick and show him who's boss," Emmet says.

"No. Give him line and tire him out," Tad counters.

I glare at the peanut gallery. "Do you mind? Catch your own fish. I sacrificed my phone for this. This one's mine."

They laugh, which makes me more ornery.

By the time I get back to my catch, the line is slack, and I have nothing. "Now look. He got away."

Reeling my line all the way in, I lift it from the water and frown at my empty hook. "Okay, one of you overly helpful fishing experts needs to worm me up again, or I might lose my shit."

Aiden is about to come, and Nikon waves him back. "Druids keep fishing. Like Fi says, there's no prize for the Greek or the human."

"Was that a shot?" Kevin looks at Calum.

"I think it was." Calum feigns insult.

"It wasn't a shot." Nikon picks a big juicy one and rolls his eyes. "So touchy. Human isn't a bad word."

Kevin huffs. "Says the immortal Greek god."

"Not a god," Nikon snaps.

We all chuckle. He hates it when we say that. "How about the immortal Greek god-like human," I say.

"I suppose that's better."

Standing this close and staring at him while he works on my hook, I sigh and let go of my annoyance. If he can smile after centuries of being stalked and persecuted, I can take the high road after something as stupid as dunking my phone.

Then it strikes me. "Hey, dude. You're aging."

"What?"

"You are." I push his long, blond hair back and examine the sides of his eyes and the line of his jaw. "I know it's only been a month, but I swear, your expression is maturing."

"You think?" Excitement cracks his voice. "Seriously? You wouldn't fuck with me on this, would you? I mean, that would seriously piss me off."

I cup his jaw and turn his face one way, then back the other. "No. I would never. I really believe you look older."

"Noice," Emmet says. "Congrats, Greek."

"You say that now," Aiden counters, "but will you still say that when he's old and wrinkled?"

Nikon shakes his head. "Nah. Everyone in the Tsambikos bloodline stops aging at thirty-one. That's when Papu gained his immortality. I'm not worried about getting too old. I'm just tired of looking like I need to borrow my dad's car to get lucky this weekend."

"Well then, congrats." Dillan holds up an empty hand as if he's holding a glass. "If we had liquor, we'd toast to life after puberty for you, Greek."

Emmet waves his hands under his eyes and pretends he's tearing up. "They grow up so fast."

Nikon flashes my brothers his middle finger and kisses my cheek. "Thanks, Red. You made my year."

CHAPTER FIVE

"There ye are." Sloan rises from the couch as we return after four long hours of fishing. He sets the notebook he's reading face down on a stack of books and steps around my snoring bear sleeping on the rug.

"It's well past dark. We were gettin' ready to send out a search party," Gran says.

Sloan's arms close around me, and I melt against the heat of his body. "Och, yer chilled to the bone, *a ghra*. Ye should've come back sooner."

"We couldn't. We needed the fish. Besides. It wasn't bad. We had *Internal Warmth* to keep us cozy for most of the time."

He arches a manicured brow. "Yer hands are like sheets of ice. Ye don't feel a bit cozy."

I reach up and kiss his cheek. "Thank you for worrying. I'm good. My phone was the only potential casualty of the day, but thankfully, it's waterproof, and Dillan's lightning reflexes saved its Android life. Have we heard anything from the kidnappers? Did Bruin find out anything? Was he able to find the truck that took Granda?"

"No, no, and no," Sloan says. "He was gone a long while because he didn't want to come home empty-handed, but he wasn't able to track them down."

As if in response to Sloan's comment, Bruin lets out a labored snore.

"Ah, my poor boy is tuckered out."

"He is," Sloan says. "Now, how did the fishin' go?"

The excitement in the room shifts to Emmet holding up the prize of the night. "I caught the fish we need."

"Of course ye did, ye talented wee man." Gran rushes to take the fish from his hands. "Och, and ye cleaned it, so it's ready to cook."

"Nikon cleaned it and took care of the head and tail." I smile at Sloan as he drapes a blanket around my shoulders. "The Greek's a fisherman from way back."

"*Waaaay* back," Dillan adds.

Gran rushes toward the kitchen, and the rest of us fall into the procession. "Did Tad not come back with ye?"

I open the faucet over the kitchen sink and wait for the water to run hot. Grabbing the dish soap, I squeeze a puddle into my palm and get to cleaning and warming. "Tad took the fishing gear back to his friend's marina, then needed to *poof* home for a bit. Ciara and Iris Doyle have gone over to the Perry house to work on scrying for the location. He's taking them something of his father's and coming over."

"Do they want something of Lugh's?"

"I asked that. Tad said Iris has one of his books about druid transfiguration that the twins borrowed."

Gran sets the fish on a wooden cutting board and looks at me. "Is there a particular way to cook it?"

"Not that Fionn mentioned. When he fed it to me, he pan-fried it over a fire in the ring of Drombeg Circle."

She nods. "Then I'll forgo herbs and anything else and keep it unsullied. I don't know how the magic of the wee creature works."

"Sounds good. Neither do I."

I peel away from the sink, and Emmet takes my place to wash up. "Where's Da, Gran?"

"He's at the shrine lookin' through Lugh's texts. Sloan's been doin' the same here."

"Did you find anything?"

Sloan tilts his head from side to side. "A few possibilities. Let me grab yer father, and we'll see what he's come up with as well."

I nod, and he *poofs* off.

A few minutes later, the greasy sizzle and *pop* of the meat snap in the air, and my stomach growls. We missed dinner, and the scents are triggering my need to feed.

Da walks in from the living room and casts a glance toward Gran cooking at the stove. "A successful day on the river then?"

I nod. "After a bunch of false catches, yeah."

Dillan snorts. "She kept insisting that when we caught the right salmon it would glow with magical promise."

Kevin nods. "There were a dozen caught and released that didn't fit the bill."

"By our thirteenth fish, we were ready to discard that theory and take whatever salmon we caught," Aiden adds.

I step in beside Gran and breathe in the aroma. "Then Emmet lifted this guy out of the water, and the moment he held him up against the darkness of the night sky, he burst into a champagne brilliance like the one I saw Fionn catch in my vision."

"Well done, son." Da pats Emmet's shoulder. "Well done all of ye. Perseverance paid off."

Unwrapping myself from the blanket, I fold it up and set it on the bench by the side door. "So, what did our two researchers find out?"

Sloan fills the kettle and sets it into its base to boil.

Da takes the lead on filling us in. "We stayed with the assumption that there has to be something coming up that involves the elders that the kidnappers either need them to do or not do."

Sloan takes the seat next to me and laces his fingers with my hand on the table. "Several things are happening this week, so there's quite a list. Last night was St. Patty's, so we started on March seventeenth."

"If we weren't supposed to go out and drink our faces off, they struck a day late on that one," Dillan says.

Sloan nods. "Beyond the modern significance of drinking green beer and celebrating, St. Patrick's Day was traditionally a Catholic holy day. The tale goes that St. Patrick used the three-leafed shamrock to explain the Trinity of Christian dogma. His followers adopted the custom of wearing a shamrock on his feast day. They celebrated him for many things but among them, for driving the snakes out of Ireland—although symbolically speaking—many believe the term 'snakes' refers to pagans."

"Rude," Dillan says.

"Does that mean we've been celebrating our historical persecution?" Calum asks. "That's shitty."

Em frowns. "Damn, I loved St. Patty's Day, too."

I wave that away. "We're in the green beer and shamrocks camp. Last night, I celebrated Patty—my Patty—and the Men o' Green. Intention is everything."

Da nods. "So, yesterday didn't seem to hold any significance to why they kidnapped the elders."

"On to today's holiday." Sloan stands when the kettle clicks off and signifies the water is boiling. After pouring it into Gran's big Brown Betty, he brings the teapot to the table. "March eighteenth is the feast of Sheela-na-gig. The pagan symbol of Sheela-na-gig has a bald head, a skeletal body, and a gaping vagina that alludes to the power of the Mother Goddess. She's part of the fertility of spring celebration."

Emmet makes a face at the gaping vagina part of the description. "Do the elders do anything for Sheela day?"

Sloan shakes his head. "Nothing that I know of and nothing we could find in Lugh's notes."

"All right, then what's next?" I ask.

"March nineteenth holds no pagan holiday but is recognized as a transitional time between winter and spring in the Northern Hemisphere. It's believed that during the Pisces Moon, yer to drink a cup of mugwort tea and the messages you need for the months ahead will come to you in your dreams."

"Or eat a chunk of Salmon of Wisdom," Emmet interjects. "We already know that works from when Fi did it last summer. I vote on prophetic fish over trippy tea."

Sloan chuckles and points at the pot steeping in front of us. "It doesn't have to be either-or. We have both."

"None of this sounds promising for why they kidnapped Granda," Dillan says. "Are we sure it's based on the calendar and not a vendetta or an angry sect of fae?"

Da shakes his head. "We're lookin' at it from all angles, but we must start somewhere."

"What's next on the calendar approach?" I ask. "I never realized there's a pagan significance for almost every day this week."

Sloan nods. "Aye, there is. Now, March twentieth brings us to Alban Eiler, the Spring Equinox. The ancient Celtic calendar only had three months, but in 1752 it was reconstructed with four months and eight holidays. In the more modern calendar, the Spring Equinox is one of our two 'balance' holidays, or when night and day stand in equal balance."

"The other being Alban Elfed the Autumn Equinox in September," I say.

"That's right." Sloan winks at me. "The Spring Equinox marks our step from the dark half of the year into the light half of the year. This is the time when we recognize the importance of planting, growing, and nurturing new life."

"It's Ostara's time of fertility and baby chicks and bunnies and eggs," I say.

"Could that be what this is about?" Aiden asks. "Are there any belief systems or prophecies about the druids being the gate-keepers to usher in the light?"

Da frowns. "Ye think someone wants to keep us in the dark half of the year?"

Aiden shrugs. "Just throwing out the question."

"Well, maybe this will help with the answer." Gran sets a steaming plate of pan-fried salmon on the table. "Who's hungry?"

I stare at the pink meat and my mouth waters. "Is it better for a couple of us to have a good helping or for all of us to try and see what we get?"

There doesn't seem to be a clear consensus on that.

"Well," Kevin says, "after trying to capture all the thoughts and details Fi spewed the last time, I think at the very least you need to stagger who's eating it. Nikon and I can only write so fast, and if all of you are jabbering on about important stuff, it'll be too much."

"Fair point," Sloan says.

Emmet grabs the roll of paper towels and heads to the table. "I caught the magical fish, so I want to try it, and I think Fi eating some is a no-brainer. She's the Fianna rep and resident expert."

"Represent!" Dillan says.

My shield starts to tingle, and I press my hands flat on the kitchen table. Ignoring the buzz of my family, I focus on an odd presence brushing my mind. I can't quite get hold of what it is, but the nape of my neck heats with the sensation of being watched.

When it persists, I hold out my hands to stop the conversation. "Hold up…I'm getting something."

The kitchen falls to a hush. My Spidey-senses are tingling like crazy. Looking over to Sloan, I squint. "There's something here. It's perched at the edge of my awareness, but it's here. Activate your ring."

"My ring usually activates itself." Sloan frowns but does as I ask and brushes the ring with his thumb, spinning the bone circle around his finger. He scans the room, searching for whatever it is that has set off my warning system. "I don't see anything."

Weird. "Bruin?" I call toward the family room.

"Yeah?" Bruin's voice is deep and heavily drugged with sleep.

Sorry to disturb you, buddy. I say, reaching out to have a private conversation with him. *Can you spirit around the house and see if you pick up anything? My shield and my instincts say there's someone here, but I can't figure out who or what.*

I'll do my best.

I read the curious gazes around the room, but it doesn't do our stealthy search much good if I announce that I sent my bear to search the place.

Changing the subject, I pull a large chunk of fish onto one of the serving plates. "Emmet and I will get the digestion of information started. When I ate with Fionn, he gave me a piece this big, and it worked fine. Once we confirm it's working, I'd say the rest is fair game."

"Should we maybe freeze some for another disaster waiting to happen?" Kevin asks.

I snort, skimming the meat away from the skin and forking it into my mouth. Like the first time I ate it with Fionn, it's hot and oily and very good. "Can you food prep a magical prophetic fish?"

Kevin shrugs. "No idea. It was a thought."

"A good thought too." Da opens the drawer where Gran keeps her freezer seal bags and pulls out a box. "We'll save a piece as big as Fi indicated and freeze it for a future experiment."

Spatula in hand, he slides a chunk inside and zips it closed. With a black marker he finds in the junk drawer by the door, he writes Mar 18 - Salmon of Wisdom.

I laugh. "And the winner of, 'What is the weirdest thing in your fridge' is..."

Emmet rips off a strip of paper towel and dries his fingertips and mouth. "When will we feel it?"

I smile at the curious faces watching us in wait. "We're going to need scribes because when it starts, it's a tidal wave. Emmet? What do you know about druid transfiguration? Why did you turn into a kangaroo?"

Emmet's green eyes widen, and I can practically see the gold flecks bursting with knowledge. "Wow, that's incredible. It's like an encyclopedia of fact is downloading into my mind. This is crazy."

"Someone scribe for Emmet and keep him on track. I'll need the same."

Gran rushes over and hands Calum her grocery pad and a pen as Da jogs back from the living room and hands Sloan a notebook.

"Close yer eyes, *a ghra*, and tell me what comes to ye. Why were the elders kidnapped? What's this about?"

I close my eyes and draw a deep breath. The first thing I see is… "It's the black wolf again."

"Where are ye, Fi?" Da asks.

I look around, taking it all in. "I'm standing at the entrance to a tomb. It's a massive, rounded mound of earth set on a river. The walls are white stone, and there are heavy boulders engraved with swirls and patterns all around. It's old…like, really old."

"It sounds like Newgrange," Da says. "Or maybe Knowth or Dowth."

"Where is the wolf, *a ghra*? Twice today you've seen the black wolf. What does that mean?"

"He's not part of this…not really…but he is. He's watching me…readying to approach. It's almost time."

"Time for what?"

"I don't know.

"Fi, tell us about the tomb," Kevin says. "Last time, you had me draw the floorplans of Fionn's fortress…is this like that? Are you supposed to get the layout?"

"Maybe." I describe to Kevin what I see as I head into the

tomb. "There's a sixty-foot stone passageway that leads into a central chamber with three small circular alcoves. The walls are carved out of huge boulders rolled up from the river and set in place. It took the ancient civilization decades to build it."

"That sounds like Newgrange," Sloan observes. "It's older than Stonehenge and the Egyptian pyramids and took several generations of Irish farmers to build."

"People know it's a tomb and think it was a place for rituals, but they don't realize it's the gateway for fae purgatory."

"What does that mean, Fi?" Da asks.

My gaze skims the deep chamber hidden beneath thirty-six feet of earth and stone. "I see the echo of a great battle fought here. Animals are fighting, clawing, and tearing at a downed foe —a huge stag, a jungle cat, and an alligator are attacking a bloody and bleeding man. The three are tired but vicious."

The battle seems to go on endlessly, and adrenaline pumps in my veins. The grunts and whines of animals in pain fill the chamber, and yet they don't relent.

"Beaten, the man collapses, panting against the sandy floor of the tomb. The animals shift and take human form. The jaguar is a wild-looking female warrior, the alligator is an Asian man, and the stag—" My mind fritzes the instant he takes form. "The stag is Fionn. He led the attack on the man in the tomb."

"Who's the man they're fighting, *mo chroi?*"

"I don't know."

"Ye betrayed the oath," Fionn says. "We are Hunter-gods. We swore to protect nature's innocent and secure the balance. For yer treachery, we banish ye to the Neitherlands."

The three surround the downed man and raise their palms to create a triangle between them. They murmur a long string of words in a language I don't recognize.

The chanted words dance like a song, the rhythm creating a magical vibration in the air. The pulse builds, snapping with magical potential. They continue to chant, and the hair on my arms stands on end.

I repeat the chant with them.

The cadence and pronunciations tire my tongue to get it right, but I continue to say it with them.

The vibration builds and the chant dances on.

I don't understand the words, but the meaning of their intention resonates deep in the marrow of my bones. It's a pledge to protect the balance of nature against anyone who acts against it—no matter the cost.

I look down at the man bleeding onto the sandy floor. There is no remorse in his gaze, only a promise of vengeance. His lips curl with hatred, and his body shakes with power.

"The gods send nuts to those who have no teeth and punish those who wish to chew."

I'm still considering that when a bolt of magic zaps from Fionn's palm. It streams into the woman's palm and through her to the other man and back around to Fionn. When the connection is complete, a blast of power explodes between them.

I raise a hand to shield my vision from the flare of brilliance. When the light dims, the three of them lay strewn around the chamber, and the man is gone.

Fionn lays in a heaving heap for a long time before he pushes up to his knees, then stands to help the others to their feet. "I regret this, my friends—the blood on our hands, the innocents lost, and the betrayal of our oaths. Let this be the end of it."

The vision fades, and my focus returns to my family sitting in Gran's kitchen looking worried. My pulse thrums hard and fast through my veins, my body vibrating with the adrenaline unleashed from my trip back to ancient battles fought.

Sloan and Da each take one of my trembling hands and anchor me until my heart rate slows.

"Are ye all right, *a ghra?*" Sloan asks.

I swallow and draw a deep, steadying breath. "That was

intense, but I'm good. I also know why you haven't had much luck finding the information on what we're dealing with."

"Oh?" Da says. "Why is that?"

"Because it's not Granda's notes we need to search for the answers—it's Fionn's."

CHAPTER SIX

I rise from the table and realize the household has divvied up for the salmon download. Nikon, Sloan, Da, and Kevin are in the kitchen with me while Gran, Dillan, Calum, and Aiden are in the family room with Emmet.

I'm not sure what kind of info-tripping Emmet is enjoying, but he's standing on the coffee table waving his arms and speaking in Irish tongues.

Usually, I'd pull up a chair in the front row, but I've had enough excitement for the night.

Besides, Dillan has his phone up and is recording it.

Emmet—PVR'd for later.

Granda's office is part business and a bigger part library. As a historian and the Keeper of the Shrine for the Ancient Order of Druids, and with his primary discipline being knowledge, past, present, and future, he's a bibliophile through and through.

It's probably one of the reasons he and Sloan get along so well. They're two sides of the same ancient silver coin.

"Where are the written works we brought home from the Fianna fortress?" I ask.

Sloan strides around the desk to the credenza and cabinet behind. He swings open the two doors above his head and pulls down a box to set on Granda's desk.

"I give Fionn credit, even though he was in power long before journaling became a thing, he recorded a lot of useful information for us."

Some of it is longhand writing…some of it is more pictogram with a few words scribbled here and there. Either way, he gets his point across.

The five of us each take a couple of journals and find a quiet spot to sift through the ancient pages carefully. As delicate as the parchment and pages seem, the first thing Granda did was spell them to remain strong enough for handling. It's a good thing, too. Some of these pages are seven hundred years old.

"Here's something that might relate," Da says twenty minutes later. "Fionn talks about being betrayed by one of their own. He writes, 'Mingin left us no option but to banish him. The others think me rash, but with Jaladhi dead, the choice was made. We swore the oath of the Hunter-gods to secure the balance of light and dark. Mingin betrayed us.'"

"Hunter-gods," I repeat, looking at Sloan. "Do you know that term?"

Sloan shakes his head. "I never heard it until tonight, but I'll look into it."

"Fionn talked about being the Hunter-gods securing the balance. That could mean we're right about it relating to the equinox ritual and the balance of the light and dark halves of the year."

"Or a statement of good and evil," Da offers.

"Or vanilla and chocolate," Kevin adds. "Securing the balance could be anything. We're guessing at best." He meets my gaze and shrugs. "Sorry. In my opinion, noting light and dark isn't enough to go off in one direction over another."

I sigh. "No, you're right. We don't have enough to go on yet to make any decisions."

Shouts of excitement from the family room make me jump up and bolt out the door. When I get to the end of the hall, my socks slide on the hardwood floor as I put on the brakes.

What. Is. Happening?

Dillan and Calum are laughing and trying to get an alpaca off Gran's coffee table.

"What the hell? Is that Emmet?"

Dillan has his arms wrapped around Emmet's long neck, trying to tug him to the floor. "Yep. Emmet stoned on salmon wisdom is even crazier than normal. He spouted off a dozen spells and said he finally understands how to unlock transfiguration."

"And voila, Emmet's a llama," Calum says, pushing at his furry rump.

"That's an alpaca," I correct them. "They're smaller and more amenable than their llama and camel cousins."

Sloan frowns at the scene and steps in to intervene. "Where do ye want him?"

"On the floor would be a start," Calum says. "Gran, I don't suppose you have a livestock paddock, do you?"

"Och, yer not puttin' my wee boy out to pasture. He's fine in here, just perhaps not on the furniture."

Sloan *poofs* Emmet to the floor, and I rush over to scrub the fleecy fur on his head. "Poor guy. First a kangaroo and now this. Are you in there, bro?"

"Clomp your hoof once for yes and twice for no," Dillan says.

I frown. "Why would he clomp his hoof twice for no if he wasn't in there? If he's not in there, he won't understand he's supposed to stomp at all."

"Good point."

"Och, he understands ye," Gran says. "He needs a moment to focus. He's workin' on changin' back."

The room quiets down, and I feel the surge of energy before Emmet shifts form again.

"Oh, much better," Aiden says.

I bite back my laughter and stare at the red panda blinking up at us. He's the size of a large cat and has a creamy mask and the innocent face of a teddy bear. "Oh, so cute. Ohmygoodness, how adorbs."

The little red ball of fur stands on his back feet with his hands in the air and lets out what sounds like a huffy-quack.

"Is that him getting pissy or did he hack up a furball?" Dillan asks.

Emmet shifts his masked face toward Dillan and gives him a furry middle-fingered salute.

"Rude." Dillan chuckles. "Okay, furball, give it another go. Em-met! Em-met! Em-met!"

Emmet drops onto all fours and glares.

"All right, all of ye shut yer gobs so he can focus," Da snaps.

A moment later our cute and furry ball of red panda bursts into a purple, leather-skinned hippo.

With a grunt, he staggers back and flops down on his big ass. The *crack* and *snap* of wood mark the end of Gran's coffee table.

Aiden winces. "Sorry, Gran. It survived the alpaca, but there's no coming back from a hippo attack."

Dillan nods. "Well, hippos *are* considered the most dangerous land animal."

Gran steps forward and presses her hands on the sides of Emmet's massive jaw. "Och, that table was old and chipped anyway, luv. Don't give it another thought. Now then, I realize ye must be tired, but try coming back to us as yer true self. One last effort, sweet boy."

The hippo flicks and twists his little ears and closes his eyes. When nothing happens, I sigh, my heart going out to him. Emmet-roo was around for days before he shifted back. Having a hippo in the house won't be nearly as easy.

"Why don't you *poof* him out to the gazebo, hotness? I'll grab a sleeping bag and sack out on the hammock with him to keep him company."

"Nah." Dillan waves that away. "You look beat, baby girl. You and Irish take the spare bed. I'll hang out with the hippo. Who knows, maybe the equinox full moon will give him a power-up, and he'll change back."

That's Dillan. He's a giant pain in the ass. He's snarky and the first one to throw down, but he's also as sweet as they come.

He's right. I *am* beat.

The adrenaline rush from the fishing expedition and the quest for wisdom have taken their toll. "I'm not going to argue. I'm calling first in the bathroom to get ready for bed. I'm done."

Sloan presses his lips to my forehead and smiles down at me. "You get some rest. I'll get Emmet settled and stay up for a while longer to see what else I can find out about Hunter-gods and what it means to be banished to the Neitherlands."

Calum frowns and does a double-take. "You think they banished the elders to Holland? What have the Dutch got against druids?"

I chuckle as I wave over my head, leaving Da and Kevin to explain the difference between the Neitherlands and the Netherlands.

It's a fitful night. My mind burps up all kinds of convoluted images of black wolves and fields of tulips and cloaked figures chanting ancient rituals to welcome the darkness. I understand the need for balance, but I am solidly a "light" girl myself.

When I stretch and roll over in the morning, it's not Sloan who's sleeping beside me. It's Aiden. I smile at how peaceful he looks when he's at rest.

There's no sign of the stress of providing for a growing family creasing his russet brows. The lines beside his eyes aren't tense with the worry of money and safety for those he loves.

He looks as young and happy as ever.

His breath saws in and out in easy pulls.

How many nights did I crawl in with him after our mom died? Da had to get back to work and Aiden was the oldest. At sixteen, he took on a lot of the responsibility for securing our family in those early years.

He has always been my rock.

"Why are you watching me sleep, baby girl?" His eyes are still closed, and his voice graveled with a husky morning voice.

"Just loving my big brother."

He half opens one eye and smiles. "Your big brother loves you too."

I never doubted it. "Spread out and go back to sleep. I'll wake you if anything is happening."

I scoot to the bottom of the bed and grab my hoodie off the back of the chair where I flung it last night. By the time I round the mound of brown grizzly bear and make it to the door, Aiden has fallen back to sleep.

"Good morning, *a ghra*." Sloan looks up from Granda's desk. "Did ye sleep?"

"As well as I sleep when there's trouble brewing."

His brow lifts, and his smile softens. "So, no. Ye battled worry and woes all night, did ye?"

"How could I not? Granda is missing, and we're no closer to finding him or figuring out what to do to get him back."

Sloan tilts his head from side to side and smiles. "That's not quite true. I may have a few insights to add this morning."

I shake off my exhaustion and take in the dark rings under his eyes. "Have you been up all night?"

"I stayed up fer most of it, but I did lay down to unplug when I couldn't keep my eyes open."

He points at Granda's recliner in the corner, which a lovely lynx curled up tightly into a furry gray ball currently occupies. Somehow, I think Manx got the lion's share of the rest between the two of them…or the lynx's share I suppose is more accurate.

"Come see what I found."

I round the end of Granda's desk, but before we get into the chaos of what is sure to be another crazy day, I tap his shoulder. "I'd like a proper good morning before the world invades our lives."

Sloan straightens, and though he doesn't exactly tower over me, he's quite a bit taller. "Even better." He chucks my chin with the side of his finger. After he presses a chaste kiss on my lips, he hugs me and presses his cheek to my head. "Good mornin', Cumhaill. I missed lyin' next to ye last night."

I squeeze him tight and ease back. "I was asleep before my head hit the pillow, but I'm sure part of me missed you too."

He kisses me again, this time with a bit more heat, then pulls back and winks. "How are ye feelin' after yer Salmon of Wisdom adventure?"

"Fine. Once the adrenaline fades, there's a bit of an energy crash, but no real aftereffects once that's over."

"Good. After I show ye what I've come up with, we'll go out and check on Emmet and see if we can help him reclaim his form. Lots to do today and I don't want to be down our buffer and number one distraction."

I smile, thankful my boyfriend genuinely loves my brothers for who they are. I'm protective of Emmet because although he's grown and able to defend himself, he has the truest, purest sense of joy I've ever known.

That's a hard characteristic to nurture in today's climate, and I hate it when people try to make him conform to what they think is appropriate.

Emmet *is* joy.

Or, at least, that's how I see him.

Snapping my attention back to the point at hand, I turn to see what Sloan's working on. "What's this?"

I read the notes he's written on a pad of paper aloud. "When dark overtakes light and the day remains night, the gate between worlds will align, and the portal will open. Into this world will spill the legions of evil banished by the Hunter-gods."

Huh, there's that phrase again.

"Where did you find this?"

"I asked a history buff friend of mine who gives tours at Newgrange if he could send me shots of the carved stone in the main chamber. From what ye described seein' in your vision, I was fairly sure that's where Fionn banished the bloody man."

"Hokey-doodle, what time were you texting the poor guy for pictures?"

"Och, it was goin' on two this mornin'. I owe him a bottle or two of very expensive whiskey to make up fer that, but he was amicable enough."

"Excellent. So, he had photos to send you?"

"He did." Sloan opens a folder near the corner of the desk and pulls out half-a-dozen printed pictures of rocks with swirls and nicks and rudimentary animals carved into them.

"These hieroglyphics gave you that statement about the evil escaping the Neitherlands?"

"Not at first. I couldn't read the meaning behind the inscriptions until I figured out that the cipher's base was an ancient druidic language that died out in the early 1500s. Once I had that, it was simple enough."

I chuckle. "Once you recognized the symbols of a dead language were the key to unraveling an encrypted missive chipped into the stone of a tomb thousands of years ago, it all fell into place."

He straightens. "Are ye makin' fun of me?"

I roll my eyes. "I am absolutely *not* making fun of you. Hearing you explain how your mind gets from A to Z short-circuits my gray matter. I'm in awe of you, and it makes me laugh because most times you don't even realize how spectacular you truly are."

The crease in his brow smooths out, and he stands a little taller. "Och, well, thanks. That's lovely of ye to say. I appreciate that ye think so."

"It's one hundy percent true. Now, back to the message. Do you think it's describing the equinox? Do you think someone's trying to make it so the light half of the year doesn't take over from the dark somehow?"

"That's my take on it, yes. Or something to that effect." He flips his page and shows me what looks like three advanced spells. "Yer father and I reverse engineered the ritual preparations I made with Lugh every year to try to discern how that might work."

"Did you get anywhere?"

"With the preparations made, we narrowed it down to three possible rituals fer this time of year. One we eliminated because it's a dawning sun spell and I know fer a fact the elders performed the equinox ritual from the zenith sun until the zenith moon."

"Twelve until twelve, all right, I'm with you. So that left you with two."

"Right. We discounted a second possibility because it requires the blood sacrifice of a white bull."

"Ritual sacrifice? I can't see Granda involved in that and certainly not as a yearly event."

"Agreed. I can attest that there were no ceremonial blades involved and, when I cleaned up the stones of Drombeg circle the next morning, there was never any blood mess. Besides, I think

Lara would take them all to the mat if they slaughtered a white bull each year in celebration of spring."

"True story. She'd kick their elder asses."

Sloan grins wide. "Yes, she would."

"So, you're pretty sure you have the annual ritual to usher in the light half of the year."

"I do."

"Do you honestly think if the Elders of the Nine Families don't perform the ritual, we'll lose the balance and the darkness will reign?"

He makes a face at me. "Of course not. That's silly. Nature is powerful and does wondrous things without the intervention of well-meaning or even ill-meaning men."

Okay, good. Just checking.

"So what's the kidnapping about?"

He holds up his finger. "That, I think, is where Tad saved the day."

"Tad? He came back after I went to bed?"

"He did, and when I asked him if he'd ever heard of the Hunter-gods, he said he had and flashed home to bring me this." He moves a couple of Fionn's scrolls to uncover an ancient book.

It's lying open, and I scan the pages. "I don't understand the language, but the pictures are cool."

"Check out the front cover."

I flip the book closed and trace my finger over the tree of life symbol burned into the leather of the front cover. The symbology is similar to the Fianna mark on my back, but it's different, too.

This tree sits on top of a closed circle pentagram, and at each of the points, there's an engraving of an animal.

At the top point of the pentacle star, in the position of spirit, is a stag with a broad and pointy rack. Moving around the circle to the right, in the place of water is a dragon, bottom right in the position of fire is a jungle cat, at the bottom left in the role of earth is a wolf, and in the top left place of air is an eagle.

"These are the animals I saw in the chamber. Fionn was the stag."

"That makes sense. From what I've been able to understand from the text, when the darkness aligns and there is a threat to the containment of evil banished to the Neitherlands, five individuals with the blood of gods are called forward to prepare to defend the Earth realm."

"So, Fionn was a Hunter-god because his grandmother was a goddess of the Tuatha De Danann."

Sloan nods. "That blood runs strongly in another of the Cumhaill line."

I blink. "Me? You think I'm supposed to step up as one of the five Hunter-gods?"

"I think ye already have, *a ghra*. We've always assumed it was Fionn who marked ye with the Fianna crest and awoke the powers of yer lineage within ye. What if that's not all of it? What if the threat of the evil of darkness escaping activated ye somehow?"

"Awesomesauce." I sit back on the edge of the credenza and let that sink in. "I was getting used to the idea of being Fionn's successor and leading druids back to their roots as Fianna warriors. What am I now?"

He rubs my upper arms and squares off in front of me. "I don't know the answer to that yet. I do know, however, whatever gets thrown yer way, ye'll handle it with the same skill and tenacity as always."

I sigh, my head spinning with images of dark and light and animals snarling in the bowels of an ancient tomb. "Why can't I be boring old Fi?"

Sloan chuckles and steps forward, pulling me against his chest for a hug. "It's not fair, I know, but if the universe never gives ye more than yer able to handle, I'd say the powers that be have great faith in ye."

I roll my eyes and draw a deep breath, soaking in the rhythmic thrum of his heart beneath my ear. "Well, that makes one of us."

CHAPTER SEVEN

Sloan and I head out to the kitchen to say good morning to everyone, and I'm happy to see Emmet has returned to being the cute red panda. Not only is he small enough to be allowed back in the house but there's a chance we'll be able to fill his appetite. Sitting on the kitchen counter, he smiles up at me and waves a little paw.

I go over to check on him and can't help but kiss his cute little ear. He's way too cute. Gran's cutting apples and washing grapes for him while he happily chews the leaves off a bamboo stick.

"Where'd we get bamboo?" I ask.

"Ye've got a true friend in that man, luv." Gran tilts her head toward the kitchen window. Nikon's outside, chatting with Calum and Kevin.

I gasp. "He cut his hair."

Gran looks at me like I've lost my mind.

"No, that's a big deal. In the past, Hecate never allowed him to alter his appearance from what he looked like when they were together. He cut his hair, and it's still short. That's huge."

"Och, well, it's a fetching style on him."

It is. It's shaved up the back of his neck and with a medium-length fringe up top styled forward to look a little messy. "He must be so happy."

The three of them are smiling and emptying a party pack box of Timbits.

"He's a sweet young man. He brought those bite-sized donuts fer everyone to enjoy, then popped over to Nepal to get us a supply of bamboo fer yer brother."

I snort. Popped over to Nepal.

My life is amazing.

Nikon must sense us talking about him because he looks up and meets my gaze. I point at his hair, then heart my fingers against my chest. He waggles his brow and winks before refocusing on his convo with Calum and Kev.

"He's a keeper, all right." I hand Emmet a branch. "I'm truly blessed in the amazing men category of life."

Gran rinses her fingers and dries her hands. "Aye, ye surely are, luv. I can't tell ye how proud yer Granda and I have been watchin' ye grow into the woman we hoped ye'd be. It seems ye've gathered some good souls along the way."

Da comes in looking a little worse for wear, and Sloan pours him a black coffee without hesitation. "Thanks a million, son." Da takes it to sit at the table. "So, where are we and what do we know?"

I knock on the window and wave for the others to join us. As we wait for them to file in, I text Tad and invite him to join in for the debrief.

When the boys file in, Da hikes his thumb over his shoulder. "Calum, go wake Aiden and Dillan."

Calum shuffles off, and I rush to hug Nikon and brush my fingers over the velvety softness of the freshly cut hair on his neck. "I lurve your new look, Greek. It's sassy and suits you."

"Thanks, Red." His grin is dazzling. "After you said I aged a bit, I wondered if I could get a haircut and so far so good. I'm really jazzed."

I squeeze his hand. "I'm so happy for you. With all the crazy worry right now, I'm thrilled to have something to celebrate. You look amazing."

"You can do better than that. Hot as fuck is what Calum said."

I giggle and lean closer. "I'm not touching that, and you know it. Now, be good. You look great."

A moment later, Tad *poofs* into the backyard, and I wave him in. When he steps in, he eyes Emmet panda on the counter. When my brother grins and waves a little paw at him, Tad looks confused.

"Emmet's having a little trouble with animal transformations at the moment."

"Och, got it. Shall I give him a hand?"

"Have you got hidden guru skills in transfiguration training, McNiff?"

Tad grins. "Maybe."

He leans close, cups his mouth around Emmet's little round ear, and whispers something to him.

Our red panda's eyes widen, and Tad shrugs. "Just sayin'. It works for me."

Emmet holds up his fuzzy arms, and I set him down on the floor. He drops to all fours and scampers out of the kitchen, his ringed tail bouncing along behind him.

Sooo cute.

A moment later, he strides back into the doorway looking whole and nakey, with a blanket wrapped around his hips. "All good. Once I find my duffle and get pants, I'll join you."

I laugh. "Okay, McNiff, what did you say to him?"

Tad shakes his head. "Trust me. Ye don't want to know. It's crude and not appropriate fer mixed company, but it worked fer me when I was a teenager and learning to shift forms."

"I didn't know ye could shift," Sloan says. "It's never been one of my skills. Da thought it might have been a tradeoff fer my wayfarer ability."

Tad shrugs. "Sorry. I don't use it much, but I can if the need arises. I prefer to portal over shifting forms."

Emmet returns, dressed and in good spirits. He studiously avoids eye contact with Tad, and that makes me even more determined to know Tad's mental trick.

"So, what wisdom of McNiff's brings you back to us, Em? Inquiring minds want to know."

The fast flush that mottles his cheeks makes my curiosity burn. Before I can pester him for details, the late risers join us and Da brings the gathering to order.

"All right. Let's try to focus on the muddle we're in. Sloan and I discussed things at great length last night, and we believe we have two or possibly three separate events working against us."

I roll my eyes and snag a few chunks of apple Emmet didn't get to. "Oh, goody. Why give us one battle to fight when you can give us two or three, amirite?"

There's a male grunt of agreement around the room, and Da continues. "First, we believe we've tracked down the druid ritual performed by the elders and understand why the kidnappers took them."

"Why is that?" Gran asks.

"The Sacred Oath of Ostara is a ritual we found in one of Da's texts in the shrine. It's a welcoming of the season of light. It's also a potent fertility spell that blesses the land with lush health and fruitful abundance."

I brighten. "Are you saying it's the druids that put the emerald in the Emerald Isle?"

Sloan nods. "According to notes connected with the ritual, the original Heads of the Nine Families gained the favor of Ostara back when people forgot the celebration of spring's rebirth. The Jewish celebrations of Passover, as well as Christian communities adopting the pagan celebration of Easter, led to a mashup belief of what had traditionally been Ostara's holiday."

"Those druid leaders back then remained true to the worship

of Ostara," Da says. "Our ancestors recognized the significance of the Spring Equinox, and the Alban Eiler became our dedication to nature's rebirth."

"Yay, us." I finish Emmet's apple slices and go for the grapes.

"Yeah, yay us," Da says. "The rub of it is that not only do the elders give the land the blessing for the coming season of growth, but we've learned many of the fae species attend the ritual for an added oomph to spring fertility. They see it as a reaffirmation of our place as nature's guardians."

I choke on the grape and pound my chest. "What? We boost the fae sex mojo at a spring orgy?"

"We should invite Dionysus," Dillan says. "I'm sure he'd help on that front."

Da frowns. "Not a fae orgy. By the look of the spell, it's a potency charm. They come for the blessing. They leave for the consummation."

I pop in another grape. "Oh, much better. Might as well cancel Dionysus's invite."

Calum frowns. "So, if the ritual doesn't happen, not only do we not give Ostara our devotion and the land our blessing, we also lose face in the eyes of the fae?"

"That's the gist of it, yes," Da says.

"So, we need to find Granda and the others and get them back in time to perform the ritual," I say, more determined than ever.

Da dips his chin. "That's the plan, but Sloan and I think it best to initiate a Plan B."

"Which is?"

Sloan shrugs. "I think the Heirs of the Nine Families need to prepare for the ritual as a safeguard."

Tad's scowl mars his handsome, frat-boy features. "At the same time we're trying to locate our parents, ye need us to rally and be ready to do a mastery-level ritual by the day after tomorrow?"

Da nods. "That's the idea, yes."

Tad runs a hand over his jaw and exhales. "Well then, I guess we better start makin' arrangements."

My mind immediately stalls out on the heirs who are not on our WhatsApp group. "What about Seamus, Lia, Reagan, and Brian. The oldest of them is twelve. Can they get the days off school? Will they be allowed to perform a fertility ritual? Do they even have the oomph to affect the magic of the spell?"

Da shrugs. "As I said, things are workin' against us on this."

"How does the 'heirs' detail work for rituals?" Calum asks. "Technically, we're all heirs. Can we fill in for the kids?"

Da and Sloan both shake their heads, but it's Sloan who elaborates. "Traditionally, it's the firstborn who takes the appointment as the Head of the Nine Families. I don't know that it's a set rule or not, but it must be one from each of the nine. It has to be Reagan, Lia, and Seamus who join us."

"Is it me, then, or Fi?" Aiden asks. "I'm the oldest, but she's the family phenom."

The look that passes between Da and Sloan speaks volumes. It's obvious they've already had this discussion, and I don't think they agreed on it.

"We think it has to be Aiden," Da says. "With what's happening with the other problems we're facin' we think it's best if Aiden works on the ritual with the heirs and Fi helps to locate the elders."

I extend my knuckles to my big brother. "You'll kill it, dude. Besides, you're a natural leader and will give the kids the confidence they need to getter done."

Aiden nods. "Okay, I'm in. Whatever I can do."

Da smiles. "Excellent."

Tad raises a hand from scrolling through a text on his phone. "Ciara has news about scrying for the elders. She said they got a general area, but someone shut them down before they could zone in. They worked on it most of the night and all morning, but that's the best they can do."

Gran nods. "Best efforts are always enough."

"Could we invite the adult heirs here to go over things?" Tad asks. "We've all been exposed to a different knowledge of druid life. One of the others might be able to contribute something we missed."

Da nods. "That's a fine idea, son. Go ahead and invite them over."

I groan, thinking about Ciara and the others seeing me straight out of bed. "Since more people are coming and I haven't brushed my teeth yet, can I ask for a ten-minute break to get dressed and pull myself together?"

Da frowns but relents. "Fine. Ten minutes. Everyone get yer shit sorted. We have plenty more to talk about."

***

Growing up with five brothers and one full bathroom, I know how to hustle. In the ten minutes Da allotted, I've showered, my hair is toweled and braided, and I have a fresh pair of undies on, so hey, I'm ready for anything.

When I get back out there, the meeting of the minds has moved from the kitchen into the family room, and the rich aroma of tomato sauce and bacon makes my stomach growl.

"Yesss! Pizza for breakfast." I rush in to claim a couple of slices. "Whose feet do I need to kiss for this?"

I notice the writing on the box, and there's only one person here who would've skipped back to Toronto to grab five large pizzas from our favorite pizza parlor. "I heart you hard, Greek. I'm serious. You rock my socks."

Sloan chuckles. "That's my girl...declaring her undying devotion to the man who brings her Hawaiian pizza fer breakfast."

"Pineapple on pizza is sacrilege." Jarrod Perry makes a face.

I take a big bite of savory goodness and grin. "Then consider me the least repentant sinner on the planet. Hawaiian is the way to go."

"It's just wrong," Eric Flanagan says.

"It's *Canadian*, you mean." Dillan pulls two more slices from the top box. "Food of the gods…delivered by the Greek god of sass and ass."

Nikon snorts. "Are you saying I *am* an ass or I *have* a nice ass?"

"Och, ye have a lovely ass." Ciara smiles around a bite of pepperoni.

Nikon nods. "Thank you for noticing."

Normally I'd get chippy and warn Nikon against Ciara's flirtations, but the last few visits to Ireland have shed light on another side of her. Sure, she and Sloan used to hook up, but despite that, I've started to like her.

I think the change in our relationship began when I got to punch her during our fistfight performance at the witch's bar at Samhain.

I've always admired the way guys can be pissed at one another, punch it out, then go back in the bar and have a beer together.

There's limited seating in Gran's family room, so I snag a couple of pieces for my plate and sit on the floor between Sloan's knees. "Have you guys been caught up on the ritual plans?"

Jarrod nods. "Yer brother, Tad, and I will talk to Mrs. Dempsey and Mr. Scott this morning. We haven't gotten in touch with Mrs. Mac Craith, but my mam and she are friends, and she'll keep tryin'."

Da comes back from wherever he's been with Gran and opens his palms to the group. "It's good of ye all to rush over. As I was explainin' to the others before ye got here, Sloan and I figure we have a battle on at least two fronts if not three, so it's all hands on deck."

He lifts the lid of the top pizza box and claims the one slice left as his. Straightening, he takes a bite and locks in. "Our first challenge is the kidnapped elders. We need to find them and, at the same time, prepare for the equinox ritual in their stead."

"Aiden, Tad, and Jarrod are working on coordinating the kids for that," I say.

Da nods. "Good. Emmet, ye'll need to be part of the ritual team. Help boost the connection of the wee ones and ensure Ireland remains green and fertile."

"The fae too," Calum adds. "I'm not sure what you have to boost on that fertility front, but I'm glad it's you and not me."

Emmet scratches his jaw, giving Calum the finger, and smiles innocently at our father. "Sure thing, Da."

Da finishes the saucy part of his slice and hands me his crust. It was a long-standing thing for me to steal his crust. Somewhere over the years, he gave up the fight and simply surrenders it to me now.

There's a reward for persistence.

In this case, it's pizza crust.

"Next," Da says, "there's the business of why someone wants to hinder the fertility and growth of Ireland and the fae."

"Rude," Dillan says. "That's plain rude."

"If we didn't know what the elders were doing, how did these people know?"

"Another good question for which we have no answer, *a ghra*." Sloan squeezes my shoulder from the couch behind me. "Until we figure out who they are, we won't know how this plot of theirs took form."

Emmet waves that away. "Screw them. We're going to kick this ritual in the ass, and I'm going to super-boost fertility. We're going to have bumper crops of sheep and wildlife and fae babies coming out our ying-yangs."

I snort. "I don't think sheep are considered crops."

"I'm not comfortable with fae babies being anywhere near my ying-yang," Ciara says.

Emmet rolls his eyes. "You know what I mean."

I laugh. "Yes, we do. Yay you. Go, buffer, go!"

"What about the Hunter-gods stuff?" Tad asks. "How does that work into this?"

I draw a deep breath and take the floor. "We think that might be another possible reason my Fianna mark appeared, and I became the magnet of mayhem."

"How so, baby girl?" Aiden asks.

"Tad's father had a book that talks about five warriors with god blood that banish evil from the empowered world. Legend states that when the need arises, five warriors will be called upon to fight the darkness."

Calum's jaw drops. "You think they drafted you as one of the five?"

I check with Da and Sloan and all three of us nod. "It looks that way. Boann and Dionysus both said they sense goddess blood within me, and that's a prerequisite. Fionn was one. I saw that in my salmon vision."

Dillan frowns. "So, someone's trying to damage Ireland, make us look bad in front of the fae, disturb the balance, at the same time there's a glitch in the matrix, and the banished baddies of the empowered world are planning an escape? That can't be a coincidence."

"No," Da says, "we don't think so either."

"Who benefits from the downfall of Ireland and darkness reigning supreme?" Jarrod asks. "Who's gunnin' fer us?"

No one has an answer to that.

"His name is Mingin," a tall, Native American man says, standing in the front entranceway.

I move to launch to my feet but get nowhere. A panicked gaze around the room confirms everyone else is suffering the same restriction of movement.

The intruder holds up his hand and steps into the house. "He was banished centuries ago because he chose to draw his strength from death and darkness and betrayed his oath as a Hunter."

"How exactly do ye know so much about this?" Da asks, his gaze murderous.

"I know a great many things. I am Samuel Wright, one of the five Hunter-gods, like your daughter, and Mingin was my ancestral grandfather."

CHAPTER EIGHT

Samuel Wright releases his hold on us and raises his palms in surrender. "Forgive my intrusion. It took me some time to track Fiona after running into her on the astral plane. I shouldn't have intruded, but I am anxious to speak with her. When I sensed the discord of the energy in this house, I knew there was no time to waste."

Wiry-fit and dressed in black jeans and a light-blue button-down, the guy gives Sloan a run for his designer hottie title. He has ebony hair, oddly golden eyes, and tribal tattoos inked on both hands and encircling his left eye from forehead to cheekbone.

"There's a thing called a doorbell dickwad," Dillan snaps. "Use it, and you won't need to immobilize people, and in turn, they won't jump up and kick your ass."

"Which is still on the table," Aiden says.

"Damn straight," Calum says. "This is our grandparents' home. You overstepped by inserting yourself into a conversation that has nothing to do with you."

The stranger doesn't look the least bit abashed at his behavior. "I explained my intrusion. In truth, I'm not here to make friends.

I'm here to make amends for my ancestor's betrayal and to unite the five Hunter-gods to keep him contained in the Neitherlands."

He strides toward me and extends his hand. "Fiona, I am Samuel. Time is of the essence. We need to go. The others are gathering, and there are preparations to be made and skills to be assessed."

I glance at the proffered hand but don't take it.

Something about this guy feels way wrong. He brightens a room with his outer package, but I've met enough pretties since being exposed to the empowered world to realize they ain't pretty. They only look that way.

Samuel is this to the extreme.

It's as if someone picked my brain, took all the things I find the most attractive about a man, and made him for me—that would be Samuel Wright.

"Sorry. I'm not buying whatever it is you're selling. I don't know you, and I don't recall meeting you on the astral plane. Besides, the first thing you did when you got here was bind us… which is exactly what happened to the Elders of the Ancient Order before your ancestor's minions kidnapped them. Coincidence? I think not."

He frowns. "I arrived in Ireland only hours ago. I don't know anything about your elders or what happened to them or who my ancestor's minions are."

"You don't know? You just arrogantly told my father you know a great many things."

"Not about kidnappings."

"That's convenient."

There's a knock on the door and Gran moves to answer it. Da shakes his head and gestures for Dillan to go instead. My brother strides forward and comes back with two guys in their thirties and an extremely tall, brunette woman that looks as fierce as she does stunning.

"I saw you," I say, drawn forward toward the woman. "In my

vision of Mingin's banishment in Newgrange tomb. You, Fionn, and an Asian man who shifted from an alligator were fighting together."

The woman studies me and her expression softens. "That was a very long time ago. You possess the same aura as Fionn. Fearless...stubborn...skilled...and I would guess too compassionate for your own sake."

"Um...thank you?"

She grins. "I am Melanippe of Scythia, but you may call me Melani. This is Ahren, and that's Quon Shen. I see that Samuel's already subjected you to his charms."

Between my family and the heirs and the new arrivals, there's quite a crowd. I feel a little overrun with quizzical gazes.

I decide to disperse the group. "Aiden, Jarrod, and Tad, you start working on the kids. Ciara, Eric, and Emmet, you're on the ritual. Dillan, Calum, Kevin, and Nikon, you work on tracking down Ciara's scrying area and find our elders. Gran, it's your house, you can help whoever you want. Da and Sloan, you're with me and the new arrivals outside."

Without waiting to see if anyone listens, I grab my shoes and head toward the door. Drawing a deep breath of morning air, I stop on the cobbled patio and try to center myself as the group closes ranks.

"Do you know why we are here, Fiona?" Melani asks, standing opposite me.

I meet her direct gaze and nod. "I'm a Hunter-god sleeper agent activated to protect the gate that contains a mythical traitor. He chose the dark side, and now he wants out of the Neitherlands and wants to free all the other big baddies too."

She nods. "That about covers it."

I hear the cadence in her voice and smile. "Are you from ancient Greece? I was there last month, and your accent is very much like the goddesses I spoke to."

Her eyes widen. "You were in ancient Greece last month?

How did you manage that? That is an incredibly distant time-frame to project yourself."

I shake my head. "No. I was physically there. My friend had a bit of a run-in with Hecate, and she dragged a few of us back."

"Hecate is a bitch."

"No argument here."

"To answer your question, I have lived a long time, and my beginnings are rooted in what you consider ancient Greece. Ares is the father of my line, but I am an Amazon. If you know your history, Amazons and Greeks aren't the same."

I frown. "Obvi, I don't know my history because I thought Amazons came from the Amazon, not Greece."

There's a deep-throated chuckle behind me, and Nikon joins us. He comes to stand next to me, but his attention is on the Amazon female in front of us. "No, Red. The Amazons are a race of warriors who dwelt in an area that is now part of Ukraine."

"Huh, I did *not* know that."

"Melanippe." A wry smile tugs at the side of Nikon's mouth. "That was the name of one of the three daughters of Ares and Otrera. Are you she or a descendant of hers?"

Melani straightens and lifts her chin. She is fierce, over six-and-a-half feet tall, and has the rockin' bod of a woman who has kicked someone's ass every day of her life. Her long, chestnut brown hair catches in the breeze, and when she arches her brow, the movement exposes a scar through her right eyebrow.

When she opens her mouth, she speaks in an ancient dialect. I don't understand the words, but the tone is sharp, and the words clipped.

They exchange a few volleyed sentences, then Nikon grins and holds up his hands in surrender. "Well then, I'll leave you to the business at hand. Good luck, Red." He kisses my cheek and snaps out.

Melani's gaze narrows on me. "Who was that?"

"Nikon Tsambikos of the Isle of Rhodes."

"When is he from?"

I shrug. "That's his story to tell. Let's just say you might've known some of the same people back in the old neighborhood."

"Exactly how much time are we going to waste here, ladies?" Samuel snaps. "Tick-tock."

Melani sends him a scathing glare. "Watch yourself. I sent the last Hunter from your line into oblivion. I have no problem sending you to join him."

I meet the concerned gazes of Da and Sloan and shrug. "Fun, eh?"

It's the Asian guy in navy fatigues who gets us rolling. "Hey, Fiona, I'm Quon Shen. What do you know of the term Shamanism?"

I gesture to the circle of stone benches around the firepit and head over to take a seat. "Native nations have shamans. They're like medicine men."

He nods. "They can be. In our case, it's something a little different."

I'm about to ask what 'our case' means when he lifts a finger to pause the interruption.

"A shaman is a man or woman who enters an altered state of consciousness—usually at will—to utilize a hidden reality to acquire knowledge, power, to help, or to banish others. Additionally, he or she has at least one spirit in his or her service."

I swallow, my mind trudging along with all the vitality of a pregnant sloth in a heatwave. "All right. I can retreat into myself and have done so to gain knowledge and help others, but—"

"And there's Bruin," Da interjects.

All heads turn my way.

"Who's Bruin?" Samuel snaps.

"He's my spirit bear companion—my bonded warrior guard."

His eyes widen as the corner of his mouth twitches. "Then let's meet him and see what you've got."

Yeah no, I don't think so. "It's a little early in the relationship to air our spirit totems. How about we get to know each other better first? Go on, Quon Shen. You were talking about Shamanism."

Samuel settles back in his seat as Quon Shen continues. "I'm sure you're aware Celtic lore is flush with examples of heroes traveling between worlds on quests for magical rewards, knowledge, or power."

Sloan nods. "It's known in old Irish as *immram*. The word refers to a voyage by sea as the literal translation is 'rowing about' but can be a journey through any part of the triadic Celtic cosmos."

I blink at Sloan. "What's a triadic Celtic cosmos?"

"The trinity of the cosmos is sky, land, or sea. Though it could be any of the three, it's still perceived as a water voyage."

"What does that have to do with me?"

Quon Shen takes it from there. "Shamans typically undergo exceptional ordeals in their quests. In fact, the very nature of the shaman's suffering and trials place him outside of the norm of society. Usually, the so-called 'normal' people watching from a distance can't fully comprehend such dangerous questing."

I shrug. "I've gone through a lot, but my family and friends have been right there with me. It's not like I'm on the outside looking in or anything."

"Exactly like your namesake," Melani says. "Fionn mac Cumhaill is the quintessential shamanic figure in the old Gaelic sagas. Outlaw, poet, craftsman, and seer, Fionn was raised in exile in the wilderness by two mysterious foster mothers—"

"His birth mother, Muirne, and his father's sister, Bodhmall."

"One was commonly said to be a druid."

"That was Bodhmall."

Samuel tilts his head to the side. "How can you be so certain? There are many myths and bard tales that keep Fionn's early years vague, to say the least."

I chuff. "Not to him. He told me himself."

Samuel's golden gaze narrows on me, and the hair at the nape of my neck stands on end. "You've communicated with him?"

"On numerous occasions."

Melani leans forward on the bench. "You've had exchanges... not just observed him during a vision?"

"Yes, I've communicated with him. We've had fireside chats and shared a room in a castle in Arthurian time, and he's visited us in Toronto. The others have seen him and spoken to him too."

Melani scans Sloan's and Da's reactions, and they nod their agreement. "That's exceptional."

"Can you summon him?" Samuel asks.

I sit back. The guy's energy is a little too eager for my liking. Before I answer, I check the gazes of the other three. They look curious but not greedy for the info. "No. He comes to me when he has something to say."

"Have you ever tried to summon him?"

"Summon him, no. Yesterday I tried to connect with him, though. I wanted to say hi and ask him something about the kidnapping involving my grandfather."

"When you got stuck in the meadow," Samuel says.

Okay, now it's me who's eyeing him up. "You know an awful lot about a girl you just met."

He rolls his eyes. "I told you. We met on the astral plane. I was the one to lead you to Fionn. You only made it halfway there, and I guided you to your target."

"You're the black wolf."

He nods.

"You've been haunting me, haven't you? You're the one triggering my shield's warning. You're the creepy stalker."

"Sounds about right," Melanippe says.

"What are you talking about?"

"Last night. We were in the kitchen, and I got the overwhelming sense of your presence. That *was* you, wasn't it?"

Samuel shakes his head. "There's no way you sensed me.

You're a fledgling at best. What do you mean, trigger your shield's warning?"

Sloan raises his hand and sits forward. "Yer awfully interested in Fi and her gifts, but ye've yet to share yer skills or what ye want from her."

Good one, hotness.

"This is your business how, druid?"

I chuckle. "Because Sloan and my family and friends come as a package deal. Have you ever heard the saying, We the Druids? Well, it's a thing. There are t-shirts in production."

I'm about to launch into a diatribe about how my crew rolls when Emmet rushes out of the house. "Sorry to break this up, guys, but we have a lock on the kidnapped elders. I was able to boost Ciara's scrying ability, and now it's time to bring them home."

"Amazing job, Emmet." I jump to my feet as Da and Sloan do the same. "You the man, bro."

"Where are you going?" Samuel asks.

"My grandfather was kidnapped yesterday along with eight other druid elders. They've found them. Now we go to get them and bring them home."

"We need to prepare for Mingin and what we'll face during the equinox. We need to train and get a sense of our collective fighting skills."

"Then get off your butts and come with. There's about to be a battle with real bad guys. Let's go kick some ass, and you can start assessing."

Melani jumps to her feet and smiles. "That's a great idea. A practice run against earthbound foes. Good plan, Fiona. We accept the invitation to your battle."

CHAPTER NINE

Ten minutes later, we arrive at a private estate outside Tipperary. I want to make a joke about it being a long way to Tipperary, but it's not the time. Sad face. It would've been funny too.

The house is a classical, eighteenth-century Georgian mansion built to take advantage of a riverside view of the River Suir. There's a large cluster of trees on the property, and that's where we congregate to make our plan. We're far enough from the house to see what's happening but remain unnoticed.

After taking in our surroundings and releasing Bruin to check things out, I kneel with the group. "The bad guys have style. I give them that. This place is snazzy."

Emmet nods. "At least Granda wasn't held prisoner in a drippy, damp cave or an old dock warehouse that reeks of fish guts. These kidnappers have a bankroll."

"Okay, Da," Dillan says. "What's our play?"

Da frowns at the size of the group. There are sixteen of us with the heirs, Nikon, and the Hunter-gods added to our numbers. We know there are at least twenty-four of them. That's not terrible odds with Bruin on our side, but we don't want to be caught in the fight while a couple of the bad guys move the elders, or even worse—take them out.

The air stirs with the familiar scent of pine and outdoors, and Melani and I catch our hair. She senses Bruin's presence as he returns from his intel gathering, but I haven't introduced them yet. "What have you got for us, buddy?"

Bruin manifests at my hip, and I scrub my fingers through the fur on his shoulder. "The elders are in the east wing on the second floor. There are six guards on that floor, four patrollin' the perimeter, and another dozen at least millin' about through the house. And guys...they aren't random kidnappers."

That turns a lot of druid heads.

"What do ye mean?"

"Those boys are Barghest. They're takin' another run at us."

"Fuckety fuck," Dillan snaps. "Those dirty piece of shit necromancers gotta learn to step off."

Quon Shen shrugs. "A foe you faced before?"

I nod. "Yeah. They considered themselves druids but lost touch with the balance and decided that desiccating groves and torturing powerful fae creatures gave them more of a boost than cherishing nature."

"Yeah, they're pretty much the nightmare scum of druid past," Dillan says.

"They're exactly the kind of followers Mingin would draw to his cause," Ahren says.

It's the first time he's spoken, and I'm taken back by his iconic deep voice. He has a Sam Elliott raspy bass, and I wonder if maybe that's why he doesn't say much.

It's very distracting.

"We thought the kidnapping and Fi's vision of the banishment connected somehow," Da says. "I guess that means we were right."

"I wonder if Droghun's behind it?" I say. "That weasel hasn't been to more than two Guild Governor's meetings since I had him ousted as druid leader back in September."

"Doesn't matter," Aiden says. "Barghest don't seem to realize that 'We the Druids' won't roll over and let them foul up our relationship with the fae powers."

"Sucks to be them."

Da points toward the house. "Sloan, I want ye to portal Calum and Emmet to the flat roof section of the main building there. They'll be our lookout and sniper. Tad and Nikon ye'll go too. Locate the perimeter guards from above, and the three of ye flash in behind them and take them by surprise. Eliminate them as quickly and quietly as ye can. Calum, if anyone else comes out, or thinks to join the fight, take them down."

"Got it."

"Bruin, spirit yerself into the area where they're holding the elders hostage. If the Barghest catch wind that we're moving in, protect the elders at all cost."

"Yes, Da."

"Sloan, Nikon, and Tad, when you've eliminated the perimeter guards, flash back and gather groups of four to take to the house. Sloan's on the back door there in the shadows. Tad, take the service door on the side of the greenhouse. Nikon, yer on the front entrance."

Nikon nods and puts his fist in. "Everyone, be safe."

All of us close enough to bump puts our fists in. The hunters look confused. Maybe they haven't learned what fighting with family feels like.

They don't seem like the close-knit type.

"All right, boys, off ye go. Safe home."

Sloan squeezes my hand and kisses beside my ear. "Don't be too brave, Cumhaill."

I wink as he eases back. "Same goes for you, hotness. Love you."

"Back at ye."

Calum and Emmet stand and put their hands in for Sloan to *poof* them up to the flat section of the roof. Tad and Nikon stand

and nod that they're ready as well. The moment they're gone a small part of me holds its breath.

Be safe guys.

While they're off to take care of the perimeter guards, Bruin lifts his snout, slaps my cheek with his long, pink tongue and spirits away to position himself between the Black Dogs and the elders.

Going into battle with people you trust is one thing.

Going into the same situation with strangers, or worse, people you *don't* trust is something else entirely.

I catch Samuel staring at me and return the hard glare. Melani frowns at us both, but I don't care. My shield wakes up, and the tattoo on my back burns against my flesh. Is it paranoia or is the threat real?

The fact that a black wolf descendant of an evil betrayer shows up in my life on the same day Barghest kidnaps Granda and the others doesn't feel like a coincidence. The only thing is... I'm not sure what his game is.

Before I have time to think about that more, Nikon, Sloan, and Tad flash back.

"Perimeter guards are down," Sloan says.

"All right," Da says. "Everyone move out. Right and tight. Good luck."

I lace my fingers with Sloan's and squeeze as Da, Eric, and Melani join our squad. The moment we have our group, Sloan *poofs* us to the back of the mansion.

The moment our feet solidify on the ground, Eric moves to check the door and Da reviews our sightlines to make sure we're good. There's a downed guard stuffed behind the boxwood by the door, but other than that, there's no sign of Barghest.

Yet.

"There's a Ward of Warning on the door," Eric says. "It'll trip if we force entry."

Da shakes his head and sticks his hand back out. "Sloan, portal us inside. Ye see where we need to be."

Sloan completes the connection and *poofs* us into the back mudroom of the house.

Once inside, Da calls his staff, I call Birga and my armor, and Eric draws a scimitar out of the air somehow.

Cool trick.

The four druids in our group move like a tactical team, which makes sense. Two of us train with Da and, by extension, the Toronto Police Department. Eric matches us. Slightly crouched, we move forward in a tight line, checking our path forward and back as we clear room by room.

While we're crouched, Melani strides behind us, her expression displaying equal parts curiosity and entertainment. I suppose, like Nikon, once you've lived as long as they have, danger doesn't weigh as heavily.

The back hall is clear, likely because of the guard stationed on the door. We move deeper into the house, listening for signs that the occupants have realized we're invading.

So far, so good.

There are at least three voices in the room we're about to breach. By the sounds of how the voices bounce around, it's a large room, with the men fairly spread out. Da pauses at the first doorway and waits. Eric taps my shoulder from behind.

Before I tap Sloan's, I cast a silence spell.

Air around us stay silent and still,
No whispers shared, no secrets to spill,
Nothing is heard beyond the quiet,
Our actions here remain private.

The slight popping of my ears means it worked, and for the next few minutes, our attack will remain hidden.

I tap Sloan's shoulder, and he reaches forward and taps my father's.

When Da knows everyone is accounted for and ready, he signals for us to go.

The incursion is textbook, our precision a credit to our teachings. Still, the men we're up against aren't average perps hanging around in their hideout. Barghest soldiers are a well-trained, well-equipped group, and the moment they see us the world erupts.

Birga sings in my hand, excited for the blood of these men. My enchanted spear hasn't forgiven them for mistreating her and forcing her against me at the altar of the Toronto stone circle.

The five of us spread out in the vast space of a great room. The back wall of the house is glass, and I'm thankful to have a cone of silence to work within.

Da and Sloan take the closest two. Melani, Eric, and I race past them to the others. I thought there were three in here, but nope, there are four.

Surprise!

It's disorienting to see a fight break out and men crash over sofas and hear no sound.

It's also a little funny.

Ignoring that, I focus on the guys swinging automatic weapons at us.

Rude. Any druid with an ounce of honor or pride in our sacred abilities would choose nature magic and traditional weaponry over guns. It only proves how far out of the druid realm they've strayed.

I swing Birga in a downward arc. The wicked-sharp point of her spearhead slices through one man's arm. The limb *clunks* onto the powder blue area rug as the gun falls against his chest, caught by the shoulder sling.

I move in to disarm him, but another brute tackles me and knocks me onto my back. I barely feel the impact with my armor engaged, but he pins me. Two more men have rushed into the room and taken up arms.

Something wild within rages, and pulling a move straight out of National Geographic, I call on my saber-tooth self.

The shift to a massive auburn cat comes easier this time. I'm not afraid. There's a massive jumble of power, instincts, and emotions in this form but I welcome the hellcat to surface.

She is me, fiercer, wilder, and maybe a little more aggressive than I allow myself to be in my everyday life.

Pinned on my back, I get my back paws between us and score his belly with my claws. As he shrieks and throws himself back, I launch to all fours and pounce.

A hard swipe of my right paw pivots his head and snaps his neck.

When a golden jungle cat bounds past me, I can't fight the urge to follow. I've seen Melani's cat fight before, and she's magnificent.

The two of us race through the main floor and find Nikon's group taking on heavy resistance in the front hall. Jarrod is down and looking dazed, protected under a magical dome Ciara erected to hold off incoming attacks.

Nikon is locked in hand-to-hand combat with a skin-head Gigantor. It's funny. Even though I know he's ancient and skilled and able to defend himself, my first instinct is that a mountain of a brute like that shouldn't pick on a kid.

Honestly, there's no need to worry.

Nikon moves so fast in such practiced movements that I can barely track his strikes.

My attention is drawn to Samuel facing off against two men at the base of the stairs. He produces two black and smoky blades from thin air, and I can't help but wonder what kind of magic he possesses.

The whole place carries the silent and deadly stench of rotten eggs, but that's mostly from the Barghest fighters using dark magic. I can't tell if Samuel's magic is light or dark.

Samuel fights with single-minded focus, advancing with never-relenting aggression. He's damn impressive, and despite myself, I'm rooting for him before I catch myself. Studying him isn't our goal.

Turning away from that battle, I race up the wide staircase on all fours. The grip of my pads is amazing, and I feel the strength of my beast powering my muscles.

Damn, this could get addictive.

Rounding the banister at the top of the stairs, I bank right and find Tad, Dillan, and Aiden fighting to get into a room at the end of the hallway. Melani's jaguar matches my pace, and though she's a foot shorter than me on all fours, she's far more coordinated and deadly.

Racing forward, she leaps into the air, shifting back into her Amazon warrior form. With the momentum of her run, she flips and stretches out her long legs as she cuts through the air.

Her boots connect with the guard's chest and knock him flying backward. That eliminates the last line of defense between us and the door.

It's a move straight out of a Marvel movie, and I make a mental note to up my game so I can be that badass. She's graceful and precise in her movements.

She's beyond spectacular.

I giggle and dial back my girl-crush to save for later.

First, we need to get the elders.

Melani grips the Barghest guard she knocked stupid and delivers a brutal backhand to the side of his face. When his eyes roll back, our attention turns to the door.

My first thought is to shift back and enter as Fiona, but I'm not one hundy percent sure I'll have clothes on. Battling nakey in front of my grandfather, father, and brothers isn't my favorite plan. Not to mention the other elders.

The other time I shifted back from my saber-tooth panther, Dionysus held me in the Fountain of Peirene. He may well have put my clothes back on me.

Dionysus putting clothes *on* someone is almost an oxymoron, but beneath that bravado is a good guy.

Deciding to wildcat it until I know for sure, I press my front paws against the wood panel of the door and push out with my druid abilities.

Bestial Strength. The door is no match for my connection, and it splinters and falls out of my way.

I jump into the room and come face-to-face with my grizzly boy. Scanning the room, my brain fritzes out. *Bruin? What the hell? What's wrong with them?*

The elders are there, lounging in the room, three propped up on a couch and three lying shoulder to shoulder on each of the two beds. They're there…but also they're not.

What did they do to them?

I don't know. They were like that when I got here.

I find Granda sitting up at the end of the sofa and shift back to look at him. Yep…I'm naked.

I was afraid of that.

Grabbing a blanket off the end of the couch, I wrap it under my arms and return my attention to Granda. "Hey, oul man. You in there?"

There's no indication he's aware. His eyes don't dilate, and his muscles don't move. He's locked in place.

Seeing him like this tears my heart into jagged pieces. I push down the panic rising within me and try to breathe.

"Okay, Granda. It's okay. We'll get you home and figure this out. The most important thing is that you're safe now. We've got you."

Without knowing what's wrong with the elders, there's some disagreement as to what we should do. Normally, we'd take them to Stonecrest Castle and have Sloan's father examine them. Except Wallace is suffering from the same state of catatonia as the rest of them.

"Gran might be able to figure out a remedy." Emmet frowns.

After he takes a quick moment to check on the elders, Sloan reaches behind his head to the collar of his Polo shirt and pulls it off. Shifting me to face him, he hands me the shirt and takes control of the blanket while I pull his jersey on and cover myself.

"Lara would have to know what they suffer from to prepare a remedy," he says. "I think we're still best to take them to Da's clinic regardless. At least there, we have enough recovery rooms to get everyone situated."

"Maybe his staff can assess the problem," I suggest.

Sloan nods. "I think that's our best option."

Da nods. "Agreed. Boys, help Nikon, Sloan, and Tad get yer granda and the rest of the elders settled at Stonecrest. After that, I need Tad to gather the spouses and tell them what's happened. Bring them to the clinic but make sure they understand that there's a spell on the nine preventin' them from active recovery."

"What about the ritual?" Ciara says. "Even if we get the elders back on their feet, there's no way to know if they'll be fit to perform a ritual in twenty-four hours."

"Right ye are," Da says. "Now that we've foiled the kidnapping, our focus shifts back to the ritual."

"No, it doesn't," Samuel snaps. "Your equinox problems aren't a priority. We wasted our time to help get your people back. Now we need princess druid here to get her ass covered and ready for the real battle."

"Screw you, fucktard." Dillan surged forward.

Sloan's right with him, hands raised and snapping with energy. "Ye don't talk about Fi like that, asshole."

Bruin beats them both though. He launches from over by the

door, spirits through the room, and rematerializes as he hits Samuel's chest.

The guy flies backward like a scarecrow hit by a hurricane. Only...he doesn't hit the floor.

His body freezes mid-air and rights itself, hovering for a moment before he lowers back onto his feet. "Touch me again, Bear, and I'll skin you and hang your pelt on my wall."

Da arches a russet brow and offers what my brothers and I call the "dead man walking" look. "I realize ye have yer own priorities, Mr. Wright, but if ye threaten or insult anyone in my family again, ye'll be *joinin'* yer piece of shit ancestor in purgatory rather than securin' him there."

Samuel's mouth quirks up at the side. "You have no idea who you're dealing with, Irish."

Da grins. "Och, I think yer the one who's under the misconception of grandeur, young man. There's an Irish sayin', *Ni he la na gaoithe la na scolb.* It means, 'The windy day is not the time for thatching.' Today has been a very windy day filled with chaos, worry, and adrenaline. Perhaps ye should think twice before ye take a stab at one of us."

"There is no excuse for Samuel's outburst or behavior, Mr. Cumhaill." Melani casts him a derisive glance. "The urgency of his words, however, is accurate. We must prepare for the battle on the horizon."

Da nods. "Fair enough. Yer warlock here needs to understand Fiona isn't a princess. She's a fuckin' queen. She doesn't need us to defend her—she can do that all on her own—but if he has a lick of sense he'll take heed lest he falls."

Samuel rolls his golden gaze and lifts his chin.

Dillan meets the aggression with his own. "Despite your self-image, you're not that impressive. Wolf plus warlock. What kind of bastard does that make you anyway? A warwolf?"

"Or a Werelock," Calum adds.

Dillan shrugs. "Either way, find your manners and learn how

to speak to our sister or you'll have more battles on more fronts than you bargained for."

I meet Melani's amused gaze and shrug.

Whatevs. This is us.

"Okay, boys, point made. Bruin?" I pat my chest, and he returns to his resting place behind my sternum. "To recap, boys who portal take the elders to Sloan's. Heirs work on the ritual. I'll go with the Hunter-god four and bond with the crew. We'll reconvene later and compare notes. Love you all."

"Greek," Da says. "Yer not involved with the equinox ritual or the revival of the elders. Can I ask ye to escort Fi and watch her six?"

"Consider it done, Niall." Nikon grins at me.

Oh, this is going to get good.

CHAPTER TEN

Nikon helps with portaling the elders to the clinic, then comes back for me and snaps me to Gran's and Granda's to get dressed. "Gran? Did you hear?"

Gran rushes out of the kitchen looking haggard but relieved. "Yer da called me a moment ago, luv. He said ye found them and they're at Wallace's clinic."

"Did he mention they're spelled and in a state of non-response?"

"He did. I'm not so bothered by that. We'll figure it out. Whatever Barghest can do, we can undo."

Gran's animal companion, Dax, waddles around the corner and frowns up at me. "Hello, Fiona."

"Hello, skunk. Finally decided to get your lazy ass out of your den, did you?"

"It's called hibernation, but I suppose a girl raised in a city wouldn't know a thing about the natural order."

I roll my eyes. "Better be nice to me. I can turn into a saber-toothed panther now, and I might eat you. You've missed a lot, furball."

"Did I miss the part where it became a thing fer a lady to tour the world wearin' only a man's shirt? Then again, ye've never been much of a lady."

Stupid badger. "No. I shifted forms, and Sloan was kind enough to cover my bits."

"Thank the goddess. No one needs to see that."

"Enough, you two." Gran frowns. "Fi, perhaps while ye get yerself dressed, I might take advantage of Nikon's generosity and ask fer a quick portal to Stonecrest Castle to see fer myself Lugh is whole?"

I send a questioning look toward the door to where Nikon is standing. "That's fine, Lara. Grab what you need. I'm happy to take you."

While they sort themselves out, I hustle into the spare room and dig into my duffle.

When it became obvious life would never truly settle down, we agreed that having a packed go-bag was a good idea. Yeah, it came in super handy for this latest disaster. We were out the door within minutes after Gran called about Granda's kidnapping.

I finish getting dressed and pull out my old sneakers. Sitting on the edge of the bed, I slide my feet into them and pull the heels.

If transforming into a massive mythical saber-toothed panther obliterates everything I'm wearing, I'll have to try to kick off my shoes before I do it. I can buy and pack undies, yoga pants, and t-shirts in bulk, but shoes are heavy and need time to break in.

Huh, these are things I never thought of as a kid watching superhero shows.

By the time I've put myself back together, Nikon is eating cold pizza in the family room.

"Oh, brilliant idea, Greek." I flip the box open and grab a slice. "Thank you. I want you to know how grateful I am for you and for you being here for us."

Nikon snorts. "It's only pizza."

I arch a brow at him and smile. "I wasn't talking about the pizza, and you know it."

Nikon shrugs. "I'll never stop being grateful."

I grab a second slice for the road and hold out my hand. "Me either. I still think you're the amazing one."

He takes my hand and chuckles. "All right, we'll agree to disagree."

***

Nikon snaps us to an area of green countryside. It's flat and green, and curious sheep bleating at us through a wire fence and cows further down by the river occupy parts of it. Taking in the surroundings, I lock onto the grassy mound behind me and recognize Newgrange from my vision.

"Yeah, this is the place."

Nikon nods. "Irish had me bring him and Tad last night. He wanted all of us able to get here at a moment's notice in case things went sour and you needed us."

The lump in my throat makes it hard to swallow my next bite of Hawaiian. "He stayed up all night researching and worrying and wouldn't have said a thing about the extras he does when I'm not aware."

The Greek smiles. "He loves you like crazy, Red. He's a total goner."

I grin and look down at the beautiful platinum Claddagh band on my finger. "Yeah, that goes both ways."

Swinging an arm around me, Nikon urges us forward as one toward the Newgrange tomb.

"From what I learned via an internet search, the mound is forty-three feet tall and two hundred and seventy-nine feet across. From what I saw in my vision, there is one entrance that leads down a long corridor to the main burial chamber, which is a circular space with three smaller, round alcoves branching off it."

The inside might not be huge, but the outside is—and it's impressive to know it predates some of the most recognized historical monuments on the planet.

"All set for your playdate with your new friends?" Nikon asks.

"Yep." I swallow the last of my pizza. "Ready and able to kick butt."

The other four Hunter-god shamans are already here, so we head over and join them.

"Dressed and reporting for duty."

"Glad to have you aboard, Fiona," Quon Shen says, his smile easy and genuine. "It'll be nice to have an optimist join us. It's probably a shock, but things can get a little tedious and dire with this bunch."

When his gaze slides over to Samuel, I force myself not to react.

"So, Melanippe of Scythia," Nikon says. "What now? How do you five intend to keep the wolf betrayer and his minions on the dark side?"

Melani frowns. "This is none of your business, Nikon of the Isle of Rhodes. Stand quietly to the side or spirit yourself away."

Nikon chuckles. "Well, all righty then. Consider me a fly on the wall."

I grin, catching the friction and sparks flying between the two. It feels more like flirting on Nikon's side and threats of death from Melanippe, but it's lively, whatever it is.

Melani turns to me, and I tighten up and lock down my inner Cupid. "The red panther you shifted into this afternoon. Is that your primary animal form? I am aware that unlike us, druids can take many forms."

"That's true, but so far, my wildcat is my only animal form. That was the second time I shifted, so it's all still new for me. I was wondering, do I have to be an elk like Fionn? If so, I'll have to work on that."

"If the panther is your animal form, that's fine."

"You've only shifted twice?" Samuel's brows come down, and he's about to say more when Ahren lifts a pointing finger and stops him.

"Don't. You've said more than enough for one day."

"Agreed," Melani says. "Samuel, run the perimeter from the ground while Ahren covers it from the air. Quon Shen, join one of the tours into the tomb and assess the state of things inside. Fiona and I will start here and you three can join when you return."

As mouthy as Samuel is to everyone else, he doesn't argue with the Amazon. That only proves he's not a complete moron after all.

When they're gone, I smile. "Thanks for that...and thanks for the four of you joining to help rescue Granda and the others."

Melani shrugs. "I am pleased they are safe for your sake. In truth, I agreed to it less for the rescue and more to assess your skills, your attitude under pressure, and because your mind wouldn't have been on task until you recovered your grandfather."

"That's cool. You helped, and that's what matters."

Sparring with and against Melani, Ahren, Quon Shen, and Samuel in human form is both humbling and exciting. Druid against druid makes for even odds. I understand what's coming at me: the spells cast are all sourced from magic I understand and have a feel for, and the abilities coming at me are similar to mine.

That's not the way of things against these four.

Melani is a fierce and skilled warrior. Her towering height and millennia of experience make her a true force to be reckoned with. She strikes fast, has clean, precise movements, and is a cunning strategist on offense or defense.

Ahren fights very much like the eagle he shifts into. He's aerodynamic and darts and swoops in his attacks. He's also incredibly light on his feet and has this strange vibration about him that makes my legs rubbery and my arms feel heavy.

Melani calls it his resonance and says I have to learn to block it out so we can battle effectively together.

Quon Shen is a fun guy, and at the risk of stereotyping, he's the Bruce Lee of our time. He's taller than me but shorter than the others, and his stature only enhances his lethality. He's a martial arts phenom, and when he comes against an attack, he moves like water around a stone in a swift current. He's graceful, fluid, and deceptively unalarming.

Then there's Samuel. I saw a bit of what he can do during the rescue in Tipperary this afternoon. He's a solid fighter, has advanced and powerful warlock skills, and the aggression to be a dangerous enemy…but, in my opinion, he's the weakest link on all fronts.

Funny enough, he has the same opinion of me.

That's fine. Haters gotta hate.

I jump the sweep of Ahren's leg and get another rush of wonky-woo as his resonance hits. Fighting to plant my feet on the landing, I narrowly miss getting clocked by a bolt of magic Samuel throws at me.

Throwing my body back, I flip and land crouched on all fours as the rollercoaster in my head settles. "No offense, Ahren, but I need a bit of space or I'm gonna hurl."

"Of course. Sorry."

I'm breathing through my nose and trying to stop the butter-flies in my stomach from violently migrating north when another bolt of power catches me in the shoulder and blasts me off my feet and onto my back.

"Samuel!" Melani snaps. "That was uncalled for."

"Was it? From where I stand, it was perfectly in line with what needed doing."

I roll to my feet and check my balance. Nikon has moved in and looks like he's about to go full Greek warrior. I hold up my palm to stop him from stepping in. "I've got this Greek."

Samuel grunts. "Your father, your brothers, your bear, your friends...maybe if you fought your own battles, they wouldn't need to swoop in for your rescue. What we're readying for isn't a skirmish with a couple of dozen druids gone bad, little girl. The seam of the Neitherlands is splitting, and if that happens, it'll leak evil into this world like you've never imagined."

I chuckle. "Stop trying to blow my mind with what's coming. You don't know me or what I've faced. From where I stand, you are by far the most underprepared for what's to come."

"You're delusional."

"No, I'm not. My dad taught me that you have to drop your ego and lock down your emotions to win a fight. If you're angry or upset during a conflict, you're out of balance. If your emotions are in play, your opponent can manipulate them. You are one gigantic combustible ball of ego. You're dangerous to us, yourself, and the success of this battle."

Samuel glares at me, but he doesn't argue.

I'd be a fool to think that indicated he heard my concern and is processing it.

Nah, I'm no fool.

The chip on his shoulder weighs so heavily on him he probably doesn't even realize he's dooming himself to fail.

Straightening, I bypass the hostility and head straight for Ahren. "Do you think you and I could spend some quiet time? I need to get a handle on the effect you have on me."

The eagle hunter nods. "Many women have tried, but few can fight it."

I grin. "I'm not most women. I'm sure I'll get the hang of it."

Samuel huffs and stomps off.

I don't even care where he's going. Honestly, my only parting thoughts are about what Quon Shen learned earlier on the tomb tour, and leaving Nikon with Melanippe.

I look back at where he's standing vigil and reach out to talk to him privately. *Play nice with the Amazon, Greek. The two of you would make beautiful babies.*

Nikon laughs and shakes his head. *I think she'd break me in two.*

That might be fun too.

You're incorrigible.

She's probably tough on the outside with a soft and gooey inside. Think about it: Greek heritage—check, immortal—check, gorgeous—check, chemistry—checkity-check-check.

He arches a blond brow and gives me a look. *Seriously, Red. You, better than anyone, know how my last Greek goddess love affair ended.*

True story...but when you fall off the horse....

Are you implying she's a horse?

Only in the sense that I think you'd enjoy mounting and riding her.

He chokes and throws his arm out to the side. "Go, practice not puking with your new friend."

I laugh and gesture for Ahren to lead the way.

Mischief managed.

Ahren and I find a spongy patch of grass and cop a squat. Sitting opposite one another, I try to recall something of Sloan's training that might help me in this situation. "From where does your resonance mojo get its oomph?"

He considers that and shrugs. "I'm not sure. I don't feel like I'm doing anything, but when enough empowered people tell you that you're affecting them, you stop arguing the point. All I can say is that I don't control it or mean to do it."

So, if he doesn't feel it and doesn't mean for it to happen, it must be part of his natural harmonics. Nature is all about resonance and balance, so his normal frequency must be slightly out of phase from the rest of us.

That makes sense if part of the Hunter-gods shaman thing is the ability to access an altered state of consciousness or reality. Maybe it's a matter of finding the harmonic frequency he's on and dialing myself in so we stop getting static.

"Okay, so, do you mind if I touch you?"

He chuckles in that deep Sam Elliott baritone. "I don't suppose any man would say no to that."

My blush heats my cheeks, and I roll my eyes. Normally, I could quip my way out of a comment like that, but we only met a few hours ago. "Sorry, what I meant is would you mind if I make contact with you to see if that makes things worse?"

He shakes his head and holds out his hands. "It's fine. I was only teasing. Has anyone ever mentioned you have the cutest flush when you're embarrassed?"

"That's the Celtic curse of pale skin. Freckles cover my face in the summer, and I blush red as a beet when something embarrassing happens. It's horrifying."

"Horrifying isn't the word I'd use, but you're entitled to your opinion."

To end that convo, I shift my hands to hover over his. The wave of nausea answers my question before I even get close enough to touch him. Okay, maybe a spell instead. I think about what's happening and come up with one on the fly.

Magic mend the resonance burn,
Damage end and health return,
Strong and steady, no ill effect,
End discomfort, no more blech.

I give the spell a moment to take hold, then reach forward again and wait for nausea to set in. I still sense my body's reaction to whatever it is that weakens empowered people near him, but it's much better. "This I can live with."

"Better?" he asks.

"Much. How about we try a little gentle hand-to-hand and see if I can learn to suppress it even more?"

He nods. "Sounds like a good idea."

The two of us rise, and I shake out my shoulders and arms. "So, how long have you been a Hunter?"

He smiles. "Since early last summer. One night, I walked my dog down on the lakefront trail near where I live and felt like my skin was burning away from my bones. I managed to shuffle home and drag myself inside my apartment, but when I still felt like something was electrocuting my body a couple of hours later, I got really scared and decided to call for help."

"Wow. What happened?"

"Nothing. When I reached for my phone, I realized I didn't have arms. I had talons. It was the first time I shifted forms, and I pretty much lost my mind. I'm not sure if I zoned out or passed out, but the next thing I remember is waking up on my kitchen floor wondering if it was a horrible dream."

"I had the crazy summer night thing, too. The next morning I found the beginnings of this surfacing." I lift the back of my t-shirt and turn for him to see the Fianna mark on my back. "That's when I tracked down Granda and learned about my druid ancestry. That's also when my world exploded into the chaotic wonder it is now."

Ahren chuckles. "Chaotic wonder. That's a good way to put it."

The two of us spar a while longer, and it seems thoughts of our past and present envelop both of us.

Now and then, I glance over at Nikon and Melani.

It seems Nikon has volunteered to be her sparring partner while Quon Shen watches, and she's not taking it easy on him— not that it looks like he minds.

When Quon Shen beckons us over, Ahren and I head back to hear what he has to say.

"The main chamber is the largest point of concern. The seam of the veil is pulling apart, and the fissure openings are weakening. I have no doubt that if Mingin has any power behind him, he will have the strength to force his way free of his imprisonment."

"Awesomesauce. So, how do we stop it?"

Quon Shen's face drops. "You don't know? Fionn was the all-knowing leader last time around. We depended on you to have all the answers."

I blink at him, my eyes wide. "Dude, I don't know how to seal the stress fracture of the Neitherlands. Some days I don't even know how to get gum off my shoe."

When his face relaxes, and he starts to laugh, my heart starts to beat again. "Okay, you suck. That was well played, but you totes suck."

Nikon chuckles. "I think you need to introduce Quon Shen to the concept of the Oh! Henry bar family challenge. It seems he might be a new player."

I grin. "He might be."

CHAPTER ELEVEN

With the promise to spend another couple of hours training after dinner, Melani lets me go to check in with my family at the clinic. Stonecrest Castle is a beautiful stone mansion up in Galway. It overlooks the Atlantic Ocean, and if I didn't know better, I would be jealous Sloan grew up in such a wondrous setting.

I text Sloan when we arrive in the courtyard of his castle and inquire if the coast is clear for me to enter.

He's at the door, inviting us inside and offering me an apologetic smile a split-second later. "Of course, yer welcome to come inside. Even if Lugh and yer family weren't here, *I'm* here and we're a package deal. This *is* technically my house."

I reach up on my toes, meet his kiss, and sink against his chest for a much-needed hug. "How are things here?"

"We've made some improvements," he says, stepping aside as we enter. "Come, I'm sure ye'd like to say hello to yer granda."

"Say hello? He's up and about?"

"To some degree, yes. The elders are responding to treatment, but it's been a bit of a slow process."

I lace my fingers with his and double-check that Nikon is

with us. "Responding is great news. Have they been able to communicate what happened or who was heading up the Barghest planning?"

"Unfortunately, their kidnappers subdued them pretty much from the time they took them from their homes."

I shake off my disappointment about that. "It's enough that they're alive and responding. Let's be thankful for that."

When we arrive at the part of the castle used for Wallace's clinic, it takes me a moment to wrap my head around all the people. It makes sense...nine elders with at least one or two family members worried about them and Wallace's staff.

"Wow, it's a full house."

"It is at that." Sloan points toward the back left corner of the clinic. "Lugh's in Recovery Three. Yer Gran and Calum are in there now."

I stride forward, and he releases my hand. The loss of the connection stops me, and I turn back. "Aren't you coming?"

"No, no. Go have yer visit. I popped in and out all afternoon. Now that yer here, I'll check on the heirs and see how the preparations for the Ostara ritual are comin' along. I promised the parents of the young ones I'd get them home at a reasonable hour."

I sigh. There's so much I want to tell him about my afternoon with the hunters, but as usual, the universe has plans for us. "All right, you do you, hotness. Where are the heirs practicing? We'll meet you after I finish checking in with the fam jam."

"At Drombeg." He shifts his tired gaze toward Nikon. "Ye'll have no issues finding the location online. It's the main attraction here."

Nikon holds out his hand and the two clasp palms. "I'll get her to you as soon as she's ready."

"Thanks, *sham*. Bonus points if yer able to keep her out of trouble."

Nikon chuckles. "That's a big ask, but I'll try."

"Har-har." I step close to hug Sloan. "Don't think for a moment I haven't noticed the circles under your eyes or forgotten that you stayed up all night researching. The moment this day is over, you and I are claiming the spare bed at Gran's and closing our eyes. Tomorrow is a big day. We need to be in top form."

Sloan looks down at me and chuckles. "If ye think it's a threat to say yer takin' me to bed first chance, yer wrong. Although, I'm not sure we'll get the bed two nights in a row. Yer da and Aiden were on the couches last night, Dillan had the hammock, and Kevin and Calum got the floor. We *all* need to be in top form."

I sigh. "Poop. Well, no matter. The first chance we get, we sack out even if it's on a patch of grass in the grove out back."

"Agreed. I'm lookin' forward to it."

"Knock-knock." I lean into Recovery Room Three and find Granda looking pale but awake on the twin bed. "I heard there was an oul man in here causing trouble."

Gran smiles. "Come in, luv. We were wonderin' how yer day was goin'."

Calum stands when I step into the little room with mint green walls. He offers me his chair, and I gladly accept. "Thanks, bro."

"Not a problem. You look like you're about to fall over. Long day?"

"Yeah. On top of yesterday's long day."

Calum squeezes my shoulder as I slump into the little uphol-stered chair. "I hear you. If you guys are good for a bit, I think I'll find Kev and bribe Nikon to pop us home for a nap while the house is quiet. I'm beat and am not going to make it until bedtime before I crash. Are you okay with that, Greek?"

Nikon is standing at the door and nods. "No bribery necessary. Fi, I'll be back in a flash. Don't get into any trouble while I'm gone. You know how I hate to miss anything."

I laugh. "Take your time. I'm sure I can fend off disaster for ten or fifteen minutes."

He nods. "Done deal."

When Nikon and Calum leave, I settle in at Granda's bedside and squeeze his hand. "I'm glad you're back where you belong, Granda. We were scared there for a bit."

He smiles at me, his eyes not as bright as they usually are. "Ye'll not have to leave yer city to be the Shrine Keeper just yet. I think I have another decade or two in me before yer called to serve."

I chuckle. "Not what I meant, and you know it."

Granda sobers. "I do. And, while I appreciate the concern, I'd much rather be in my bed at home and not have people comin' in and lookin' at me like I'm hangin' on by a thread."

I know that feeling too well. "Any word on when you can blow this pop stand?"

Gran straightens the sheet across Granda's chest and smooths it down. "They said he's free to go once full mobility returns."

"Mobility? What's not working?"

Granda rolls his eyes. "It's all workin' but with the cogs still a little fuzzy, the gears are a little slow to respond. Don't worry. I'll be kickin' yer ass before ye know it."

I've never known Granda's mental cogs to be fuzzy, and I don't like the thought of him being confused one bit. "I'll even go easy on you when you try."

He chuckles and closes his eyes. When he opens them again, it's obvious how much his current state is worrying him.

I squeeze his hand and smile. "The fog will clear soon, and when the clouds part, there will be nothing but sunny skies in that magnificent mind of yours."

"That's what yer Gran keeps sayin'."

I reach across the bed and squeeze Gran's hand too. "Well,

good, then. I'm glad we agree. A smart man knows when to listen to the women in his life."

Granda chuckles. "Och, there's no doubt about that. Now, tell me about this Hunter-god business and what ye learned about since ye arrived."

I spend the next five minutes recapping my meditation vision of Fionn banishing Mingin in the Newgrange tomb and meeting the other four hunters. I tell him about Melanippe, Ahren, Quon Shen, Samuel, and the training we did today.

"It doesn't sound like ye'll start a fan club fer Samuel anytime soon."

I grin. "Only if I base it on creative ways to torture and kill him. I could get behind that."

Granda chuckles. "One thing ye learn as you navigate life is that when yer on a committee or part of a group of folks set on a task, ye won't mesh with everyone. All ye can do is bite yer tongue and focus on yer portion of what needs doing."

"I'm not convinced Samuel's one of the good guys. His ancestor is the one who betrayed the hunters way back when. Maybe he wants Mingin to escape. Maybe he's part of Barghest and is reclaiming his heritage. I've seen his wolf. He is *literally* a big black dog."

"Och, luv, ye can't judge a man by his ancestors or by the anger ye hold fer Barghest. People deserve to be weighed on their own merits."

"Yeah, but so far, his own merits haven't been all that impressive."

"From you comin' into the situation at the last moment, maybe. What do the others think?"

I draw a deep breath.

Granda's calm, reasonable tone makes things sound simple, but after two minutes with Samuel, I want to ram Birga's spear tip into his stupid face.

Gran chuckles. "It's unkind to wish him harm, luv."

I blink. "Are you psychic, Gran?"

"No, but I can read yer expression clear enough. Takin' yer frustration out on him won't solve the problem at hand."

"It would make me feel better."

"I'm sure it would, in the short term."

Granda looks at me and leans closer. "Do ye think I like all the elders, *mo chroí?* We have a few eejits and a few more that are worse than that."

Riordan McNiff comes to mind in an instant. Tad's father is a pompous, power-hungry dick.

"No, I don't suppose you do."

"Yer right, I don't. However, it's not my place to stand in judgment. I focus on my part of the Order process and do my best to support my counterparts for the greatest outcome."

I exhale and let that sink in. "Adulting is hard."

Gran chuckles. "It is, at that."

"Okay, I'll try harder. Promise."

"Good girl." Granda opens his arms, and I stand to lay over him and accept his hug. He wraps his arms around my shoulders and strokes a hand down the length of my hair. "Yer a strong and skilled warrior, but always remember there is strength in unity."

I straighten as the rocking chair lady's words ring in my head. "Ní neart go cur le chéile."

Granda looks surprised but nods. "That's right. Now, stop hangin' around here wastin' time chattin' with old men. Go do what needs doing."

I squeeze his hands and run my gaze over his face.

When I first met Granda, he was unwell, but it didn't show much. Then he thrived after I assumed the family sparks. Now he looks tired and weak again.

Seeing him like this is hard on my heart.

"Feel better. I'll check in with you later. Love you."

"Love ye too, *mo chroí.* Safe home."

The hustle and chatter in the clinic rumble as loudly when I exit the recovery room as when I entered it fifteen minutes ago. I glance around for Nikon, but either he isn't back yet, or he tucked himself in a corner somewhere to stay out of the way.

Heading up the hallway, I notice Janet leaving Recovery Room One. She comes into the hall and turns toward the clinic proper. She totally misses seeing me walking up the corridor behind her.

I take that as a win.

When I get to the door to the room she exited, I glance in and see Wallace sitting up in his bed. Sloan's father is tall and fit, like his son, and possesses the same chiseled features, although his skin is a great deal darker than Sloan's warm mocha brown.

Things have been strained between the four of us in the past, but over the last couple of months, Wallace has made great efforts to warm to Sloan and me being in love. He's adjusting to his son's stance on what he wants from life, and that's good enough for me.

I tap my knuckle against the frame and tilt my head into view. "Howeyah. What's the craic?"

"Howeyah, Fi." Wallace's expression softens as he meets my gaze. "Not much craic, I'm afraid. Sloan's not here if yer lookin' for him."

"I'm not. I'm off to meet him in a few minutes. I thought I'd pop in and see how you're feeling first."

"Och, that's kind. I'm better, thanks. Lookin' forward to gettin' out of this bed."

"I bet. You're not used to being on the patient side of things. I'm sure you'd prefer to be the one performing the healings rather than lying around waiting for the healing to take place."

"Yer not wrong."

The air falls quiet, and it's a little weird. Usually, it's him checking on me after one of my ill-fated adventures. It's odd having the bedside tables turned. "Well, I won't wear out my welcome. I just wanted to say hi and let you know how thankful I am that you're on the mend."

"That's sweet, Fi. I appreciate it." He strokes a hand down the bedspread and picks at a piece of lint. "Sloan invited me to help with the expansion of the grove once the ground freeze is over and things warm up. If yer all right with it, I'd like to stay a few days."

"Awesome. Yes, we're looking forward to pulling up the fence dividing the properties. It'll double the grove size. You're more than welcome to join the fun. We'd love to have you."

"I look forward to it."

I glance back to see if Janet's coming. She detests me. As much as I'd like to build a relationship with Sloan's parents, this likely isn't the time or place to engage his mother. "Well, feel better. I'm sure we'll be back to see you tomorrow or soon after."

Wallace nods. "Good luck with everything. Sloan mentioned the world is coming at ye once more. Please know I wish ye strength and good fortune in yer battles to come."

I lift my hand and step back with a small wave. "Thanks. I appreciate that."

Nikon is standing outside the clinic, holding up the stone wall of the castle when I make my way out. I stop in front of him and wait while he finishes with his text and pushes forward to greet me. "How is your papu?"

"Good. He's not moving much and says he's still a bit foggy, but he's alive and awake, so there's that."

"There is definitely that."

"Did you get a chance to Google Earth the location of Drombeg Circle?"

"Yep. Ready when you are." He holds out his hand, and when I set my palm against his, he squeezes my hand. "Are you okay, Fi? You look tired."

I draw a deep breath and let it out.

Why is it that you can be holding it together fine until someone who cares about you gives you a worried smile? As Nikon's compassionate gaze gauges my state, my foundation erodes, and I start to crumble.

"I'm better at handling chaos when it's me in the cross-hairs. Having Granda targeted and knowing I can't help my family and friends with the Ostara ritual sets me on edge. On top of that, shifting to my wildcat shakes loose emotions I keep locked down." I swipe at my cheeks and groan as traitorous tears leak free. "I'm not that girl. I handle my shit. I don't do weepy."

He pulls me against his chest and hugs me tight. "Don't be so hard on yourself. You're whatever girl you are in this moment— no judgment. Sometimes emotions sneak up and smack you in the face. I've got you."

I accept the grounding comfort of Nikon's hug, and it doesn't take long before I've compartmentalized things again and I'm locked down. Stepping back, I swipe my cheeks with the sleeve of my shirt. "Sorry about that."

"Don't be silly. My papu is one of the most important people in my life. If something happened to him—and if he wasn't immortal—it would rock my world too."

I tilt my head from side to side, and the hollow *pop-pop-pop* of vertebrae realigning seems to work both physically and mentally. "All right. Drombeg Circle to check in on the ritual, then home for a quick bite to eat, then to Newgrange to continue training, then back home to fight for a couch so I can get some sleep."

Nikon makes a strange expression, but I'm not sure what it's about. "Maybe since Calum and Kevin are claiming the bed for a few hours now, you'll be able to snag it tonight."

I shake my head. "Nah, Sloan was right. Mattress rotation is only fair."

He frowns. "How about I zip you guys home to King Henry for a solid eight hours and bring you back in the morning?"

"As tempting as that sounds—and it does sound tempting—I have to pass. When shit's hitting, we can't afford to be so far away. If something happened and I wasn't there, I'd never forgive myself."

He holds up his hand and offers me a sad smile. "Then, until someone comes up with a better idea, I guess it's the air mattress on the floor for you and Irish."

"Yay. Lucky us."

CHAPTER TWELVE

Nine months ago, when Fionn first transported me back to Drombeg Circle, seventeen stones stood in a megalithic formation considered The Druid's Altar. Standing with Nikon now, thirteen stones remain. It's as majestic as ever, and even though I'm not involved in the spellcasting of the ritual, I feel the druid magic in the air.

The two of us stand to the side and watch as my father, Sloan, and Aiden work with the other heirs. They are spread out around the inner edges of the stones, focused on the ritual procedures they're learning.

Part of me wishes I could be part of celebrating life and light instead of battling death and darkness.

However, you play the hand you're dealt.

"Those kids look scared shitless," Nikon whispers.

He's not wrong. The three junior druids don't look at all comfortable. "It must be intimidating for the little monkeys. Their house gets broken into, masked men steal their parent, and they have to come here and learn how to be druids as the timer ticks down on them."

"How old are they?"

"Seamus was twelve last summer at the junior trials so he must be thirteen now. Brian and Lia are eight or nine, I think."

"Crazy."

"Yeah."

Sloan sees me from across the circle and winks. When he doesn't come chat, I figure he's too busy to break away.

I'm about to suggest we leave when he straightens and addresses the ring of druid heirs facing him. "Today, as we celebrate the balance of light and dark, and the first days of spring warm the grass, leaves, and soil, we recognize our path is not one we walk alone. Goddess of rebirth, Ostara, Persephone, Flora, Cybele, hail and welcome."

"Hail and welcome," the others repeat.

"Animals, awaken from slumber," Jarrod says. "Yer long months of hibernation and slumber have come to an end, hail and welcome."

"Hail and welcome."

Tad straightens and speaks next. "Green life rising through the earth, blooming and blossoming from deep within the rich, dark soil, hail and welcome."

"Hail and welcome."

Now it's Aiden's turn. "Summer birds returning from long journeys to the south, seeking warmth and light during the season of darkness, hail and welcome."

"Hail and welcome."

Da nods and points at Ciara. Wearing a beautiful green velvet robe, she moves across the center of the circle. Emmet holds her hand like a gentleman escorting her onto the dancefloor of a fancy ball.

When they reach the altar stone in the middle, Ciara stands before the stone plinth decorated with a bountiful gathering of flowers, seedlings, and bulbs. There are two cotton-tail rabbits and birds settled in grass nests. There are wide pillar candles and baskets of eggs in colorful bowls. There are spirals of soil with beetles and worms and other crawly things enjoying the dirt.

Ciara runs a hand over one of the rabbits and smiles.

As she shifts in place, her bare legs peek out from under the robe. I get the sneaky feeling she's nakey under there.

Thankfully for the youngins, it looks like that's as *risqué* as this pagan ritual is getting.

Pressing her hands against the altar, Ciara closes her eyes and speaks. "May the soil of our lands be blessed with fertility and abundance, with rains of life-giving succor, with the heat of the sun, with the raw prana of nature's bounty. May the womb of the land be blessed and become full and fruitful bringing forth life anew."

I have to admit, Ciara is a stunning woman and makes the idea of being fruitful and multiplying even more appealing.

I'm sure the fae will agree.

Emmet stands behind her and as she speaks her part, the other eight heirs lower themselves to kneel in their places. Spaced evenly around the circle, they press their palms to the ground.

Sloan sends me an apologetic glance, and I blow him a kiss and wave goodbye.

"We'll catch up on things tonight. Let's grab a quick bite to eat. Then I'm expected back at Newgrange for another round of Hunter-god fun."

"Your wish is my command, Lady Druid."

———

It's not that much fun after all. It's close to nine p.m. when Samuel's golden gaze narrows on me as his latest offensive spell falls useless at my feet. His frustration with me has been building over the past three hours.

I don't have to be a warlock to sense the intention of the

magical mojo he's giving off. His hostility and disapproval of me are hemorrhaging from his pores.

Whatevs.

"Nice try, wolfman. In case you haven't figured it out yet, nature-based spells aren't effective against me. I'm a druid." I'm not sure if I should spell that out for him, but after Granda's pep talk, I've been trying to believe we're on the same side.

"Don't act so smug, little girl. Even a broken clock gets lucky twice a day."

Noice. "Hey, I think I rank higher than a broken clock. We've been at this for hours, and I've held my own. How do you think the Hunter-god drafting process works, anyway? I'm not here solely on my good looks and witty charm. I've got game."

He grunts. "This *isn't* a game."

I hold up my palms, too tired to deal with him anymore. Granda may have given me the pep talk to try harder, but Samuel didn't get the memo.

Ignoring his stink eye, I step back. "I get that this is critical. I haven't given you any reason to think I'm not taking this seriously. You need to back down and back the hell off."

Ahren sighs. "We're on the same team here. There's no way the two of you will be able to hold your astral forms with this much animosity. Pull it together."

That takes some of the hot air out of Samuel's sails. He grunts again and moves to step away. "I don't like you, Cumhaill, and I don't respect you."

"The feeling is mutual, but thankfully we're not dating, so who the fuck cares? We're here for one reason. Stick to the script, and we'll be away from each other by tomorrow night."

Releasing Birga, I send her back into her resting place. The moon is full and rising higher with every drill Melani puts us through. I've exceeded exhaustion and am well into cranky pants, limp-noodle territory.

"Melani, I'm done. I'm getting sloppy and might kabob the Werelock if he grunts at me once more."

"Fair enough." She shifts back from her golden jaguar form and straightens. "I think we can safely say we fight relatively well with a synchronized rhythm."

Thank the goddess, my air mattress is calling.

"Now, let's shift focus and work on our connection on the astral plane."

Hubba-wha? The Taurus redhead in me wants to balk and dig my heels in. I'm done. I'm tired. I want to go home and snuggle with my guy and pass out.

Despite what Samuel thinks, I know what's at stake and respect the danger. With a deep breath and a heavy sigh, I force myself to plod on for the team. "I don't know how much more I have in me."

Melani smiles but doesn't seem sympathetic. "There's work to be done before tomorrow night. Samuel, give us a closed pentagram to work with, please."

Samuel swings his hands in a slow circle muttering in tongues. When he lifts his palms toward the night sky overhead, a glowing orange pentagram appears in the grass at our feet. It has the tree of life in the center and looks just like the image branded into the front cover of Wallace's book.

Despite the satanic image that modern television and media brand on pentagrams, an upright, five-pointed star has been a symbol of strength and goodness as far back as 300 BCE.

It has been claimed by nearly every religion, from being recognized as a symbol of Jerusalem, to representing the five wounds of Christ, to numbering the five senses, and celebrating the five elements.

It's found in ancient temples and churches and seen on tombstones hundreds and even thousands of years old in Europe, North America, and as far away as Africa.

With many things in life—intention is everything.

I move to take my place at the top point of the star, and Melani shakes her head. "Wait until the circle is closed and the energy contained before you approach."

I stop, my body swaying with the effort to remain on my feet. I know that. I'm simply too tired to focus on the details.

When a circle of orange magic travels from each of the star's five points and encloses them, Melani nods. "All right, take your places."

Rounding the circle, I wait at the top point while the others get set. Quon Shen is to my left, then Melanippe, then Samuel to my far right, and finally, Ahren.

When Melani lowers herself to sit on her knees, we all do the same.

When she lays down and turns to place her head at the point of the star with her feet facing out toward the field, we do that too.

"Relax your body and set your mind free. You are a shaman, a Hunter-god, a healer of the realm. Expand your mind beyond the physical plane and reach out to the universe that surrounds us."

I draw a deep breath and make a concerted effort not to fall asleep and start snoring during this drill.

"There is dark, and there is light, and the balance must be maintained in order to flourish."

I sink heavily against the ground, the hypnotic tone of Melani's voice reaching into me from where she lays across the pentacle as well as from inside my mind.

It's not like when Nikon speaks into my mind. It's not so much a conversation inside my head as it's the energy of her words filtering through my cranium.

It's trippy, actually.

"Shamans are healers. Some human shamans heal the body and others heal the soul. We heal the natural world. We keep the balance and ensure the integrity of the physical and astral planes continue to thrive."

I try to connect with the astral world and recreate the sensation I had when Sloan helped me meditate into my vision to find Fionn.

I've never been much of an 'otherworldly woo-woo' girl, but after getting drawn into the past a few times by Fionn, I can't deny he had a gift.

It's bizarre to think he passed it down to me, but it does explain how I retreat to my inner sanctum. I've tried to teach Calum and Sloan to do it, and they can't get there without me taking them.

Breathing slowly in and out, I let my body drift.

Drift… drift…

I jolt awake as the energy of Ahren's eagle soars past me on the mystic plane. He brushes me with a feather touch of his wing, and I refocus on the training.

I'm good.

I'm awake.

"Allow your state to alter and become one with the ether. Send your essence across the green field and into the chamber of the ancient temple. Feel the energy of the ancient power."

Quon Shen whooshes by in a great cresting wave. His spirit form is a cool Chinese water dragon and is the embodiment of liquid and fluid motion.

"Before this monument was named Newgrange, before the ritual circle of Stonehenge was erected, and even before the construction of the Great Pyramids of Giza, this monument stood here. It is our past and our future."

That still blows my weary mind. This little-known monument, built on the green hills of Ireland in the bend of the River Boyne, has existed for over five thousand years. Cray-cray.

"Gain a sense of understanding for the boundary of the plane. Test the tension at the seam between realms. Feel the strain of what it takes to hold back the darkness of the Neitherlands."

I yawn. Stretching myself, I push into the darkness of the

tomb. I'm not sure I feel the strain, but I definitely feel the darkness. It seeps into me like a cold oil spill creeping underneath my skin.

Ew, not only is it cold, but it's cloying and invasive.

The burning of my shield awakens, and I stiffen.

I don't doubt that danger abounds. We're in an ancient tomb that acts as the portal rift between this world and the realm of banished baddies. Of course, my shield wants to warn me to proceed with caution.

The deeper I go into the dark space, the more my heart burns in my chest. Is this normal? Is it supposed to feel like someone is torching me with a flame-thrower from the inside?

I throw out my feelers, hoping to catch the energy of one of the others so I can buddy up in case I become the first shaman to burst into astral flames.

Fi? What's wrong? What's happening?

I don't know, buddy. It's some kind of side effect of the vision quest, but I don't like it.

Then stop. Wake up or get out. Stop whatever this is.

I'm with you. This sucks ass.

I try to withdraw and return to my physical form. I don't get anywhere. Fight and flight take hold in a rush, and since I can't take flight, I go with fight.

I start to scream, but a hand clutches over my mouth before I make a sound. I try to grasp at the hold, but I can't move my arms.

A second hand pinches my nose. The strength of my tormentor presses hard, and my lungs burn with the lack of oxygen.

Adrenaline fires in my veins as I panic, eyes wide.

My gaze locks onto the golden glare of a black wolf. Fury races through my veins like lit gasoline. I'm a living Molotov cocktail about to explode.

My vision narrows as the suffocation takes hold. Gone is the tomb and the world beyond. All I see are those two golden eyes filled with smug retribution.

Samuel-motherfucking-Wright.

Fighting with all I have, I will myself to breathe. To draw oxygen into my burning lungs. It doesn't help.

I scream, and the sound ricochets in my head.

Dark spots form and dissolve in my vision.

I can't open my mouth. I can't move.

Sound tunnels into my eardrums.

Darkness wins the battle.

I rise from the depths of unconsciousness long enough to recognize the snarling fury of one very pissed-off mythical grizzly. I attempt to open my eyes and calm him, but I've got nothing.

The good news is, I'm not dead.

The bad news is someone else might be soon.

CHAPTER THIRTEEN

The next time I wake up, I'm lying in a comfy bed with Sloan's arm draped protectively over my hip and the warmth of his breath gently brushing my cheek. Lying in his arms, I realize I'm totally St. Bernard drooling on his arm. Classy.

I draw a deep breath and roll back, wiping my slobber with my hand. After clearing my throat, I blink up at him and try to put the pieces together. I don't get far. My mind is heavy, and my head is pounding.

"What happened?"

"Ye overdid it, and we nearly lost ye to the darkness of the Neitherlands."

I wipe my hand on my shirt and take another beat, trying to access the memories floating around in the recesses of my mind.

When the vision of the assault comes back to me, I focus on that cold, golden stare. "Neitherlands my ass. That was one-hundy percent Samuel Wright. That fucktard suffocated me and enjoyed every moment of it."

Sloan frowns. "Not exactly. They told me ye got caught up by Mingin, his dark and dangerous granda. Melani said it was Samuel who pulled ye back from the brink and saved yer life."

I try to reconcile that with what I remember, and the two accounts don't mesh. "Not how I remember it."

"At this moment, I don't care. All I need is yer word that despite another brush with death, yer all right."

Giving his question the respect it deserves, I close my eyes and take inventory.

Wriggling my toes, I make sure my motor skills are still intact. Then I stretch and make sure my bones and muscles are working as they should. "I'm a little sore from a long day of battle and training, but I'll give myself a nine-point-two out of ten."

He looks relieved. "Good enough. Now, we've only got another hour or so before I need to be back at the stones and yer expected at Newgrange. Sadly, what happened doesn't excuse either of us from what we must do today."

I frown. "Do you think we can hold the seam shut with four out of five Hunter-gods? Like, say…if one of them gets struck by lightning and fried extra crispy? Asking for a friend."

Sloan brushes my hair away from my face and kisses my forehead. "No. The balance of the five elements isn't there without earth."

I sigh. "How do I look at that wolf dickhead and not want to kill him? Can I at least throat punch him?"

His amusement shakes the mattress. "I'm not sure that will enhance bonding in battle, but I'm sure ye'll figure something out."

I'm *not* sure, but I refuse to dwell on that. "Where's Bruin? Is he okay?"

"He's fine. He's gone for a toddle in the forest with Manx. The two of them have become the best of friends and enjoy running off into the woods together. They said they'd stay within earshot in case we need them."

I chuckle. "I don't even want to know what kind of trouble the two of them get up to when they're off on their own."

"Is us turning a blind eye wise or negligent?"

"I think wise. Parents aren't supposed to know everything their kids are doing. Man, if Da knew half the stupid stuff we did as kids, he'd smack our adult asses and lock us in our rooms for a year."

Sloan arches a brow. "We'll revisit that at a later date. I'd like to hear the tales of the ill-advised adventures of the children Cumhaill."

I grin. "If we only have an hour, we don't have nearly enough time to get into that."

"Agreed. I want to be able to savor the debacles of your life."

"Um...thank you?" More awake now, I sit up, and my curiosity grows. "Where are we? Why am I nestled in a Posture-pedic cloud of comfort instead of lying on an old air mattress over a hardwood floor?"

Sloan arches a brow. "Come. It's something yer gonna have to see to believe."

I chuckle and let him tug me onto my feet. The room we're in is bigger than my childhood bedroom but smaller than our shared master bedroom. It has lovely plank wood floors with butter-colored stucco walls and the bare necessities for furniture. There's a bed, a dresser with a mirror, and an upholstered chair by the window.

I frown at the view out the window.

Streaks of light are making it through a cluster of branches and leaves...but it's not like the house is near the tree. It's more like the house is *in* the tree.

Turning back to Sloan, I try to figure that out. "Are we in a luxury treehouse?"

"Just wait. It gets better." He's grinning like a fool as he opens the top drawer of the dresser and points at my clothes. "Get dressed. I'll wait fer ye outside."

"Why are my clothes in the dresser of a treehouse? Is this a dream? Am I dead?"

"No and no."

"Oxygen-deprived and locked in a coma?"

"No."

"On a drug-induced trip after my near-death darkness experience?"

"No, *a ghra*. Get dressed. It'll all become clear once ye come out and see. There are people out there so ye'll not want to be in yer underthings."

My mind is still spinning when he steps out and shuts the door. "People? What people? Who got invited to my treehouse hallucination?"

I yank my clothes out of the drawer and am pulled together in record time. Sitting in the club chair, I slide my shoes on and lace them up.

At home, I don't undo laces, but obviously, Sloan took these off me last night because my anal prince charming would never dream of toeing off shoes without unlacing them.

As I pull myself together, I try to figure out the mystery. The clothes in the dresser are the ones I brought in my go-bag, so I think we're still in Ireland, but honestly, with wayfarers and immortals, you never know.

When I get both shoes done up, I lean back in the chair and look out the window.

Bizarre. We are definitely in the canopy of a tree.

"Tarzan!" I jump out of the chair and cross the bedroom floor in a rush.

Sloan opens the door as I get there and leans in. "I'm sorry, what?"

"I was wondering who would be in this treehouse of my delu-sion. It's Tarzan, isn't it? And he's hunky and in a cheetah-skin loin cloth looking all buff and sexy."

"Nailed it," a male voice calls from a distance.

Sloan rolls his eyes. "Och, I hate to see what ye did just now."

I giggle, recognizing the voice of Dionysus. Easing past Sloan,

I step out into the hall and shake my head. "Seriously. What is happening?"

Sloan and I slept in the end room, and as I walk up the hall, there are two more furnished bedrooms on either side. A five-bedroom treehouse?

When I get to the main living room, Dionysus is standing at the end of the hall sporting a spotted loincloth, his brown curls hanging loose over his bare shoulders. I giggle. He's ripped and godly and everything I described.

"Did someone call for Tarzan? I love to roleplay." Stepping forward, he grabs me around the hips and pulls me to his chest. "Me, Tarzan. You, Jane."

I burst out laughing and push back. He lets me go without issue, and that's when I see Dillan recording this on his phone.

"Nice. Thanks, D."

"My pleasure. Seriously. I'm going to enjoy making posters of you and Tarzan here and plastering them everywhere."

Awesomesauce. I turn and take in the rest of the Cumhaill gang laughing in the spacious family room and kitchen combo.

"Okay, someone has to catch me up. What is going on? Where are we?"

Calum hikes his thumb over his shoulder to where Nikon is standing behind one of the couches. "It's all the Greek's doing."

"The Greeks plural," Emmet adds.

Nikon flashes me an unrepentant smile and points at Dionysus. "I may have mentioned that your family gets stacked floor to rafters when you stay with your grandparents. I wanted to do something nice for all of you so you don't have to sleep on the floor while you're busting your butts trying to save the world."

I stride over to the open door opposite the breakfast bar island and look outside. We're in the forested area that borders the open backyard of my grandparents' property.

We're opposite the grove and only about six hundred feet

from their cute Shire home with the floppy-hat thatched rooves with the tree coming out the top.

"You *poofed* us a magical house?"

Nikon shakes his head and points at Dionysus. "That's above my pay grade. I merely mentioned that it would be nice for you all to have beds."

"I am all for beds," Dionysus says. "What fun can you have on your grandparents' floor?"

I hold up my finger. "No one answers that. That was a rhetorical question and not a lead-in for filthy minds."

My brothers laugh, and I take another look outside. There's a long, wooden porch and ladders down to the ground below. "We're the next-gen Swiss Family Robinson."

Aiden nods. "Yeah, the Irish Family Cumhaill."

"Gran is good with this?"

Nikon nods. "I spoke with her first, of course. She told me where she wanted the guest house and is fully on board."

I hold up my hands and make the sign of my brain exploding. "Mind blown."

Drawing in a deep breath, I close the distance to hug Nikon. "You are a thoughtful man, and I heart you hard."

He winks. "Right back at you."

Next, I move to give my thanks to Dionysus. He waggles his brow and opens his arms. I give him his hug but ease back quickly to avoid extended contact with his loincloth. "This is incredibly generous of you. How did I ever get so lucky to call you my friend?"

He grins. "I believe you were being persecuted by a witch bitch goddess and I saved your beautiful ass."

"You absolutely did."

His gaze drifts, then he's not looking at me so much as around me.

I turn and look around. "Now what? What am I missing?"

He chucks my chin and holds my gaze so I'm facing forward.

Moving his hand along the outside of my head and down my body, he smiles. "You have a stunning aura. Women glow differently when they're loved right and treated properly. It's obvious you're blessed because your glow takes my breath away."

"Wow, that was slick." Dillan taps his thumbs against his phone. "I am abso stealing that, dude."

I laugh and give Dionysus my full attention. "Thank you. That was a lovely thing to say. You're a charmer."

"Yeah, yeah." Emmet strides past us. "Now, the only question that matters is whether or not you two stocked the fridge? I'm starving."

After a quick breakfast in our new digs, we leave Dionysus to work on his vine-swinging and head across the back lawn to the main house. We all want to check on Granda before our day starts and since he refused to stay at the clinic overnight, he's inside the house.

"Tad brought him home late last night," Calum says.

Sloan nods. "Yer Gran finally relented and agreed Lugh was well enough to come home. I think they both needed time in their climate to unwind after the events of the past few days."

"I bet."

"We didn't mention yer brush with darkness last night. Nikon brought ye to us, and we figured they had enough to deal with. The danger had passed, and we knew ye would be fine by morning, so we left it unsaid."

"Okay, good, but honestly, I'd like to understand more about Shamanism and how my astral self works. How did Samuel's or Mingin's attack affect my physical body? How is it that I can see the seam when I'm in that form but not normally? While I'm asking questions, why is the seam weakening? Are we patching it or fixing it?"

Dillan frowns. "No idea. You're going to hang with the Fantastic Four today. Maybe ask them."

"Yeah, if only I trusted them."

"Good point," Calum says.

"Well, Kev, Calum, and I can try to find some info while Aiden does the heir thing and Emmet does his fluffer thing."

"Buffer, you asshole," Emmet says. "I'm sick of your porn jokes. I'm enhancing the potency of the fertility spell not participating in a giant fae orgy."

"Buffer...fluffer...same diff." Dillan ducks, laughing as Emmet's fist swings through the air.

"No, it's not the same diff."

"It is when your efforts end in the skin-slapping dance of twenty toes."

"I don't think all fae have toes," Sloan adds.

"Not helping, Irish." Emmet scowls.

"No. That was a good point." Dillan dodges Emmet and zig-zags across the grassy yard. "How about horizontal hijinks? Screw. Bang. Bone. Ride. Score. Root. Shag. Insert the P into the V."

Aiden's laughing and shaking his head. "Face it, Em. Like it or not, you're the fae wingman tonight."

Calum pulls Kevin out of the way as the radius of the skirmish widens. "No worries, Fi. We'll help Dillan and see what we can learn."

Kevin nods. "We'll give you the CliffsNotes version later."

I laugh and jump out of the way as Emmet takes Dillan to the ground. "Awesome, thanks, guys. That would be a huge help."

I'm still laughing about Emmet being a fae fluffer when it hits me. "Hold on. Dionysus is the god of fertility and wine, and he's already here." I turn back to the trees and press my fingers under my tongue. "Yo, Tarzan, you busy tonight?"

He flashes right in front of me and grins. "Why? What have

you got in mind? Are your closed doors opening? Are you and Sir Serious ready to let loose?"

I laugh and wave that away. "Would you be interested in partaking in a fae fertility ritual to honor Ostara and keep Ireland green and reproductive?"

Dionysus arches a brow. "Will there be nakedness?"

"From what we understand, yes. Rumor is, the fae will come and partake in the spirit of the ritual. If we're right, there will be fornication in abandon."

"Then I am in. I'll bring the wine."

Aiden grins. "Awesome. The fertility part of the ritual will be after dark at Drombeg Circle."

"I'm looking forward to it."

I laugh at the glee in his eyes. "Glad to have you on the team, Dionysus. You rock."

Nikon, Bruin, and I arrive at the bend of the River Boyne below Newgrange a few minutes before ten in the morning. The other hunters have already assembled across the open, grassy plain. Melanippe is lying in the grass, soaking up the sun while Ahren and Quon Shen chat, and Samuel sits off by himself staring at the mound of the tomb in the distance.

"I hate that guy." I stretch out my shoulders.

"I hear ye, Red." Bruin plods along beside me, his massive paws flattening the grass as we walk. "Normally I wouldn't argue, but it did seem like he was genuinely bustin' his balls to pull ye back from the clutches."

"Maybe Mingin altered your perception during the attack?" Nikon asks. "Maybe he was able to make you see what he wanted you to see."

Bruin grunts. "It would be a great way to undermine the unity of yer quint."

I stare at the man and frown. "I'm not sold."

"Fair enough."

"Try not to let this become about him," Nikon says. "The reason you're here is bigger than both of you. There is a true and imminent danger and only a finite amount of time to pull yourselves together as a team."

My phone buzzes in my pocket and I smile at the shamrock on my screen as I accept the call. "Hello, Patty. How's the craic?"

"Tons o' craic this mornin'. Are ye in town, Red?"

"Yeah, there's been a development, but we're here. I would've come to check in, but I can't afford to lose the hours in the dragon lair time-suck at the moment."

"Oh? What kind of development?"

I give Patty the highlights of the past three days and flash a thumbs up to Ahren when he waves me in.

"Lugh's all right now?"

"Yeah. The elders are all still a little discombobulated, and Barghest disrupted their connection to their magic, but they're doing okay."

"Do ye think I'd be any help with the ritual at Drombeg?"

"I'm not completely sure what your magic affects, and I already enlisted Dionysus to help."

"Och, well, he's the slam dunk fer a fertility ritual, I suppose. Let me know if ye need me for anythin' else."

"Will do. Your support is always appreciated."

Quon Shen whistles and I nod, holding up a finger. "The Hunter-gods are waiting on me, so I have to go. If all goes well, I'll pop in tomorrow. Does that work?"

"Och, that's why I was callin'. Dartamont is agitated. He senses ye nearby and wants to see ye. He has the others good and riled up too."

I continue walking toward the group, so they see I'm coming. "He senses me?"

"Aye, it happens like that sometimes with dragonborn. They

can form a bond and get quite attached to their human, especially if they think there's something wrong. His worry is spreadin'. They need to see ye and the sooner, the better."

I think about my blue boy and his siblings. "Well, that goes both ways. I'm quite attached to them too and miss them terribly. Tell Dart I'll be there as soon as I can and not to upset his siblings. Tell him there's nothing wrong. I'm good, and I love him."

"All right, but don't wait long. A juvenile dragon is tough to parent at the best of times. Twenty-three is worse. If they don't get what they need soon, things won't end well."

I imagine a dragon tantrum is something to avoid at all costs —especially if it's a twenty-three-dragon tantrum all at once. "I'll come the first chance I get."

"Also, try not to get upset. That only makes things worse on this end."

"I'll try my best."

"That'll have to do. Safe home, Red. *Slan.*"

"Thanks. See you soon."

I end the call and take the last few steps to close the distance to the Fantastic Four. I chuckle to myself. It's going to be hard *not* thinking of them like that now.

Thanks, Dillan.

"Are you finished chatting with your boyfriend now? Can we get started?"

I meet the golden gaze of Samuel, and my insides boil with fury. He tried to kill me. There's no doubt in my mind it was him and not an illusion or deception. Now he has the balls to stand here chastising me?

Thunder rolls overhead and the clouds begin to gather. It would be so easy to call a lightning strike.

Maybe one little bolt aimed right...

"Fi?" Nikon's touch on my arm brings me back.

I shake out my hands and release the potential energy building above me.

Play nice. Seal the rift. Fry the wolf.

Looking forward to phase three in that plan I force a smile. "That wasn't my boyfriend on the phone. That was a dear friend who warned me that my dragon brood is ornery and if I don't get over to see them soon, there will be trouble on yet another front of my life."

"Dragon brood?" Quon Shen repeats.

"Yeah. I'm the honorary mother of twenty-three juvenile dragons. They know I'm in town and they're getting antsy about me not making time for them. The man on the phone, Patty, is their Man o' Green guardian. He called to warn me things are getting dicey at the lair."

Quon Shen barks a laugh. "A leprechaun called you to say your two dozen dragons are getting pissy?"

"Yeah, that's the gist of it. Welcome to my world."

CHAPTER FOURTEEN

"Before we begin the astral training, I think it would be best to clear the air," Melani says. "Last night, we nearly lost Fi, and that shouldn't have happened."

"No. It shouldn't," Nikon snaps from the sidelines. "She expressed to all of you that she was exhausted, and you negated the weight of that and put her in danger."

Melani sends him a scathing look but turns to speak to me directly. "The immortal interloper may not have any business being here, but he's not all wrong."

"I'm not at *all* wrong." Nikon strides forward with Bruin at his side. "You put Fi in a dangerous situation knowing she was burnt out from working to recover her papu. You are the leader of this merry band, and you opened her up to the attack."

Melani's gaze narrows. "Beware the toils of war."

He shakes his head. "Upon the conduct of each depends the fate of all."

"An army of sheep led by a lion is better than an army of lions led by a sheep."

"The strong do what they must, and the weak accept their fate."

As the two of them push up in each other's faces and switch to slinging their insults in their native tongue, I blink and look at Ahren and Quon Shen. "Do you feel like we were scrolling through Greek mottos on a Pinterest page?"

Ahren shakes his head. "It's more like we're voyeurs of the foreplay for very vigorous Greek hate sex."

I reassess my perspective and nod. "Yours is better."

I'm not sure if the two of them hear us or simply pick that moment to turn their attention back to us. Melani arches a brow and glares at me. "Please ask your escort to step back and allow us to begin our day. There is much to do, and I won't have him disrupting what is already a tenuous bond between us."

I grin at Nikon and speak privately to him across our mental channel. *You really liiiike her. You think she's sexxxy. You want to kiiiiss her. And get all schmexxxy.*

You're ridiculous, he says, his cheeks flushed, his chest rising and falling as he catches his breath.

It's amazing how often people say that to me—it doesn't mean I'm wrong.

After I was so nice to you. Rude.

I chuckle. *You know I love you, but your Amazon heartthrob isn't wrong. You're causing tension—steamy sexual tension—but still tension. Why don't you snap back to the treehouse and check on the others? I'll text when I'm wrapping up.*

I promised Sloan I would stay. I'll retreat to the river bend and stay out of sight. I'll be close should you need me.

If you get bored, feel free to leave, and I'll text you later.

Won't happen, but thanks.

When Nikon snaps out, I make a concerted effort not to glance toward the River Boyne. He's there, but Melani doesn't need to know that.

No distractions necessary.

"Okay, that was fun."

Melani arches an elegant brow. "I'm sorry your friend drew

me into an argument. What I was trying to say was that I was justified in pushing for excellence. Where I erred was in underestimating your sensitivity to the darkness and how someone could exploit that due to your inexperience."

Funny. This apology feels more like criticism and justification. Seriously?

"I'm sorry too. I followed blindly and ignored my instincts when I was exhausted and knew I was at a point of making mistakes. I should've stood my ground. My weakened state opened the door for this black dog dickwad to cut off my oxygen supply and almost kill me."

Samuel grunts and rolls his eyes. "Unbelievable. I was the one who saved you."

"Bullshit. I looked right into your piss-yellow eyes and saw the same smug superiority I see now. You tried to snuff me out, and we both know it. Still, I'm here. Like it or not, there's a job to do, and I don't run from a fight. Just know that I've got your number. You won't get another run at me. I'm ready for you now."

"Don't make me out to be the bad guy here, kid." Samuel prowls forward. "If I wanted to take you down, I'd come straight at you. Do you really think I was the one who attacked you?"

"Without a doubt. The dishonorable betrayer gene runs deep in your family. You must be so proud."

One thing I learned from the hours of battle training yesterday is Samuel has a tell. Right before he launches a physical attack, his lip twitches up in a crooked sneer.

When I see that twitch, I ready for the incoming force of what's been boiling to a head. Calling Birga to my hand, I activate my body armor and brace for impact.

Instead of evading the attack, I spin Birga in my hands and crack him across the jaw with the staff end of the spear. His head pivots on his spine.

The dazed look of indignance is gratifying.

The purple bolt of power that knocks me off my feet is charged to cause real damage, but thanks to my *Tough as Bark* protective layer, it doesn't.

"The two of you, stop this!" Melani snaps.

Samuel doesn't slow his roll, so I don't either.

As much as I want to skewer him, I haven't lost sight of the fact that we all need to be alive to fight the Mingin battle tonight.

A few bruises won't affect the mission, though.

Whether the others believe me or not, I looked into the darkness of this man's soul, and it wasn't his ancestor or the darkness of the other realm. It was a pompous dick wolf that has a secondary agenda.

It wouldn't surprise me if he were here to release Mingin and not reinforce his prison.

I dive to duck the next two bolts and crack him with Birga. It's a hard and fast strike into his ankle, and the *snap* of bone has him pitching to the side. He catches himself as he hits the ground and bellows.

I go in for a follow-up strike, and he rolls onto his back and hits me point-blank with another bolt.

The air whistles in my ears as it throws me back thirty feet. Hitting the ground, I press my palms to the dirt. *"Erupting Earth."*

The ground beneath us trembles as the earth breaks open. It catches Samuel in the crumbling of his footing. When only his head and one shoulder are still visible above ground, I release the earth spell and secure him.

"Hold Foe." I stand tall and flip my hair out of my face. *How do you like feeling immobilized and helpless you pompous piece of shit?*

The air builds with a vibration of power, and I fight to keep his magic contained within the earthen tomb I've trapped him in. He is exceptionally strong.

Too strong.

The crack of his spell blasting free of my entombment echoes in the air around us, and I cup my hands over my ears. Samuel rises out of the ground, and he's gone feral. Good.

The others need to see who he truly is. Looking at him there's no way to miss the darkness and violence.

There's a glowing spell wrapped around the ankle I broke, bracing his weight as he storms forward. "You'll pay for that, bitch."

He throws his hands forward and—

A shriek of fury rents the air and the field around us erupts. Slashes of red, green, and blue explode from the ground and drop from the air. They surround me, and Samuel is snatched in the jaws of a dragon and taken into a wide wyrm hole.

I shout for them to stop, but there's no stopping this.

Dart steps between me and where Samuel had been, and he's not the little version of my blue boy.

He's the supersized version.

Crappers. "Anyone know how to glamor a brood of dragons?"

"Casting is Samuel's skill," Quon Shen says, "but he's being eaten at the moment."

"I put up a temporal screen between the tourists at the tomb and us," Melani says. "Ahren, go make sure it's keeping this hidden."

While they take care of exposure risks, I rush to hug Dart. "I'm okay, baby boy. It's all right."

"Holy shit," Quon Shen laughs. "Did you seriously call that thing baby boy?"

"Fiona. Get control of them," Melani shouts.

Nikon is with me a moment later, and he's brought backup.

"Dillan, Scarlet took Samuel into that hole. Put your hood up and see if you and Calum can find him before she eats him. Nikon and Dionysus control Esym, Chezzo, and Green Guy before they get to that field and eat that flock of sheep. They're stress eaters. Watch out. They bite. I suggest the Hunter-gods stay back. The kids don't know you."

Thankfully, only Dart seems to have access to his full size so far. The rest of them aren't small, but they aren't massive either.

I tug on Dart's center horn and pull his nose down so I can rub his snout. "I'm good, baby. Thank you for coming to my rescue. I missed you so much."

His gentle purr vibrates in my chest.

"Such a sweet, sweet boy."

Patty appears with the Perry twins in tow, and the three of them frown at the scene.

"*Arragh!*" Patty snaps. "I was afraid somethin' like this was brewin'."

I lift my chin in welcome to the Perrys. "Welcome to hell, boys. Any help you can offer corralling these crazy kids is most appreciated."

The twins get right to work, and I'm glad Patty and the Dragon Queen have eager helpers. Druid dragon care is a lost art but with the hatching of a new generation, very necessary.

Minutes tick on. As time passes, we regain control and the frenzy of the moment dies down.

Dart shrinks from full dragon to the size of an elephant, and I breathe a deep sigh of relief. "Coming here was very brave, buddy, but also very dangerous. You have to be more careful."

He throws his head back, grunts, and lets out a stream of fire. Connecting with him, I get all kinds of images of him being sad and feeling abandoned.

Then, when he felt I was close by and didn't come, it hurt even more.

"Don't think like that. You know I love you. Bad men kidnapped Granda. I had to get him back."

He shakes his head, but when I focus on the images in my mind of Gran panicked about the kidnapping and how we found the elders drugged and locked in that mansion, he settles and forgives me.

I square off in front of him and hold his scaly jaw between my palms. "Patty told you I was grounded from seeing you, right? You know I love you and wanted to check on you after the fae realm."

He does, but it still hurt.

"I know, and I'm sorry. Let's not give your Dragon Queen mother any more reason to keep us apart, okay? We'll follow her rules and show her we can behave and not get into danger."

He seems to agree with that logic.

"All right. I have to spend some time with your brothers and sisters because they're upset too but don't worry, I'll talk to Patty about you coming and staying at Gran's and Granda's once this is over."

That wins me points, and we part on a high.

When everyone is calm and relatively well-behaved, I take some time to hug and snuggle with each one of my naughty kids. There are so many, and they're changing so rapidly, it's hard to keep them all straight, but when in doubt, I call the boys, buddy, and the girls, beautiful girl.

All-in, it takes about twenty minutes to put out this particular fire. "Patty? Any sign of the Scarlet tracking crew or the wizard she kidnapped?"

"Nothin' yet, but I'm sure it's fine. Scarlet's mischievous, but I don't think she'd resort to eating a human."

"She might play with him a bit though," a twin says.

I chuckle, imagining her tossing him up in the air and batting him down like a cat with her catch.

A better person would care if Samuel's life thread was snipped and maybe feel badly that the man became a chew toy for a dragon. I try to care but nope.

Zero fucks given.

I should be ashamed of that.

I'm *not*—but I should be.

Melani has been brooding from the sidelines but joins us once the dust has settled. "What a disaster." She glares out at the mulched field.

"Meh, it could've been worse."

Melani glares at me like I've lost my mind. "How, exactly could this be worse?"

"None of the wyverns are here. They're already pretty much water-bound. That means there are only sixteen and not twenty-three."

She shakes her head as if I missed the entire point. "I meant the general discord and the fact that Samuel is now missing."

"Oh, that."

"Yes, that."

"Honestly, I'm not sure losing Samuel is such a bad thing. He's not the man you think he is."

"I have known and been working with Samuel since last summer. We've known and been working with you for two days. Who do you think I put more faith in?"

Ouch. Whatevs. "Do the Hunter-gods have backup shamans? You know, like if someone gets hurt in baseball and gets put on the injured list, they call a player up."

Melani frowns. "No. Hunter-gods are nature-based shamans with god blood who can enter an altered state of consciousness. They need to be empowered and able to banish others to the Neitherlands and also must possess an animal spirit. It's very specific and very rare. They aren't just—"

"I'll do it."

I turn and meet Dionysus's grin. "Hey there. I was shamelessly eavesdropping and heard your qualifications. I'll pinch-hit. Fi said I'm part of the team. It's only a one-night gig, right? Will there be celebrating after?"

"You're already booked for the fertility ritual. What about the fae orgy?"

"Meh, I have orgies once a week. I haven't banished people to the Neitherlands in centuries. Sounds fun."

Melani shakes her head. "Who are you?"

He holds out his hand. "Dionysus, god of fertility, wine, and divine ecstasy. I'm an immortal god who transforms into a bull or a lion, who can banish people with the snap of my fingers, and have worked in an altered state of consciousness since the dawn of time."

"That's called inebriation," I say.

"Potato-tomato." He winks but then sobers. "Just kidding, scowly Amazon woman. Yes, I can join your fivesome—it wouldn't be my first—and yes, Fi, I can impart my fertility mojo through Emmet at the same time so the ritual is covered too. I'm a god. I can multitask."

"Amazeballs. Thanks, dude. First, I suppose we should try to locate Samuel...or at least his body."

Melani shakes her head. "Samuel has trained for this night for months. He deserves to see it through. Him surviving and rejoining us is the only outcome to wish for."

Yeah, that's debatable.

CHAPTER FIFTEEN

By noon, the Perry twins and I have the cow pasture put back together so it erases the evidence of our little dragon debacle. Then, the boys take the dragons back to the lair despite the beasties insisting they want to stay and play. It takes Patty and me a great deal longer to convince Dart to return home.

It's becoming clear my boy won't live under house arrest for much longer. The Dragon Queen will have to get over her control issues and loosen the reins.

"I have to figure out how to fit Dart more prominently into my life," I say to Nikon and Dionysus after the dust settles. "The wee monkey bonded with me and it upsets him when we're separated. I won't have that."

"Having a dragon living in downtown Toronto isn't an option," Nikon says.

"No, likely not."

"*Pfft.*" Dionysus waves his hand through the air. "Dartamont is almost old enough to glamor his presence. The biggest problem will be keeping him fed."

I groan. "I didn't even think of that."

Nikon gestures to where Melani and the others are milling

around. "You two better get back to the immediate problem. It doesn't look like Dillan and Calum are coming to the rescue anytime soon."

"Do you think your little red dragon ate him?"

I suck it up and turn on my heel. "I honestly have no idea but let's deal with one disaster at a time. Shall we?"

Dionysus chuckles and falls into step. "Is this what life with you is like all the time?"

"Pretty much, yep."

"Then I see why Nikky likes shadowing you so much. After millennia of the same old thing, the vortex of chaos that circles around you is quite entertaining."

"Well, I'm glad the sufferings of my life amuse you. If you hang around, I'm sure I'll end up as the universe's punching bag again very soon."

The two of us fall quiet as we reach the others. "Sorry about the disruption. As I mentioned earlier, there are fires to put out on more than one front in my life."

Quon Shen shrugs. "I don't know that there was anything you could've done to prevent that. I think you handled it quite well. How did you become their honorary mother?"

"That's a long story involving Baba Yaga, basilisk sperm, and a leprechaun with a Super-Soaker."

Dionysus snorts. "Oh! I can't wait to hear that one."

"Another time," Melani snaps.

I'm not keen on her tone. Dionysus is solid and a good guy here to help us. She shouldn't take her frustrations out on him. The only reason I don't make a stink about it is that he genuinely seems unaffected.

So, I let it go this once.

Today turned into a shit show. The last thing we need is to pick at one another. "There's too much happening now to let our guards down. When Samuel said I don't grasp the seriousness of what's happening, he was wrong. I grasp it fine and filed it in order of problems to address. At any time, though, I have three or four problems equally urgent and dire that I need to deal with. Don't mistake that for me not caring."

Melani frowns. "So where is the priority now?"

"Right here and right now, I'm all about Mingin and the seam to the Neitherlands. Let's do this."

The five of us lay around the points of the pentacle for the next few hours. My weakest event is surfing the astral plane, and I work hard to get up to speed. I learn a lot about how the "essence of self" works from Dionysus. Despite his crass bravado, he's quite a skilled warrior with a depth of reflection I hadn't imagined.

I think even Melani learns a few things from him—which she doesn't seem pleased with.

The Amazon truly isn't fond of Greeks.

Being in this state of consciousness with Melani, Ahren, Quon Shen, and Dionysus is incredibly different than what it felt like with Samuel last night.

There's no threat of possession. No burning darkness present. Nothing to make my skin crawl or the hair on the nape of my neck stand on end.

There's no way they can miss that…is there?

Doesn't matter.

I stated my opinion, and Melani shut me down. If she wants to believe him over me, that's her mistake. I know what I felt, and I know what I saw. As long as he stays gone, it won't matter anyway.

Dionysus is a great substitute. He is far more powerful and better-equipped.

When it's clear we have a handle on navigating the astral plane in general, Melani leads our spiritual selves into the tomb.

The experience of entering the main chamber of Newgrange is the same as last night and yet vastly different. The pervasive weight of darkness is still here, but it doesn't seep under my skin.

I allow my energy to flow freely and test the seam of the Neitherlands. The seal is straining, and that will only get worse as midnight draws nearer.

Still, we're ready, and we're strong. "Why now?" I ask as the five of us drift over the glowing tear between two worlds. "Why after all this time is the seam weakening to the point of letting dark souls out?"

Ahren flies close, and I'm pleased my visceral response to him is negligible. "We believe that while the veil between worlds thins during the hours of solstice and equinox, Mingin and his dark companions worked to weaken the seam. Over the passing centuries, he's caused enough damage to threaten a breach."

In my mind's eye, I picture prisoners scraping away at the stone of their cell with the handle of a plastic spoon. Yeah, that could take a while.

Once we've explored the tomb and the three round alcoves thoroughly, Melani leads us back to where our corporeal selves are lying in the sun in the grassy field by the River Boyne.

I reclaim my body and stretch under the warmth of the mid-afternoon sun. "I could go for a nap."

"You talked me into it, Red. Your bed or mine?"

I roll onto my side and face Dionysus. "You Greeks. Such flirts." Melani arches a brow and I auto-correct. "I meant him and Nikon. Not him and you. I get that you don't identify as a Greek."

"The Greeks were our enemy."

"That was a very long time ago."

"Not so long for an immortal. I remember the face of every Greek I slaughtered in the wars. They were passionate times."

Dionysus grins at Melani. "Passion can be consuming. That's not always a good thing."

She says something to him in their ancient tongue and a flash of something dangerous lights his eyes.

Funny, yesterday I thought Melani and I connected.

Today...not so much.

Is she annoyed that I'm a bit of a scramble to nail down? Or maybe that I spoke out against Samuel? I may have rocked the Hunter-gods boat by unleashing my mayhem on them, but I didn't mean to. Can she fault me for that? Is she annoyed I'm friends with the Greeks? If that's it, we have a real problem.

I love my friends.

She seems like the kind of woman who rules her emotions. I doubt she'll allow herself the distraction of letting personal bias and history get in the way of our task at hand.

As good as I am at reading guys, I'm not nearly as good when it comes to understanding women.

Still, she's the captain of this ship, and I respect her, so I'll mind my manners and see where things end up.

"All right. Close quarters melee," she says.

The five of us spar until dusk, then sit in a circle to discuss the various battle scenarios we might face.

"To reinforce the seam and keep the rift to the Neitherlands sealed is, of course, our primary objective," Ahren says. "If we do that, Mingin and the other dark souls stay where they're supposed to, and all is well."

"We need to consider what happens if he or another of the Neitherlands captives breaks free in a spirit form," Melani adds. "If that happens, we'll have to contain him to the tomb and battle him in our astral forms."

"What if he takes physical form?" I ask.

"If he manages to take physical form, we'll have to battle him until he's too tired to fight, then surround him to do the banishment spell," Quon Shen says.

"That's the palm-to-palm spell I saw in my vision? The one

where you stood around him and energy formed a triangle from your outstretched hands?"

"That spell almost killed us," Melani says. "It's designed for the power and balance of all five elements. When we faced Mingin, he had killed Jaladhi, so there were only three of us to perform the banishment."

"How does the spell work?"

"Fionn understood it best," she continues, "but at its most basic level, it's a one-way transportation spell. We cast a proximity spell sealing ourselves into a confined area with Mingin. Then we pushed him through the seam of the Neitherlands rift."

Quon Shen plucks a blade of grass in front of his crossed legs and holds it out for the breeze to snatch it away. "The trick is to ensure the seal remains unbroken and nothing and no one else breaks out in the process."

Melani nods. "Under no circumstances can we allow the proximity spell to come down before we're certain there aren't any escaped essences."

"And if there are?"

"We stay sealed in our bubble and repeat the process to send them back."

"So, we surround the rift, raise the proximity bubble, ensure no escapees make it through, or if they do, we send them straight back. Then, when the equinox is over, we strengthen the seam, check that we're alone in the bubble, and take down the spell."

Melani nods. "That's right."

"It sounds simple enough, but after walking this road a few times, let's play devil's advocate."

"All right. What do you see going wrong?"

I consider that before answering. "What if something happens and the proximity bubble doesn't hold? What if one of the dark-souled prisoners do escape into the physical plane?"

Melani frowns. "We can't let that happen."

"I realize that and am committed to it, but what happens if it does? Do we have a Plan B in place for the possibility?"

"Could you overwrite it?" Ahren asks Dionysus. "You're a god. I realize you're slumming it with the humans at the moment, but if things go sideways you could snap your fingers and fix it, couldn't you?"

Dionysus shrugs. "Yes and no. I have the innate ability to fix it but am not allowed to. That would be me altering the course of human lives, and as Fiona knows, the Fates—Clotho, Lachesis, and Atropos—take their domain very seriously. They don't let us swoop in and *deus ex machina* the shit out of things."

"If that's true, can you even be here?"

"Yes. I can act as one of you and work alongside you as any Hunter-god would. I simply can't stack the deck or impose my will upon what is supposed to happen. The Fates are very clear on what the members of the Pantheon can and can't do."

I chuckle. "Yes, they are. Since Atropos promised not to cut my thread before my time, I'd like to remain on her good side."

Quon Shen blinks at me. "Fi? Are you saying you've met and interacted with the Fates?"

"Yeah. Remember? I told you I spent time in ancient Greece last month."

Ahren's deep, bass laughter rumbles around us. "I think you buried the lead on that one, Cumhaill."

I shrug. "Like I keep saying. I've had more than a few challenging adventures."

My phone vibrates in my pocket, and I pull it out. "Oh, it's Calum. Hold on." Swiping green, I accept the call and raise the phone to my ear. "Hey, bro. How'd it go with tracking Scarlet and Samuel?"

"We found Scarlet but no sign of the Werelock. Whether she ate him or he got free, we don't know, and we don't speak dragon, so we can't find out."

"Is Patty there? He could find out."

"That's the other reason we're calling. Can you have Patty meet us and help us find our way home? After spending five hours meandering underground tunnels, we're really fucking lost."

"Are you wearing your Batcave pendants?"

"Yep. Don't leave home without them."

"Cool. I'll track your coordinates and send Patty to find you for a ride home."

"Thanks, Fi. Good luck tonight. We're rooting for you."

"Thanks. Love you. Safe home."

I end the call and open the app to access the tracking technology we all have within the workings of our Batcave pendants.

Calling up Dillan's and Calum's dots, I copy the coordinates and open a text to Patty. After sending them, I give him a quick call. "Hey. I sent you a text just now with Dillan's and Calum's location. They have Scarlet and need a pickup."

"Och, that is good news. I'll go straight away. Thanks a million, Red."

"My pleasure. And Patty, see if Scarlet can tell you what happened to Samuel. The boys said he's not there, but they don't know what that means exactly."

"Will do. I'll let ye know what I find out."

"Perfect. You rock. Talk soon."

I hang up and roll to the side to slide my phone back into my pocket. "My brothers found Scarlet, but there's no sign of Samuel. That could be good or not, depending on what happened to him down in those tunnels. Patty says he'll find out and let us know."

Melani nods. "We'll continue as if nothing has changed. Everyone step back for a couple of hours, get something to eat, clear your minds, then meet back here tonight, and we shall proceed as planned."

Did someone say eat? Music to my ears.

I finish washing up my dishes in the main house and set them in the drying rack beside the sink. "You okay, Gran? It's been a rough few days, and you look tired."

Gran looks up from sipping her tea and smiles. "Och, don't mind me, luv. I'm right as rain."

"And a terrible liar."

She chuckles but doesn't deny it.

"Have you had the tour of the guest house yet?" I think maybe a change of scenery might help. "Would you like to stretch your legs?"

She glances back toward the bedroom, and a worry line creases her brow. "I better not. Lugh might wake up and need me."

"Easily fixed." I bend and stroke a hand over Manx's velvety gray fur. "Puss, sweetie, will you curl up on the rug in Granda's room? If he wakes up and needs anything, let him know we're in the yard, then come get us."

Manx straightens, arches his back, and stretches out his massive fluffy paws. "Happy to help. Enjoy yer tour, Lara. I've got things covered here."

It seems odd to hear him call her by her first name, but he and Sloan grew up in this house knowing them as Lugh and Lara, not as Gran and Granda.

Wrapping her arm around my elbow, I lead her outside, and we stroll across the back lawn at a leisurely pace. "Granda's going to be fine. He's stubborn as a mule and almost as strong. He got taken by surprise with the kidnapping, but Wallace's healers say all the elders will make a full recovery."

She smiles at me and winks. "Och, the logical part of me knows that well enough. It's just...after almost losin' him last summer, I unconsciously pictured smooth sailin' from then on. Him gettin' kidnapped right out of our home and held at the mercy of those Barghest fiends has shaken me more than I can say."

"Perfectly natural." Turning my head toward the forest, then to the grove, I reach out with my gift and call the animals in the area. *Gran needs comforting little ones. Come show her some love.*

As we meander our way to where our new guest treehouse sits high in the canopy of our family forest, the creatures of the property begin to hop, scurry, shuffle, and glide in to see us.

Gran looks at the mass of little faces coming forward and looks at me. "What did you do?"

"Nothing but let them know you could use some comforting."

Gran reaches down, and a little gray mole climbs into her hand. Straightening, she kisses him and snuggles him against the fuzzy lining of her jacket.

"You give everyone around you endless amounts of love. You deserve the same TLC in return when you need it."

The two of us sit on the grass and Calum, Kevin, and Dillan step out onto the wooden porch.

"What's this?" Calum asks from above.

"Gran needs a love-in to set things right."

Dillan and Calum both step off the porch and free-fall toward the forest floor. As they near the ground, their descent slows, and they land as gently as if they dropped only a foot or two.

Kevin has to take the ladder down and laughs. "*Slow Descent* doesn't work for me."

"Yeah, it would be more like Break your Ankles," Calum teases.

"No doubt."

The three of them sit in a small circle, and the five of us spend a moment as a family. It's hard sometimes, during the chaos and stress, to remember to set aside time simply to be present with one another.

The fact that bunnies and foxes and squirrels and chipmunks are climbing into our laps as owls and hawks, and blue jays and woodpeckers land in the grass around us is magical icing on our cake.

"So, if you're the Snow White of Kerry," Calum says, "does that make us kids your seven dwarves? There's the five of us, plus Kev and Nikon."

"Seems about right." Dillan lifts his chin to gaze up to the porch above. "Get down here, Greek. You're part of this family now too."

Nikon flashes to the ground and pauses. "Are you sure? It seems like a real family moment."

Gran pats the ground beside her and smiles. "Like Dillan said. Yer family. Fi mentioned that ye miss yer Yaya. I realize yer a grown man, but maybe I can help fill that ache a little if ye like."

Nikon sits next to Gran and ducks his head a little as he nods. "That sounds nice."

We remain there, the six of us petting and snuggling with our woodland friends until Gran sits straighter and nods. "All right, now. I believe someone promised me a tour of yer treehouse."

Dillan helps Gran to her feet, and Nikon holds out his hand. "May I escort you up?"

Gran smiles. "That would be lovely, son. I'm not so old that I can't climb a ladder, but it would be unladylike in this dress."

We all chuckle.

"Then it's a good thing Greek's here," Dillan says. "I knew there had to be a reason we keep him around."

CHAPTER SIXTEEN

The two hours away from Newgrange does me good and by the time I return to meet up with the other shamans of the astral plane, I feel better about things. Night has fallen, and though it's no darker than any other night, somehow it feels like darkness is closing in.

Paranoia? Maybe.

In case it's foreshadowing and not foreboding, I send the heirs a rush of positive vibes.

Go forces of good and light. Bless the Emerald Isle. Make those fae randy and fertile. Impress Ostara with our commitment to nature.

"Where's Dionysus?" Melani looks around me as if he might be hiding behind my back.

I snap out of my mental musings and address the issue at hand. "He spent his free time at the Ostara ritual, boosting the spell of fertility and light."

When she frowns, I shake my head. "He'll be here. Like I keep saying. There are many problems to prioritize. All we can do is our best."

"What if that's not good enough?"

I stare out at the darkness and take a page out of Gran's book of faith in the universe. "It will be. Everything happens as it's supposed to in the end."

"Unless evil rears its head and screws the world and everything you love and believe in."

I blink.

"There's a real negative side to you, Amazon," Nikon says.

She frowns. "Why is it you're always here?"

"Because I'm watching Fi's back. Leaving her alone to face the world usually invites trouble. Be thankful I'm here to help."

She shakes her head. "*We* are her backup. We are the Hunter-god shamans."

"How well did that work out for her last night?"

By the look she flashes him, she didn't like that jibe. Honestly, though, he's not wrong.

"Regardless of what happened last night, this is where we are now." I hold up my hand, trying to break the tension. "Last night is over. Let's focus and get ready for tonight."

Ahren's eagle swoops down from overhead and lands in the grass beside us. When he straightens as a man, he nods hello. "The perimeter is secure. The employees are gone, and there's no one around for miles."

Melani nods. "Good. Let's move into the tomb."

As she strides off, Dionysus flashes in and joins the procession. "Did I miss anything chaotic or fun?"

I tromp through the grass and chuckle at his hopeful tone. "Nothing yet, but the night is young. How are things progressing at the ritual?"

"From what I can tell, it's going well. I gave Emmet a super power boost of sexual mojo. He'll be able to amp things up for the fae afterparty without difficulty."

I cast a sideways glance. "How much sexual mojo is in a super power boost?"

"A lot."

"Is that safe for him?"

"Sure. Why wouldn't it be?"

"No reason. I want to make sure he's able to conduct that much power without negative effect."

He's quiet for a moment, then frowns. "Would you consider being insatiably horny a negative effect? Just asking."

"It could be. Why? How horny are we talking?"

He shrugs. "How should I know? I'm the god of ecstasy and desire. I'm always horny. But I do see your point. I'm not sure how that much power will affect a human—especially one who's an empowered buffer."

"Is that something you should've maybe considered before now?"

He considers that but then shakes it off. "I'm sure it'll be fine."

I pull out my phone and text Dillan.

Distinct possibility Emmet might be a supercharged sex machine after the ritual. Dionysus power-boosted him.

Dayam. OK. Not sure how we'll get there.

Patty maybe?

K. On it.

I don't have time to get more into it than that. Nikon falls back at the tomb's entrance, and the five of us enter the passageway to make our way down to the chamber. I release my fae vision to see in the darkness and what comes back to me is cool.

I highly doubt ancient farmers with basic cutting and chopping tools constructed this stone tomb over five thousand years ago. There's too much magic in this monument for it not to have been built by the fae.

I wonder if Boann knows who and why?

My ancestral cousin is the namesake goddess of the river bordering this land. I bet she witnessed the building of the monument firsthand.

"You don't get the visceral effect of the place during an astral visit though, do you?" Ahren draws a deep breath. "It's different in person."

I agree. "Very different. Although it's not as damp and musty as I would've thought."

Quon Shen points up at the stone ceiling. "The guide mentioned that in the tour yesterday. He said it remains water-tight and dry despite being constructed so long ago."

"In a rainy place like Ireland, that's quite an accomplishment," Ahren says.

"True story," I say. "Almost magical."

"The coolest thing the guide said was that during the morning of the winter solstice, the sun angle is perfect to pass down this passage and light the main chamber. The farmers who built this place, without modern tools and over forty years of construction, positioned things so perfectly that once a year everything lines up."

"That's incredible," Ahren says.

"It makes me more convinced that Newgrange is fae built and not constructed by primitive farmers."

I'm still thinking about that when we exit the long corridor, and the interior opens to the main burial chamber of the tomb.

My fae sight allows me to see, but light would be better. *"Faery Fire."*

I toss a couple of balls of blue flame no bigger than lacrosse balls. They cling to the line of the stone ceiling and are bright enough so we're not working in darkness.

From our visits on the astral plane, I know the weakest point in the seal of the seam is a vertical tear in the veil near the far wall.

"So, where do you want us?" I ask.

Melani points at the open, sandy ground. "Samuel was supposed to conjure us a closed pentagram with the seam centered in the middle but without him here…"

Dionysus snaps his fingers, and one appears at our feet. "Annnnd, for my next trick…"

I chuckle. "Thanks, dude."

The circle is exactly as it was outside, so I head over to the symbol representing spirit. Dionysus takes his place across from me on earth. Quon Shen stands at water, Ahren at air, and Melani takes her place at fire.

When she settles, she looks at all of us and grins. "Whether you've been with us for months or days, all the training and planning comes down to what happens in the next couple of hours. We'll set up the proximity bubble, strengthen the seam, and hold things together until the danger is past."

"Just like we practiced," Ahren says.

"Just like we practiced," I repeat. I lower myself to lay in the sand in my position. "Good luck everyone."

Lying back, I stare up at the swirls chipped and chiseled in the stone above my head. I saw these designs in the pictures Sloan showed me yesterday morning…the pictures he spent all night decoding.

"When dark overtakes light and the day remains night, the gate between worlds will align, and the portal will open. Into this world will spill the legions of evil banished by the Hunter-gods."

"What's that now?" Quon Shen says.

"That's what those squiggles and swirls say."

"Dark and dramatic. How about we don't let that happen and foil whatever prophetic pessimist wrote it?"

"Sounds good to me." I draw a few deep, cleansing breaths and focus on doing that. *Are you ready for this, buddy?* I ask Bruin.

Whatever happens, I'm here, Red.

The shaman part of things, the meditation, and spiritual

projection aren't as difficult as I thought they would be when Quon Shen first explained things to me.

I release my consciousness into the astral plane and focus on the task at hand.

How are things looking? Bruin asks.

The seam is like a half-inch wide ribbon dangling in the air. It wavers in and out of focus, like focusing on something on a scorching day with waves of heat distorting your view. If I weren't looking for it, I'd miss it.

Is it worse than last night with the equinox upon us?

No. Better actually. Last night, a violently charged darkness hung in the air even with the seam closed. Tonight, that's not here.

Ye think that was Samuel?

I do. It may be an unpopular opinion, but I know what I felt, and I know what I saw. The seam was intact, and darkness overtook me on this side. To me, that means it was here with me.

Then, if everything happens as it's supposed to, I suppose Scarlet played her part in the goddess's plan by removing him from the group.

That's how I see it, yeah.

Quon Shen's water dragon brushes past me as he checks the perimeter of the main chamber. When he returns to his place on the pentacle star, he reclaims the image of his human form. "All clear. We're good to start with the proximity barrier."

Thankfully, this spell is primarily Melani's responsibility. She's done it before, and she's the expert. The other four of us are here to balance the power and represent the other elements.

The five of us stand in our positions around the seam and raise our palms toward one another. Melani speaks in tongues, and I zone out while she does her thing. *I wonder how the heirs are doing with the Ostara ritual?*

Bruin chuckles. *I wonder how randy Emmet will be afterward.*

I'm more than a little concerned about that and wish I could be there. *I should've texted Sloan and Aiden too, but I didn't want to disturb them.*

D can handle it. He has Calum and Kevin to help.

Yeah. I suppose you're right. I hope Em doesn't shift into a forest animal and make like the rabbits, you know?

Bruin's chuckle gains strength. *Now I kind of hope he does. Can you imagine that...litters of rabbits hopping around Drombeg with yer brother's green eyes and his knack for grand distraction.*

I don't want to think about that.

The *pop* of my ears reclaims my attention, and I refocus on what's happening inside the tomb. Melani has finished her spell, and I can see the shimmering body of the proximity bubble surrounding us.

She moves off her point to examine the seam.

When the skin on my back starts to tingle, my focus kicks in. "Be careful, Melani. I'm getting a warning from my shield. That's never a good sign."

She shakes her head and runs a finger against the hairline fractures in the fabric of the seam between realms. "Don't worry. Everything is exactly as I expected. It's all going according to plan."

My shield ramps up from a tingle to a full-blown warning and adrenaline starts pumping. "What are you doing? Whatever it is, it's dangerous. You need to stop and back away."

Fi? We have a problem out here, Nikon says across our private channel. *I have four trucks pulling into the parking lot outside, and I don't think they're late-night tourists.*

Are they Barghest?

Yeah...and I'm severely outmanned.

Damn it. Okay, come inside and hold the entrance as long as you can. I'm sending Bruin out to help.

I relay Nikon's conversation to my bear. When I feel him release, I turn to the other Hunter-gods. "We have a small army of incoming hostiles. Mingin's minions are here. Nikon and Bruin are holding the entrance, but they won't be able to hold it for the length of time we need until the equinox is over."

I look at Ahren and Quon Shen. They don't seem to know what we should do. Then we all look at Melani for our next move—

"What the hell?"

Melani has released the claw of her jungle cat from her nailbed and is slicing down the seam. The two sides of the rift are peeling back, and a smoky black essence is drifting through the split.

"Melani, stop!" Ahren says.

She grins and the sickening feeling of darkness and dread I felt last night returns. "Stop? Why would I do that? I told you it's all going exactly to plan."

The dark smoke seeping free from the seam swirls around inside the proximity bubble and starts to build. I don't think it has enough strength or volume to take human form, but at the rate it's gathering, I can't be sure.

Melani draws her hand through the ebony wisps as tendrils of evil and darkness coil around her. Creepy as it is, it looks almost intimate, like it's caressing her.

"Guys? Is she altered? Has the darkness corrupted her somehow?"

"I have no clue." Ahren looks stunned. "Whatever happened, we need to deal with it and send that toxic smoke back to oblivion."

Melani chuckles, using her claw to tear the seam wider. "You can't send them back. You don't know how. The only one with the kind of power and understanding is Samuel, and he's gone."

I think about earlier when I asked what we could do if there was a breach and we needed to send it back. She didn't answer, and I was too distracted to realize it.

I flip my gaze over to Dionysus. "Please tell me you can stop this."

He shakes his head. "Sorry, Red. My hands are tied. I can't interfere beyond acting as one of the Hunter-gods. I can't be my most magnificent here even though I'd love to kick her Amazonian ass."

Violence breaks out at the entrance to the cave. The rhythmic *tat-a-tat* of automatic gunfire makes me want to break through the bubble and go help my guys.

Sure, both Bruin and Nikon are kind of indestructible, but they can get hurt and bleed and die.

They don't *stay* dead, but I don't want them any kind of dead, even if it's temporary.

The cloying darkness and dread I suffered from last night are back, and I struggle to breathe.

Those creepy wisps have coalesced and are pulling together into a distorted version of a man—an inky, slightly greasy man, but a man all the same.

"Why would you do this?" I say. "You're one of the good guys. You've served your entire existence to hold back the darkness."

"What has it gotten me? You have no idea what an immortal life is like when you're alone. Mingin was my love, and Fionn forced him into the Neitherlands."

My poor little mental hamster is having such a hard time catching up. "You did too. I saw you working the spell and sending him back."

"It was the only way. Mingin knew Fionn would never stop hunting him and he'd never understand his stance. Exiling Mingin ripped my heart in two, but we knew we'd get a second chance with my immortality. He and I have been working at this damned seam every equinox for centuries. I *will* set him free."

"Then why go to all the trouble of gathering us and training us to stop it?"

She scowls. "That wasn't me. The fae universe activated the Hunter-god, and Samuel became obsessed with containing Mingin. He tracked each of us down and built this team, determined to unite the Hunter-gods of this generation to ensure the seam remains strong."

"Why didn't he come to get me?"

She grins. "He could only find us through the astral plane, and I wasn't about to volunteer that the fifth would be the heir of Fionn mac Cumhaill."

Of course.

He found me on the astral plane when I tried to connect with Fionn. "Then he found me."

She scowls. "I couldn't believe it. I had him convinced we'd have to go ahead with four. Then two days before the equinox he sensed you and was determined to have all five."

"Then why did he try to kill me?"

She chuckles, holding her hand out to the black grease splotch thing taking shape.

Yikes. Now that he's forming, it's obvious that the extra wisps are other essences of other prisoners enduring the same process.

This is bad.

"Samuel *didn't* try to kill you," Ahren says. "We told you. He saved you."

It clicks into place then. "Somehow you made me *think* it was him."

Melani's grin tells me I'm right. "I couldn't allow the four of you to gain the strength of a team that trusts one another, now, could I?"

What. A. Bitch.

And to think, I had a girl crush on her for a minute.

The *pop* of gunfire outside slows like popcorn nearing the end of its microwave time. Is that a good sign?

Bruin and Nikon fighting against four truckloads of necromancer mercenaries doesn't bode well for the good guys. Honestly, I can't worry about that.

I have my own cyclone of shit hitting.

I send Ahren and Quon Shen an imploring gaze. "Please, tell me one of you two knows how to put an end to this madness."

For the first time, Quon Shen looks wholly furious. "Samuel and Melani did all the heavy lifting."

"If this were my disaster," Dionysus says, "I would totes reclaim my physical self and focus on repairing the seam before armed madmen invade the tomb. I might also try to immobilize the Amazon. Tracking down the escaped fugitives can be a later thing but not if your body is dead. Not that I'm telling you what to do, but you know…if you asked me hypothetically what *I* would do in this situation, that's what I would say."

"You rock my socks, Tarzan." I look at the others, and they seem to agree. The three of us send our essences back to our bodies and revive at the same time Melani sits up and rolls to her feet.

Too bad.

I hoped she'd stay ghosty with her boyfriend and we *could* immobilize her. That would've been too easy. "Anyone know how to mend the seal?"

"I do."

My heart thumps in my chest at the sight of a filthy and tired-looking Samuel.

"Not dragon chow." Dionysus claps. "Yay for you, Werelock. Welcome back. Things have gotten interesting since you've been gone."

Samuel glares and points across the pentagram. "You're in my spot, Bacchus. I'm earth. Move to fire."

Dionysus doesn't seem to mind getting bossed into Melani's position. I suppose the chaos and mayhem of the moment from there will still entertain him.

Assuming his position at the earth point, Samuel widens his stance and raises his hands toward the torn seal leaking out darkness.

"No!" Melani screams, launching at him.

He shoots a bolt of magic and knocks her back while the

Mingin dementor and three half-formed smoky ink globs rush forward.

I swipe Birga through the air, but her marble speartip cuts straight through the smoke. Returning her, I take another tack. *"Whirlwind."*

I hurl a gust of wind at them, hoping they are solid enough to be blown back. Sort of. Not really.

The good news is that even though my spell doesn't work as I meant it to, it scatters the dark escapees that haven't gathered themselves into solid form and keeps them from materializing more fully.

"You two keep Melani off Samuel while he fixes this mess. I'll fight the oil spill and the tailpipe exhaust."

CHAPTER SEVENTEEN

The ancient tomb of Newgrange erupts into a close-quarters battle like something straight out of an action movie. The good news is, this is exactly the scenario we trained for the past two days.

The bad news is, Melani led those exercises and knows our strategy. She's fully prepared for the way we fight. Ahren and Quon Shen are doing their best, but she really is spectacular.

Now, that's a drawback.

Fighting evil black smoke and its gloopy grease friends isn't any easier. Every time I try to collect the smoke or force it back toward the rift in the seam, it dissolves into swirly mist and reforms somewhere else along the inner arc of the proximity bubble.

Thank the goddess that's still in place.

Pop—as the pressure in the room suddenly changes I realize what happened.

Crap on a cracker. "Totes my fault, boys. I was thinking how lucky we are the bubble was holding and *bam*—jinxed us. How you doing, Samuel?"

"Almost there."

Dionysus waves his arms in the air, and Melani turns to see what he'll do. He does nothing, but the distraction gives Quon Shen an opening. He lands a solid strike across Melani's jaw that spins her head on a pivot.

Ahren follows up with a roundhouse kick that sends her into the stone wall and staggering to the ground.

Mingin's entity pushes through my funnel of wind in a fury. I try to stop the retaliation but am ineffective.

"Repel Attack." I throw everything I have at him.

"Dissipate Mist."

He's still advancing.

"Gust of Wind."

There's no stopping it.

Inky black smoke swarms Quon Shen and Ahren and takes them to the ground.

"The smoke isn't the problem," Samuel shouts. "You're seeing the stain of evil on banished souls. It's a manifestation of darkness like oil pooling on water."

"What cleans an oil slick off a living thing?" I ask.

"Dawn dish soap," Dionysus offers. "Celebrating forty years helping save wildlife."

I blink. As crazy as that statement is, his goofy answer helps me. *"Purify."*

I focus on cleaning Quon Shen and Ahren of the impurities infiltrating their systems rather than defeating the dark ooze of Mingin and his soul-stain friends.

"It's working." Dionysus pumps a triumphant fist into the air. "Go, Fi! Do it! Do it! Do it!"

I double my efforts and focus on sanitizing them against the dark taint. Mingin wails and retreats.

His friends are quick to follow.

I rush in to check on my downed friends. Both of them are

unconscious but pumping a strong pulse against my fingers when I press to gauge it.

Mingin's temporary defeat unsettles the minions. The smoky wisps dissipate and rush toward the main corridor, retreating quickly.

"Wait, no! How do we contain them?" I rush forward, searching my mind for a way to contain smoke.

A blast of evergreen scented air rushes past me, and I turn to see what has my bear in such a hasty retreat.

"Incoming!" Nikon shouts, racing down the corridor toward us.

Gunfire cracks into the stone wall by my head. I duck as shrapnel explodes, hitting me in a dusty spray of sharp chunks.

Nikon catches my arm and yanks me along in his wake. "Time to go, people!"

Bruin takes form at the entrance of the chamber and hunches, ready for the insurgence.

Samuel shifts his focus from the seam and casts a spell toward the long passageway. A burst of light explodes from his palm and patches itself over the exit.

We're sealed in.

"How secure is that spell?" I ask.

"It'll take them hours to break through," Samuel says. "I'll stay and ensure the seam holds. You take Quon Shen and Ahren to a healer and Melanippe somewhere secure. I'll need to interrogate her."

"Interrogate her?" Nikon scans the scene and frowns, looking confused. "What did I miss?"

"Melanippe of Scythia is off the list, Greek. Hard swipe left." I work with Dionysus to shift Ahren and Quon Shen close enough together to portal out of here.

When we finish, I straighten and point at the dazed Amazon glaring at us and holding her head. "Meet the dark lover of

Mingin. She double-crossed us to jailbreak her dark daddy out of the big house."

Nikon frowns. "That's disappointing."

"Isn't it? Apparently, being alone for a lifetime drove her to it."

He rolls his eyes. "Bullshit. I got bored, sad, and lonely, but I never went Anakin Skywalker."

"Hells no, you didn't." I hold out my fist for a bump. "Great reference, by the way. Proud of you."

He grins. "I thought so. I'm learning the ways of the Cumhaill force."

"It's strong in you."

He chuckles. "Okay, so what's the plan now?"

"You take our traitor back to the detainment chamber at the Acropolis for questioning. I'll call Garnet and give him the deets."

"Where will you be?"

"If Dionysus is game, we'll take Quon Shen and Ahren to Wallace's clinic, then go to Drombeg to see if the ritual is over. He can oversee the orgy with the fae and honor the fertility season, and maybe I can steal Da and the heirs away to deal with the escaped dark forces."

Dionysus brightens. "Fun. I get to battle darkness *and* lead the ritual fertility orgy. Hanging with you is awesomeballs, Fi."

I laugh at the mash-up of my vernacular but give him points for effort. "Nikon, when you finish leaving Melanippe the Duplicitous at the Batcave, double back here and guard Samuel until the equinox passes. Text us if there's an issue and we'll bounce back. Does that work?"

"What if the Barghest portal in here?" Nikon asks.

Samuel shakes his head. "Don't worry about that. I spelled entry restriction against anyone wishing to do me or our security measures harm. If they're here to reopen the seam, they won't get in. If they're here to aid Mingin, they won't get in. You'll have no problem."

"That would've been handy an hour ago," I say.

Samuel sends me a tired scowl. "It would've been in place if a juvenile dragon hadn't attacked me and dragged me into the bowels of the earth."

I wince. "I'd like to say Scarlet is sorry for her behavior, but in all honesty, I'm quite sure she's not."

Samuel shrugs. "Forget it. This is where we are now. Get them medical care, gather your team, and return as soon as you can. We need to track the souls that escaped, and their trails will dissipate quickly after the power of the equinox is over."

Nikon nods and flashes out with Melanippe.

Before we leave, I step over to Samuel and fall on my sword. "I'm sorry. Melani manipulated me into thinking you tried to suffocate me, but I wasn't your biggest fan before that either. When I'm wrong, I say I'm wrong. I put my trust in the wrong Hunter-god."

Samuel dips his chin. "I appreciate that, and, in truth, Melani said some things that prejudiced me against you as well. I am not without fault in this."

I extend my hand, and he accepts the gesture. "You saved our asses tonight, dude. Thanks. I guess you turned out to be Mr. Wright, after all."

He arches his one brow, and the tribal tattoo around his eye distorts. "The dark souls of Mingin and countless others have escaped. Now is not the time to congratulate ourselves."

"One problem at a time. Right now, I'm thankful it's four or five dark entities and not the entire Neitherlands. Let's take that as a win."

Dionysus flashes us first to Wallace's clinic to drop off Quon Shen and Ahren, then to Drombeg to gather the troops. I'm half-expecting to burn my retinas when we interrupt an adult lifestyle, free-love event, but thankfully, I find Sloan, Eric, Jarrod, and Ciara cleaning up the circle.

"Hey, there." I jog toward the altar stone. Sloan and Eric are releasing the wildlife from their participation in the ritual and setting them on the ground to continue their night in the wild. "How'd things go here?"

Sloan turns with a smile, and his expression falters. "Dammit, what happened?"

"More importantly," Dionysus says, "where is the promised fae afterparty? I am now in charge of the festivities, and I take my duties very seriously."

Sloan points toward the forest bordering the stones. "The elves went that way, the sprites and faeries that way, the nymphs, brownies, and dwarves that way."

"Ooo, decisions, decisions. I think I'll start with elves." Dionysus grins and jogs off to join the celebration. "Don't wait up."

Sloan scrubs a hand over his face and blinks at me. "Ye've gathered the craziest bunch of friends. Ye know that, right?"

I laugh. "True story."

He turns his back on his work with the altar and grips my arms. "Now. Tell me. What has ye lookin' like ye might fertilize the flowerbed again?"

I give him the extremely short version of how the evening took a sideways tilt and look around. "I need to find out what escaped dark souls means and help Samuel track them down. Where are Da, Aiden, and Emmet?"

"Tad and yer father took the young ones home to their parents. I took Aiden and Emmet home to the treehouse straight after the closing circle. Dillan said ye believe Em might be altered by Dionysus's infusion of power and needed to be locked down?"

"Yeah. I've been freaking out about that. Thank you for getting him back and behind locked doors."

"Not an issue." He takes a laurel of flowers from under one of the nests and sets it on my head. "There now, yer a vision of spring vitality."

I chuff. "I'm sure. So, if the ritual is over and Dionysus is here to represent, are we good to gather the heirs and go back to Newgrange?"

"I suppose so, what do ye—Oh, shite. How'd he get back here?"

"Who?" I turn to follow his gaze across the radius of the circle and see the problem immediately.

Emmet is back, he's randy, and he's wrapped himself around Ciara. With one hand buried in her hair and the other splayed against the green velvet of her ceremonial robe, he's crushing her against him.

It might have taken Ciara by surprise, but she doesn't seem the least bit resistant to my brother staking his claim.

"Okay, wow, she looks as wild as him."

"Yer not wrong." Sloan sets down the nest in his hand, and we move to intercept. "She stood as the female embodiment of the fertility spell he amplified. They must've formed a connection."

"Crappers." I take off at a run. Even though Em seems wholly distracted in his exploration of Ciara's tonsils, the moment I get close, they flash out. My footing falters, and I turn and stare at empty air. "What the hell happened? Can Ciara portal?"

"No." Sloan looks equally stunned.

"Neither can Emmet, so how did they *poof* out of here?"

Sloan frowns. "Emmet's a buffer, and he did have a dip in the river of fae prana. Maybe he amplified more than Dionysus's sexual mojo."

I close my eyes against the throbbing of my pulse pounding in my skull. "So my brother is not only on an aphrodisiac high, but he also has the powers of the God of Drunk and Disorderly?"

Sloan rubs a hand over his jaw and sighs. "That's my take on it, yes."

"Well, that's not good. Emmet has impulse control issues on a normal day. Can you track him?"

"Track him how?"

"I don't know…like, follow his energy stream or something?"

Sloan screws up his face. "This isn't *Star Trek*. I'm not wired like that."

I dig my fingers into my hair and scan the empty stone circle. "What can we do?"

"Aside from sending Nikon to check our place in Toronto and me portaling into Ciara's room, not much."

There's a deep rumble of amusement inside my head as Bruin weighs in on this. *At least there won't be fuzzy woodland animals with green eyes. Ye didn't seem keen on that idea.*

"I'm not. I'm not keen on any kind of god-induced fertility when it comes to my brother." I pull out my phone and text Nikon.

While you're in TO. Can you pop into our place and see if Emmet is there sexing Ciara? He has Dionysus's ability to portal as well as his need to copulate. FML.

LOL. Just another day in the life of you, my friend.

Har-har. I wish you were wrong.

I draw a deep breath. "Okay, there's nothing to do about them right now. We need to gather bodies to help round up the escapees from the Neitherlands."

Sloan nods. "All right. We might as well bring Jarrod and Eric with us now."

"Good point. Okay, let's grab them and *poof* back to the treehouse for a team meeting."

Sloan chuckles. "I never had a treehouse before. This is kind of fun."

I roll my eyes. "Of all the adjectives I can think of to describe the night I'm having—fun isn't one of them.

Sloan *poofs* Jarrod, Eric, and me to the living room of the treehouse and startles Calum, Kevin, and Dillan. "Hey, baby girl," Calum says. "Why do you look so wound up?"

"Because the night is kicking my ass and there's nothing to be done about it." I head straight for the bar and flip a tumbler up for an offering. "I love that Dionysus built this place for us. We're as well-stocked as Shenanigans. Anyone want to chug alcohol with me for a very quick drink?"

There's a resounding chorus of: "Yes." "Hells, yeah." "Fuck, yes."

I grab the Redbreast Whiskey for myself and pour a dram. Tipping my tumbler back, I let the burn of liquid sedation take hold and savor the flavor. Rinse and repeat.

When I've lingered long enough to take a beat, I open my eyes and get back to it. "So, here's where we are..."

When I finish my account, Dillan frowns and jogs back to the bedrooms. "You're right. He's gone."

I take another sip of whiskey and swallow. "I know I'm right. We saw him and Ciara going to town five minutes ago at Drombeg before they flashed out to destinations unknown."

"Knowing Emmet, it's somewhere tropical with an open bar," Dillan says.

"What about the Bro Code?" Calum says. "Maybe he won't—"

Sloan and I both burst out laughing. "Oh, the Bro Code won't stop that train from pulling into the station," I say. "Consider Emmet and Ciara naked and indisposed until however long it takes for the mating mojo to wear off and burn out of their systems."

"Which, knowing Dionysus, might be weeks."

"Maybe they're at the house, and Nikon will find them," Sloan offers.

"Who's good at scrying?" Calum looks at Eric and Jarrod.

"Ciara." Jarrod bites back a smile. "Sorry. She's the one we go to."

Sloan waves that away. "All right. Sexual indiscretions must take the back seat fer now. We need to figure out what to do about the darkness, Mingin, and Barghest. How are they involved with Melanippe?"

I shrug, checking the time. "Samuel is guarding the seal until 1:00 a.m. Then he'll want to begin tracking the escaped souls. When we left Newgrange, Barghest was swarming the tomb. I think we should go back, secure Samuel and his efforts, and maybe we can learn something from the men there."

Sloan chuckles. "Ye mean yer feelin' powerless and are brewin' to start a fight."

I consider the hostility cycling inside me and can't deny I want to crack someone in the face. "Nut-punching someone does have its appeal. I won't deny that."

Dillan stands and grabs his cloak off the back of the couch. "Finally. Something for us to do."

Calum doesn't look quite as joyous for an outing, but he doesn't hesitate. "I really am sorry our babysitting stint ended in such a clusterfuck, guys."

I wave that away. "Not your fault. It is what it is."

He finishes his drink and kisses Kevin before jumping to his feet. "I guess we take our frustrations out on the evil of the world."

"Kev? Can you text Da and Aiden on the family channel and have Tad take them to Newgrange?"

"On it. Be careful, guys."

"Always." I finish my drink and extend my hand toward Sloan. "Manx, you coming, buddy?"

"If yer askin', I am." Sloan's lynx companion jumps off the

couch and stands on his back paws, reaching up my chest to my shoulders.

When my arms close around him, I kiss the black tuft of his ear. "Next stop. Newgrange tomb, please."

Sloan makes sure he has contact with all of us and the energy of his wayfarer gift tingles over my skin. "Yes, ma'am."

CHAPTER EIGHTEEN

Since Sloan has never been inside the Newgrange tomb, he *poofs* everyone to the area behind the mound of the monument. From there we can assess the situation without engaging the Black Dog assholes before we're ready.

"Dayam...they stink," Dillan says. "Do they realize they smell like a festering landfill on a July afternoon?"

"Add a putrid corpse buried under the heap of garbage, and I think you've got it," Calum adds.

Sloan crouches beside me after checking things out. "That's the price they pay for embracing dark magic as their source. They chose this."

I telescope my head a little higher but can't see much in the limited moonlight. We can, however, hear them and smell them.

"Life is about choices." I give up trying to see anything and bend back down. "You can worship the goddess of nature and all things good, and work for your powers *or* take the easy and powerful dark path, and smell like a dead animal trapped in a sweaty gym bag the rest of your life."

Calum chuckles. "It seems like a no-brainer when you put it like that."

"Right?"

Sloan chuckles and points at my pocket. "Text Nikon and tell him we're back here. It's almost one a.m. Samuel should be finishing guarding the seam."

I do as I'm instructed and send Tad an update of where we are as well.

The gentle flutter in my chest signals my bear getting restless. *Red, do ye mind if I stretch my legs and have a look around while we wait on Da and Aiden?*

"Sure, buddy. Have at it." I release Bruin from his resting place and smile as the air picks up around us in a gentle breeze. "Stay out of trouble."

He chuckles in the wind. *What fun is that?*

"Bruin's going to check things out," I say.

Dillan returns from his intel gathering. He's in full druid ranger mode, and it still amazes me how stealthy he is when he's doing his cloak and shadows thing.

He tips back the hood of his enchanted cloak so we can see him in the darkness of night. "Barghest soldiers are swarming in and out of the entrance like angry ants defending their colony. Whatever Samuel did to keep them out has them in a tizzy."

"Good. Them off-balance and freaking out is a good sign. Good for us, anyway."

Sloan glances at his watch again. "Their time to access the seam is about to run out."

"So, what's our plan?" Eric asks.

Tad *poofs* in with Da and Aiden and the three of them crouch and join us in the shadows.

"Welcome to the horror of our night." I gesture toward the tomb. "Melanippe was a sleeper agent and opened the seam. Dark-souled baddies seeped out as evil inky smoke. Ahren and Quon Shen were nearly killed and remain unconscious. How was your night?"

Da frowns. "Better than that. Why are we hunkered down at

the back of the tomb?"

"Barghest came to help Melanippe with the jailbreak, but Samuel locked them out. They've been trying to access the tomb for the past hour."

Da checks his watch. "The hour of the equinox is long over."

"Yeah, but Samuel wanted the seam guarded for an hour after, just in case."

"And Barghest? Why are they still here?"

"My guess is either they think Melanippe and the black meanies are still inside or they brought a seam ripper and want to let out more."

The rumble of truck engines starting has us frowning. Dillan pulls his hood on and jogs off around the gentle arc of the tomb's wall toward the front.

Da frowns and points for us to follow. "Divvy up and rush the entrance from both sides and over the top."

Calum and I choose the "over the top" option.

We climb the wall, pull ourselves up onto the grassy mound above, and make our way over the gentle arch of the grass growing on the top of the tomb.

From our perch, we watch the red tail lights of the Barghest trucks pull off the property and drive away.

"Barghest is bugging out," Calum says. "I guess they figured out the Amazon and the black meanies are gone."

"Dillan will be so disappointed."

"Yeah. He'll be pissed."

The two of us jog over the mound's crest and descend toward the entrance of the tomb. When we jump down from the lip of the overhang, we join the others.

"It seems we have the place to ourselves," Da says.

"Stupid Black Dog cowards," Dillan snaps. "Things were about to get interesting."

I text Nikon and tell him the coast is clear. A moment later, he and Samuel exit the tomb.

"The dark half of the year has officially ended," Samuel says. "Now to the business of tracking the escaped souls and sending them back where they belong."

I nod. "How do we do that? We figured you're the man with the answers, so you would know."

Samuel lists to the side and Aiden catches him under the arm as he staggers.

"Okay, sit for a sec before we continue. You probably used a lot of juice mending the rift between worlds."

"That was after playing the part of a chew toy for a naughty dragon this afternoon," Nikon adds.

Aiden angles Samuel to sit on one of the Neolithic boulders in front of the entrance. He waves away the concerned looks and shakes his head. "Just a moment of dizziness. I'm fine."

Da studies him and accepts his answer. "So, tracking the escaped darkness."

Samuel draws a deep breath. "They will be undetectable until they claim a host body to possess."

"Possession?"

Samuel looks at me and frowns. "Yes. What were you expecting?"

"I don't know...maybe them manifesting bodies?"

He shakes his head. "No. They are no longer people. They are dark spirits. Their goal will be to merge with a living being. Once that happens, we bring them back here, break their claim on their host, and banish them back to the Neitherlands."

"Easy-peasy," Dillan says, sarcasm thick in his tone.

"How do we break their hold on their hosts?" I ask. "Is this like an Emily Rose-slash-Linda Blair exorcism kinda thing or a Sam and Dean Winchester Latin banishment kinda thing?"

"Once we can get them back here it's a straightforward banishment," Samuel says. "Without Melanippe as our fifth, things will be more difficult, but with the power of Newgrange, we'll be able to return the exiled souls to where they belong."

"I get that it's old," Eric says, "but what's so special about Newgrange? The seam to purgatory is here. We have to banish the darkness here. I always considered this a mound of earth and stone outside of Dublin."

Samuel frowns. "There's a lot more to the power behind the lands of Brú na Bóinne. On this site and inside the tomb dwells the power of one of the divine triads."

"Do tell," Dillan says. "Triad of who, warwolf?"

Samuel growls at my brother before gesturing to the tomb and the land beyond. "Archeologists say local farmers built this tomb over three generations, but in truth, the Tuatha De Danann built it as a burial place for the chief god of the Irish, Dagda Mór. It's no coincidence it's found cradled in the bend of the River Boyne."

"How so?" Da asks.

"The River Boyne is considered the sacred river personified as the mother goddess, Boann."

I nod. "That's one hundy percent true."

"Dagda Mór," Calum repeats. "Isn't Boann the mother of one of Dagda's sons?"

"Yeah. Oenghus," I say. "Mythology says Dagda had an affair with Boann and sent her husband off on a journey. While he was gone, Dagda made the sun stand still for nine months to hide the term of her pregnancy. Oenghus was born in what seemed like a day, and her husband returned unaware."

"That's not precisely how it happened," a melodic female voice says.

We turn to watch the approach of a goddess striding forward from the darkness. Her hair is dark under the moonlit sky and flows like the gossamer fabric of her dress, in long, fluttering waves on the breeze.

"Myths carry some truth but bend reality as well. In the end, the result is the same. I bore Dagda a son, Oenghus, and he and his father are buried here in the tomb. Yer right about that much."

I straighten. "Sorry. I meant no offense."

She waves that away. "None taken. Merry meet, cousin. It's grand to have ye back on my river."

"I'm glad to be back, although I wish it were under better circumstances."

Her gaze drifts to the tomb behind us. "Yer talkin' about the dark energy I sense, are ye? Yer aware of what happened here then?"

I nod. "A woman split the seam to the Neitherlands and allowed half a dozen dark souls free before Samuel was able to repair the seal."

I gesture over to Samuel. It's a good thing he's still sitting on that boulder because he looks shell-shocked and faint.

"Well done, Samuel," she says. "We all owe ye a debt. If the seam to purgatory remained open, the damage to this world could've been much worse."

Every trace of Samuel's cocky arrogance is gone. Humility is a good look for him. His mouth opens...then closes...then opens again.

"I mentioned Boann is my cousin, didn't I?"

"Not solely yer cousin, *a ghra.*" Sloan tilts his head toward the others. "Perhaps ye should do a round of introductions."

"Right. Sorry. Boann, goddess of the sacred River Boyne, these are your other cousins, my da, Niall, and my brothers, Aiden, Calum, and Dillan."

She grins and dips her chin. "It's grand to meet ye. Truly. I'm blessed to have such brave and handsome kin workin' to keep the balance."

Da drops his gaze. "It's a pleasure to make yer acquaintance as well. We're sorry the duplicity of one woman affected yer lands."

She casts a glance toward the entrance of the tomb and frowns. "Sadly, that's the way of things at times."

"However, if Samuel can untie his tongue, he was about to explain how we track the dark souls and make things right again." I wave my hand in front of Samuel's face. "Hellooo, Samuel. Anybody home?"

Eventually, Samuel snaps out of his haze and focuses on what we need to do to turn around this shit show and right the wrongs of the night.

"We don't know the identities of the banished souls that escaped with Mingin, but they will carry the darkness of the Neitherlands on top of the innate darkness that got them exiled. People notice when their husband or their neighbor becomes a violent, soulless nightmare."

I snort. "You'd think."

Dillan looks at me and grins. "It sounds like something you'd notice. Honey, did you rip the head off the dog?"

Da rolls his eyes. "Is there a way to track that darkness before the dog gets sacrificed? Maybe something like Fi's fae vision that assesses levels of nastiness."

Samuel glances my way. "You never mentioned that as one of your abilities."

I shrug. "Yeah no. Honestly, I didn't share much with you. At the time, I was picking up all your dark and dirty. No offense but you were creeping me out."

"That wasn't me. That was Melanippe manipulating things, and you know it."

"So we found out." I release my fae vision, and he stiffens. "Yeah, I know. They're freaky-deaky, eh? But hey, they were a gift from Mother Nature, so I smile and remain grateful."

Tad chuckles. "No regifting those beauties."

"Mother Nature? Like, *the* mother goddess?"

"Yeah. She gifted me these when we secured the origin Source of fae prana."

Samuel shakes his head. "Who the fuck are you?"

191

Da's brow arches. "Careful. While I understand the sentiment and recognize you've had a trying night, that is my daughter yer talkin' to."

Samuel scrubs a hand over the tribal tattoo encircling his eye. "Sorry, sir. You're right. Let's get back to the situation at hand. "Yes, I can spell objects to seek out the darkness. How many entities do we think escaped?"

Everyone looks at me. I replay the night in my head and frown. "Four plus Mingin? Maybe five."

Samuel reaches down to pick up a stone off the ground and holds it in the palm of his hand for us to see. "Help me find seven smooth stones like this and I'll get us started."

The group breaks up and looks around.

Within a few minutes, Samuel has what he asked for. Seven smooth, round stones are set on one of the large kerbstones surrounding the tomb. While he works on that, I glance around, looking for Sloan.

He's off to the side of things chatting with Boann.

When I join them, they sober and Sloan wipes a hand over his mouth to hide his smile.

"Something funny?"

Sloan shakes his head. "*Och*, no. Boann noticed our bands and was askin' if we got married since she saw us last September."

I lift my hand and smile at my Claddagh. "No. Nothing as binding as that yet. I'm giving Sloan time to realize he's in love with a mayhem magnet. He needs a chance to change his mind and run for it."

Sloan clucks his tongue and holds out his hand to pull me to his side. "Not happenin'. Yer not gettin' rid of me that easily."

That still doesn't explain why they were laughing.

I decide not to pursue it. There's enough on our plates for one night. Besides, I'm tired and cranky, and I think my exposure to the darkness has made me a little hostile...or maybe a lot hostile.

Probably not the best time to question my guy and my goddess cousin on a private conversation.

"Everything all right, luv?" Sloan studies me.

"Sure. Just tired. If you'll excuse me, I'm going to check on Samuel and his magic stones."

Da opens his arm, and I slide against his side and rest my head on his chest. "Is it bedtime yet?"

He chuckles. "It can be bedtime whenever ye need it to be, *mo chroi*. There are enough bodies here to take care of things."

"Actually, he's right." Samuel bends at the waist to get a closer look at the seven glowing stones. "It'll take hours for the dark souls to gain enough strength to trigger the trace. You might as well go home and get some sleep. Tomorrow's going to be a long day."

I chuff. "Unlike today? Or yesterday? Since you came into my life, all I've had is long days."

"Okeedokee." Calum turns me by the shoulders. "Sloan, can you escort Fi, Aiden, and Dillan back to the treehouse? Da and I can figure out what tomorrow looks like and Nikon can snap us home in a bit."

I'd like to argue and stay until the end of the party, but honestly, I'm too damned tired. "I am officially not a fan of the Alban Eiler. Next year, I'm hiding eggs with Aiden's kids and staying home."

I wake with my heart pounding against my ribcage and my mind spewing up all kinds of images I don't like. Emmet wild and getting caught up in the freedom of Dionysus' insatiable pangs of hunger. Sloan brushing back Boann's hair as he kisses her neck and grinds her up against the wall. Darkness strangling Ahren and Quon Shen and me standing there, useless as their eyes bug wide and gloss over with the fog of death.

"Fi, luv, wake up." I hear Sloan's whispered words through the distortion of the nightmare, but it only hurts more, makes me angrier, makes me want to lash out.

My lungs burn from the betrayal and failure saturates the very air I breathe.

I give with every ounce of energy I have and people like Samuel judge me, people like Melanippe betray my trust, people like Sloan…

"Fi, wake up!"

I gasp and throw myself out of bed, scanning the room around me. Sloan's kneeling on the bed looking horrified, but it's me who has that right. "What were you laughing about with Boann? It was about me, wasn't it?"

He shifts and launches off the bed. "What are ye talkin' about? Yer stuck in one of yer nightmares, *a ghra*. Yer not awake."

"I'm awake." I swipe at the tears streaming down my face. "Are you planning to dump me and trade up for a goddess? Is that it?"

He has the decency to look stricken. "Never in a million years. Fi, look at me. Yer my every breath and ye know that. Snap out of it."

Anger erupts in me so hotly I swear I could set the whole treehouse on fire. "I need out of here. I can't breathe near you right now."

I stride for the door.

He shifts to match my movements. "No. Ye need to stay here. Somethin' isn't right."

"Isn't right? You mean like you flirting with Boann right in front of me? Like Melanippe betraying me and making me watch as my friends suffocate? Like my brother being out of his mind and lost with no inhibitions to keep him safe?"

I move to push past him, and he shifts to stop me.

Calling Birga forward, I tense for confrontation.

Calum and Dillan slide into the room. They look from me to

Sloan blocking the door and back to me again. "Irish? What's happening?" Dillan asks.

"Don't ask him." I point my spear at them. "*I'm* your sister, and I want out of this room. He can't keep me here. None of you can."

"What's the matter, baby girl?" Calum raises his hands and takes a couple of steps into the room.

Dillan does the same thing. "You're crying and upset. Was it one of your dreams?"

I point my spear at them. "I told you two to protect Emmet. Now he's missing. I trusted you. Why does everyone betray me?"

My body is practically vibrating with the rage building inside me.

Sloan shifts to grapple me, and I swing Birga. I catch him across the chest and leave a line of scarlet against his skin.

"Fuck, Fi!" Dillan shouts, pulling Sloan back to give me some space. "You could've killed him."

"What do I care? He wants Boann. I saw them together tonight."

"Nothing's happening between them, Fi. You're confused," Calum says. "She's our cousin. You need to get a grip, Fi. You're going to hurt yourself."

Hurt myself?

I can't imagine hurting myself more than I hurt right now. It makes me want to raze the earth…to level everyone around me.

There's a weird *snick* sound in my head and my vision flickers. They recoil, staring at me.

I take in the pain in Sloan's eyes and focus on the blood rushing scarlet from the wound I scored into his chest. Something inside me writhes against the fury. I want to hurt them for hurting me.

At the same time—with everything in me—I don't.

I can't hurt them. I mustn't hurt them.

The energy in the air *snaps* and my mind unplugs.

The world goes black.

CHAPTER NINETEEN

I rise from my heartache and lift my gaze to find Da, Aiden, Calum, Dillan, and Sloan sitting in one of the back booths of Shenanigans. Only it's not Shenanigans. The presence of the trees of my grove and Brendan tending bar tell me that much.

I'm in my special place on my subconscious plane.

They're talking and don't notice me, so I step over to my wicker swing and sit.

"It has to be the taint of the darkness," Sloan whispers somewhere in the back of my mind. "There's no way Fi in her right mind would attack me."

"It's building strength like Samuel predicted," Da says. "Calum, have ye gotten in touch with the warlock yet?"

"No. Quon Shen and Ahren haven't regained consciousness, and Fi and Samuel weren't friendly enough to exchange numbers."

"Who took the man from Newgrange tonight?"

"I think Tad dropped him somewhere."

"Then call Tad and find out where. We need to work on the banishing spell with Fi and send whatever bastard is trying to take her over back to the Neitherlands."

I track the worry in my father's voice. It should bother me that they're worried, but all I can muster is a boiling resentment that they're talking about me.

The mind is an incredible thing. When too much pain or stimulus hits, it shuts down or breaks things up into bite-sized pieces so you can deal with things without frying your circuits.

I think that's what happened.

It's hard to tell because there's a time when I don't see or hear anyone. I'm happy enough in my special place with Brenny. We have a few drinks, hang out in the grove, talk about old times... but eventually, a little something nudges me from the back of my mind.

It happens when Brenny and I are pouring drinks, and I find a bottle of two-hundred-year-old whiskey. I remember it has special meaning to me, but I can't quite remember why—nudge.

It happens when I'm sitting in my brown, wicker swing. I'm content to sit there, lost in contemplative thought, but for some reason, I stare at the empty matching chair across from me, and my chest aches—nudge.

The next time it happens, Patty stops by for a drink at the bar. Well...he almost does. I see him there, his blue eyes and puffy white, Einstein crazy hair, and crinkled brow. When he tries to speak to me, I can't hear him. It's like he's out of phase with me —nudge.

"Brenny? Do you ever get the feeling there's something important you're supposed to figure out, but you're missing the mark?"

My big brother shrugs, passing a bar towel over the pitted wooden surface. "Nope. I'm content."

"Good. You deserve to be." I take another long drink from my tumbler and pivot my barstool to look down the bar. As right as it feels to see Brenny there, it's wrong too. In my mind's eye, I see Liam back there. Tall and fit, with brunette hair and ice-blue eyes —nudge.

"I feel like I'm not all here. Does that make sense?" I rub the center of my chest. "I feel like I'm missing something big—or someone big."

"You have me, Fi," Brenny says. "You'll always have me."

"I love that. I do." I finish my drink and set my tumbler on the bar. With my hand wrapped around the glass, I catch sight of a platinum Claddagh band on my ring finger. Spinning it on my finger, I let the words catch the light. I study the traditional crown for loyalty, heart for love, and hands for friendship and return to those two words engraved into the design, *A GHRA*.

"Fi? Why are you crying?" Brendan asks.

I swipe my right hand over my cheek and continue to focus on that ring. "This is important. I feel it."

Brenny leans up on the bar and looks at my ring. "It's pretty. Who gave it to you?"

I stare at the platinum band and try to answer that one. The answer lies within me—I know it does—I'm just having trouble accessing it.

"Fiona? Are you all right?"

I turn toward the voice of a man that is not my older brother. He's Native American with ink-black hair, oddly golden eyes, and tribal tattoos inked on his hands and encircling his left eye.

"I know you, don't I?"

He dips his chin. "We met a few days ago. I'm Samuel, a Hunter-god shaman, like you. I can send my consciousness into different planes of existence—also like you."

I look around, and something about that clicks. "This is my special place."

"That's right."

"It's not real, is it?"

"It's real to you. It's a construct you use to retreat to in search of answers or solace."

"Which am I here for now? What happened?"

"That's what I'm here to find out. Do you remember being in

the Newgrange tomb and fighting the darkness that escaped the seam to the Neitherlands?"

Like magic, as he speaks the words, the images coalesce in my mind, and the story I've been trying to access begins to take form.

"The darkness infected Ahren and Quon Shen."

He nods. "The dark souls tried to kill them, but you interceded. You saved them, but in the process, you became infected. We didn't notice it at first, but it grew stronger over time."

That resonates with some of the things I've been feeling but not the most important things. "Do you know about this?" I show him my ring. "I feel like this is my anchor. Do you know who gave it to me?"

"Your boyfriend, Sloan Mackenzie. He's a druid, like you. He's devoted to you and trying to reach you. We banished the darkness that possessed you, but you didn't wake up."

"Sloan Mackenzie." The name sounds nice in my ears. "Hotness."

He nods. "You call him that, yes. He needs you to leave the safety of this place and return to him."

My stomach churns at the thought. "I can't. I tried to hurt him. I used my spear against him. I was so angry and filled with venom. I wanted to do more than hurt him…I wanted to kill people I love."

"Not anymore. You locked yourself down to keep from hurting them. It's over now. I cleansed you of the darkness."

"You're sure?"

He nods. "As you say, one hundy percent."

I chuckle, and the fog starts to clear in my head. "Hotness. I love him."

"I gathered. Now, release your sanctuary and wake up. There are other innocents to track down and cleanse. Our job isn't over. There's work to be done."

I think about that, and my mind isn't so sluggish.

Other innocents. Yeah, I don't want this to happen to other people. "You're sure I won't hurt them?"

"Positive."

I search the face of the man before me and decide to trust him. He seems like a good guy. Turning to my brother, I push my tumbler in and give him a parting wave. "Laters, Brenny. Love you."

"Safe home, baby girl. Love you, big time."

I close my eyes and focus on reclaiming my conscious self. When I open them again, I'm not surprised to be looking into the panicked gazes of Sloan and my fam jam. "Hey there," I say.

Sloan rolls his eyes and scoops me off the sandy floor of the Newgrange tomb. "Ye'll be the death of me, I swear. One of these days, my heart is simply going to explode from the stress."

I bring my arms around his back and return his hug. That's when I remember slicing him with Birga. "Oh, your chest. I attacked you."

Pushing back, I grip the bottom hem of his designer shirt and push it up his chest. His skin is smooth and unmarred and as beautifully toned and muscled as ever. "How? I didn't dream that. I hurt you."

"Ye did no such thing. Ye weren't yerself, and given the choice, ye'd never raise arms against me. That was the darkness pure and simple."

I shake my head, my gaze blurring behind a rush of tears. "No. It was me. I was angry and hurt. I thought—"

He chucks my chin. "Yer mind was playin' tricks on ye, *a ghra*. I have no designs on Boann. Yer my heart and soul. Ye know that. I know ye do."

I take a moment for a gut check. He's right. There's no jealousy or doubt in me...only the anguish of what could've happened. "Oh, hotness, I'm so sorry. What if I'd killed you?"

"Ye didn't. I easily healed the damage. I am, as you keep tellin' me, a talent in my own right."

Hot tears sting my eyes and warm my cheeks.

"All right, enough of this." Nikon grips under my arms and hikes me up to my feet. "Trust me, Irish, having been on the receiving end of Fi's anguish after hurting someone she loves, I assure you it's best not to let her slide too far down this dark path."

I look at Nikon, and his image is wavering behind my blurred vision. "What are you talking about?"

"The guilt of you spearing me got very snotty."

I bark a laugh and smack his arm. "True story. When Nikon came back from me spearing him, I snotted all over my guild robe."

"You did, so let's avoid a repeat."

I kiss Nikon on the cheek and smile at my brothers, my father, Patty, Dart, and— "Samuel, thank you for coming to get me."

"Glad to help but I meant what I said. It's been one hell of a long day, and there's more to come. Everyone, go back to bed. Get some rest, and we'll reconvene in the morning."

"What time is it now?" I ask.

Da checks his watch and frowns. "Half-past four. Everyone find somewhere to lay yer heads fer a few hours, and we'll reconvene at the treehouse at nine fer pancakes and plannin'. Got it?"

"Yes, sir." Tad sets his hand on Samuel before *poofing* out.

"You scared us, baby girl." Dillan squeezes my arm. "One minute you were wild and waving Birga around. Then you dropped to the floor like a marionette with her strings cut."

"I remember that. Part of me realized the darkness was taking me over. When I hurt Sloan and realized I wanted to hurt all of you, I kinda unplugged myself to take me off the field."

"Unplugged is right," Calum says. "It was terrifying. Please try never to do that again."

I turn to Patty and bend to hug him. "You tried to come in and find me, didn't you?"

"I did. Not that I got through to ye."

"Oh, you did. You definitely did." I ease back and hug my blue boy next. "Did my struggles trigger another wave of worry?"

Patty grunts. "That's how I knew ye needed help. The wee lad has quite a bond formin'. A dragon bond is a powerful thing, Red. I think ye need to start thinkin' about how that looks in the future."

I scrub my knuckles between the three horns on Dart's snout. "I will continue to work on that. In the meantime, can he stay at Granda's property while we're here? Our schedule is crazy, and it's distracting to know he's sitting in the lair, thinking I've forgotten him." I bend and kiss his center horn. "Which I never could."

Patty nods. "I think that's a grand idea as long as the wee man listens and minds his manners."

Dart lets out an adorable coo, and I chuckle. "Who could argue with that."

CHAPTER TWENTY

The first thing I do when my alarm goes off a few hours later is force myself out of bed and zip down the hall to check the bed in Emmet's room. I hope that, by some miracle, he came home while we were sleeping.

That starts my day off with disappointment.

Trying to ignore all the possibilities of what that could mean cramps my brain. Deflated, I go back to my room, pull on the same clothes I wore yesterday, and get ready for the day to suck.

It's uncommon for me to wake up and have Sloan still sleeping on his side of the bed. He's an early riser. Even if we go to bed in the middle of the night after a long day, he's usually up before me.

That's telling of how much my middle of the night battle with darkness took out of him. Waking up with him still sleeping next to me has only happened a handful of times in the three months we've lived together.

"Hey, sleepyhead." The mattress dips under my weight as I sit next to him. "You getting up?"

He runs his palms over his face a few times and shakes awake. "I am. Sorry."

"No apologies. I'm just worried about you."

Calum sticks his head into the room as he's heading down the hall. "FYI, Nikon brought a flat of apple fritters, warm and hot, from Timmie's. Grab one while you can. The early risers have already dug in."

I stand, unwilling to lose my shot at a warm apple fritter. "Fresh baked goods from home is a plus, but I admit, it's hard on the calorie count. What's your stance on curvy girls?"

Sloan chuckles. "Love the skin yer in, Fi. However that looks, I'm not goin' anywhere."

"I knew there was a reason I love you." I wink and give him a quick kiss before heading for the door. "Pull yourself together. I'll risk life and limb to save you a fritter from the pastry piranhas."

"My hero."

Combing through my hair with my fingers as I walk, I pull the auburn insanity back and trap it into an elastic.

"Hey." Dillan looks up from the table as I stroll out into the common area. "Did you sleep?"

I pour myself a cup of French vanilla and lift the lid of the brown Tim Horton's box. "After everything that happened, I was dead to the world. How're things out here so far?"

"As good as can be expected." Da stirs up a bowl of pancake batter. "Yer Granda went to the shrine first thing to research what dark fugitives escaping from the Neitherlands means specifically."

I sip from the edge of my mug and let the jolt of sweet delight do its thing. "Is Granda feeling well enough to spend the morning at the shrine?"

"That's what I asked, right before he ripped me a new one."

I chuckle. "What did he say?"

"He said, 'Feck off ye eejit. If I need ye to wipe my arse, I'll tell ye. Until then, keep yer nose outta my feckin' business."

"Well then. You've been told."

Dillan reaches to grab a fritter and laughs. "It's obvious where you get your communication skills."

Da arches a brow. "Ye'd be wise to shut yer gob before I shut it for ye."

Dillan laughs. "Dayam, I love being right."

The two of us are still chuckling about that when Nikon flashes in with Samuel. "Good, you're up," he says, coming over to check the selection of pastries remaining in the box. "Samuel asked me for a ride to Toronto to interrogate Melanippe."

I swallow the bite of sugary apple delight. "What about tracking down the darkness? Are you skipping out on us, Sammo?"

Samuel frowns at me. "Must everyone in your family come up with a moniker for me?"

I chuckle. "Yeah. It's kind of a thing we do. So, skipping out?"

He lifts a black drawstring bag and sets it on the breakfast bar counter between us. "These are the tracking stones. I've spelled them to find and lock onto one signature each, so if there were only four or five, seven should be plenty."

"Especially since we already took care of the one who targeted Fi," Calum says.

Nikon frowns. "What? What did I miss?"

I let Dillan and Calum tell the gruesome tale and focus on my sweet treat and happier thoughts.

"Are you good, Fi?" Nikon looks stricken. "Shit. Someone should've called me."

"I'm fine." I lick my fingers. "Even better now that I have a sugar infusion. There was no need to wake you up and drag you back here when there was nothing you could do but worry. S'all good."

Samuel nods. "The best part of last night is having one less dark soul to track down. You and your family can work at that today, and I'll try to find out what Melanippe knows."

Nikon frowns. "I'll stick close to him so we can get back to you in a snap. If there's any trouble, consider me here to help."

"I'm sure we'll be fine." Da sprays the griddle. "We can't get back into the tomb to cleanse the possessed until after the tourists clear out anyway."

"What time is that?" I ask.

"It can change if there are private tours. To be safe, we shouldn't go until after dark."

I think about that for a moment. "Before we get caught up in the chaos of the day, either Tad or Sloan needs to *poof* to the clinic with one of these stones. We need to check on Ahren and Quon Shen and make sure they aren't infected like I was."

"Good call, Fi," Calum says.

"What about Mingin and him finding Melanippe?" I say. "I thought about that last night. If they've been fighting for centuries to get back to one another, do you think he'll go after her in Toronto?"

Dillan frowns. "Do you think he'd be able to track her that far?"

"I don't know. I was posing the question."

Samuel purses his lips, looking pensive. "That's a good question. While we're there, I'll put up some safeguards to ward against that, just in case."

"Perfect. I think that's a good idea."

Nikon nods. "While we're there, I'll take another run through your house to make sure Emmet and Ciara haven't resurfaced."

Kevin jumps up from the couch and brings his mug to the sink. "Oh, if you're going to our place anyway, can I hitch a ride? Kinu is almost out of Daisy's remedy, and I have a shift at the gallery tonight."

"Yeah, grab your stuff."

Kev hustles toward the bedrooms, and I look at Aiden. "You should go too. Kinu's really pregnant and shouldn't be picking up the slack for the whole family."

Aiden frowns. "What about you guys?"

"Yer sister's right." Da scoops batter onto the heated pan. "We can track down a few dark souls, and if things go to shit, Nikon can have ye back in a blink. Go back with Kev and take care of things at that end."

Aiden studies me, and I see how torn he is. "Are you sure? I don't mind staying."

"One hundy percent. Kiss the kids and tell them we'll be home soon. Take care of Kinu and give her a chance to get off her feet. Making sure she and the babies are good is the best thing you can do for all of us."

"All right. Sounds good. Keep me posted."

"Will do."

Aiden and Calum head back toward the bedrooms, and I return my attention to my coffee. Before Nikon rushes off, I reach over and squeeze his hand. "Thanks for all your help. I'm sorry Melanippe turned out to be a traitorous bitch in love with an inkblot. She doesn't deserve to make beautiful Greek babies with you."

Nikon laughs. "You can sheath your arrows, Cupid. I just got out of a miserable twelve-hundred-year dysfunctional relationship. I'm in no rush to dive into another one. It'll happen. One of the only benefits to immortality is that I have time—lots and lots of time."

I shrug. "Fine. I'll gear down, but if I see someone spectacular, I'm going to point her out."

Nikon chuckles. "I have no doubt."

"Now, if you guys are off and we're going to be on the move, I have to go spend some time with my dragon boy. He's been struggling the past two days and is losing his mind."

Samuel frowns. "I'd rather not be anywhere near you when your dragons lose their minds."

"I am sorry about that." I bite my lip to keep from laughing. It's too soon to laugh, right? I'm pretty sure. "Okay, you guys take off and check in later."

Kev and Aiden return with their stuff and hold out their

hands to complete the circuit of Greek-powered travel. "Good luck, guys," Kev says. "Try not to get dead or possessed while we're gone, will you?"

"We'll try our best."

Nikon kisses my cheek and laughs at the sugary lips he leaves behind. "Stay out of trouble, Red."

"No promises."

I take my pancakes to go after securing Sloan's pastry and head out to the wooden porch outside the treehouse to have my breakfast with Dart. It's a damp and drizzly day, and I wonder what kind of scare-do I'll be sporting when the day is through.

Thankfully, it's a ponytail day already.

"Diminish Descent." Air breezes past me as I drop in a controlled fall to the forest floor below. My boots touch down with little more than a silent whisper as I find my footing in the moist ground cover.

Stepping under the shelter of the guesthouse to avoid the rain, I check on my boys. "How was sleeping under the stars, boys?"

Bruin and Manx offered to sleep outside with Dart to keep him company while at the same time making sure he doesn't wander off or get into trouble.

"Did you get some solid rest?"

Bruin lifts his head and yawns wide. When he stretches out his front paws, the muscles on his shoulders twitch. "More than I got before I came out. No offense, Red, but there are times when sleepin' while we're bound isn't that relaxin'."

I pull my fork out of my mouth and talk around my pancakes. "Like when an evil dark entity possesses me, you mean?"

"Yeah, like then."

"No offense taken. I don't suppose that was relaxing for any of you." Settling in the little nest of scrub they made for themselves,

I cross my legs and enjoy my after-fritter pancakes. "We have a busy day. You guys need to get something in your tummies so you're not hungry."

"Just the reason I was comin' to find ye, luv." Gran joins us. She has her rain jacket on, and a garden basket hung over the bend of her elbow. "I was transplantin' my weeds into my weed bed when I got a call from a druid family north of Dublin. Their neighbor hit a buck last night with their wee Volkswagen."

"Yikes. I bet that didn't go well for either of them."

"Right ye are. It was the death of both the car and the deer."

"Do you need Sloan to *poof* out and get the dead buck before we start?"

"No, luv. Yer father was expectin' Tad this mornin', so I asked him to fetch it and bring it when he comes."

Dart sits up straighter, his eyes bright.

"Are you hungry, buddy?"

He chirps, which I interpret as a yes.

"Well, not to worry, wee lad." Gran pats the scales on the side of his jaw. "This one is fer us to keep here. I figure Manx is likely hungry fer some red meat too, aren't ye?"

"I could eat." Manx licks his paws and cleans his cheeks for his morning bath. "Yer always so thoughtful, Lara. I appreciate it."

Gran grins and tightens the collar of her jacket around her neck. "It's a damp one today. I'm glad I got my gardening in before the sky started droppin' on us."

"If you ever want help, Gran, any one of us would be happy to lend a hand."

"Och, I know that, luv. Toilin' in the garden isn't a chore, though. It's my joy."

"It's like Kevin and his art. He can spend all day in his studio and is more at peace and energized when he leaves than when he got there nine hours earlier."

"It's a blessing to love what ye do in life, fer sure."

I finish my pancakes and set my plate down. "Da's worried

about something."

"What makes ye say that, luv?"

I point at my empty plate. "He always makes family pancakes when he's worried about one of us. I'm not sure if it's Emmet or me this time around, but I wish he didn't worry so much about us."

"It's a parent's prerogative to worry. It's a badge worn with honor. Ye'll find that out yerself one day."

"I'm sure I will."

"I think fer yer father, it's also a case of wanting to wrap things up so he can head home. He has pressing matters at work and misses his lady."

"Oh? He didn't mention anything."

"Which, of course, he wouldn't."

"No, but I wish he didn't think he needs to keep things from us."

Gran lifts her hand and smiles as a yellow and black songbird lands in her palm. "I'm sure it's more a case of him not wanting to leave his kids to deal with things while he goes off on his own."

"Sounds like Da."

She picks up a little bowl from in her basket and offers the bird some seeds. "He tells me he's seein' a woman ye all approve of."

"Shannon. Yeah, we grew up with her sort of being our second mom. We worked in her pub as our first jobs and grew up with Liam being part of our family."

"The Liam that came and stayed with us after he was hurt last fall?"

"Yep. Shannon is his mom. It's kinda nice that she and Da moved forward from being friends after twenty years and both of them being alone the last fifteen."

"Well, he seems quite taken with her. He says her people are jackeens."

I nod. "From Dublin. She met her husband, Mark, when she

was in Toronto on a university scholarship and never made it back home."

Gran bids farewell to her little feathered friend and adjusts the basket hanging over the crook of her arm. "Well, I better get to the house and wash things up while they're fresh. Do you need anythin', luv?"

"No, I'm good thanks. Just taking a breather before I engage with the chaos of the world again."

Gran smiles as if she understands completely. "A moment of quiet retrospection will never do ye wrong. I'll leave you to it then."

Gran walks off toward the main house, and I smile.

She rarely leaves this property and yet seems as content if not more content than anyone I know.

Her druid Shire looks good on her.

I wonder if I'll feel the same way when it's time for me to claim my place as the Keeper of the Shrine.

"Morning, Red," Tad *poofs* in close to where I'm sitting. He's down on one knee with his hand on the front shoulder of a large deer. "Lara asked me to bring this—"

Dart bounds past me and I wince. "Back away or you'll wear it."

Tad *poofs* under the treehouse to stand with me, and his eyes grow wide. "Wow. Is he that hungry or is that how dragons eat?"

"That's how they eat. Be thankful he's alone. The last time I delivered takeout to the lair, I flashed in with a bull, was nearly trampled by two dozen dragons, and a bloodbath ensued."

Manx gets up from the nesting area and trots over to share the meal.

"What do you want for brekkie, Bruin?"

He lifts his boxy head and sniffs the morning breeze. "Are there any pancakes left?"

"Not sure. Why don't you go up and see?"

Bruin dematerializes and breezes past me on his way up.

Before we follow, I catch Tad's wrist. "Hey, things have been so hectic that I haven't checked in with you. How's your father doing after the kidnapping?"

"Physically, he seems fine. Mentally...he's even more of a miserable asshole than usual."

"Sorry. That sucks."

"Ye can't pick yer family. Ye get what ye get."

"Maybe...but then you can pick others and build a better family if you work at it."

Tad smiles. "Don't tempt me. Say things like that and ye might end up with me on yer doorstep one of these days."

I hold out my hand and point up toward the porch. "You're always welcome. You know that."

Tad and I join the others in the treehouse, and I take my dirty plate to the sink to wash it. Jarrod and Eric are there too. "So, what's our plan? Have we got a plan?"

Da nods. "Sloan and I were thinkin' that the evil souls would want to find a host as soon as possible, so we'll start back at Newgrange and break up into groups."

Sloan points at the stones on the counter. "There are eight of us and likely four or maybe five dark escapees still out there— Mingin plus the others."

"Minus the one we banished a few hours ago," Sloan says.

Jarrod frowns. "You went hunting without us? I thought we were taking time to sleep and rest up?"

"We were." Sloan is hesitant with his words. "It was unplanned."

I chuckle. "What my beloved champion isn't saying is that while I was fighting off the darkness yesterday, I got infected and tainted. In the wee hours, I went full-dark and tried to slice Sloan in half with Birga."

The two of them blink.

"Shit, Fi. Sorry," Jarrod says.

"Nothing to be sorry for. Samuel and the guys got me back to Newgrange, and they banished the bastard to his side of the rift. We've been through the drill once and know it works. Now we rinse and repeat."

"Okay, so we're guessing four?" Eric asks.

Da nods. "We are. We'll break up into two groups of four and spread out from the tomb site. Once we identify an infected person, Samuel said to touch them with the spelled stone that is glowing, and the person will be rendered unconscious."

Sloan divides the stones into two piles. He puts half of them back into the bag and the other half into his pocket. "Tad and I will each be a wayfarer for a team. When the infected person is unconscious, we'll take them somewhere to hold them until dark."

I set my plate on the rack and grab a dishtowel. "Do we know where we're taking them?"

Tad raises a finger to take the floor. "We have a cabin in Meath, not far from Newgrange. We could put them there and leave someone to watch them."

Da nods. "That's fine. Tad, why don't ye take Sloan there now, so he'll have the coordinates to portal back when we capture someone."

Tad grips Sloan's shoulder and winks at me. "I promise, I'll return him almost as good as I found him."

Sloan chuckles. "Get on with it, McNiff."

The two of them *poof* out and are back almost instantly. Sloan comes over to stand with me and smiles. "The cabin is big enough and out of the way. I doubt the darkness will pose a threat to anyone for one day."

"Good." Da picks up the bag of stones. "I'll go with Tad, Eric, and Dillan as group one. Calum, Sloan, Fi, and Jarrod yer group two."

"We need team names," Dillan says. "Our team will be the McNifficents in honor of our wayfarer and you guys are...the Mackenzie Frenzy."

I laugh. "How come you're magnificent, and we're in a frenzy?"

Dillan swings his cloak around his shoulders and pulls his hood up. "I work with what I'm given."

Calum chuckles. "Suiting up already? We're not even tracking anything yet."

I laugh. "He doesn't need a reason. He'll take any excuse to wear his hood."

Dillan grins. "What can I say? It makes me super stealthy, sexy, *annnd* has the bonus of keeping my ears warm."

Da rolls his eyes and checks that he's turned off everything in the kitchen. "All right. Safe home, everyone."

I hold up my hand. "The Mackenzie Frenzy can't go anywhere without our bear, dragon, and lynx."

Da grunts. "Do ye think that's wise?"

"Likely not, but I won't get anywhere without them—especially after last night."

"Well, try not to look conspicuous."

I laugh. "You heard the part about me taking a dragon with us, didn't you?"

Dillan chuckles. "Maybe put a hat on him. Or do the Superman-slash-Clark Kent thing and disguise him behind a pair of dark-rimmed glasses. Then no one will guess who he is."

"Thanks, D. All good suggestions. I think we'll go the route of casting an illusion to hide his presence."

Dillan shrugs. "Whatevs. Suit yourself."

Da gathers his group and readies to leave. "Then, while yer gatherin' yer animals, we'll pop in at the clinic and ensure yer hunter friends aren't tainted as well."

"Awesomesauce. Thanks, Da."

CHAPTER TWENTY-ONE

After gathering our animal companions, the Mackenzie Frenzy *poofs* to the cow pasture below Newgrange, and we wait for the McNifficents. When they arrive, Da winks at me. "Yer friends are awake and clear of darkness. Wallace says he expects them to recover fully within the next few hours."

"That's great news."

"It is. They wanted me to tell ye that the moment they get the all-clear, they'll be joinin' in the hunt."

"Cool. Thanks, Da." That's the best news I've heard in ages. "Okay, let's get this party started."

Sloan takes a stone out of his pocket and Da takes one from Samuel's black bag.

"How do you turn them on?" I ask.

Sloan shakes his head. "Samuel didn't say. I assume once they detect a source of darkness we're on our way."

"And if not?" Tad frowns down at the inert piece of rock.

"If not, this will be the shortest quest in history."

Dillan grunts and scrapes the sole of his boot against the grass. "I didn't step in steaming cow patty delight for nothing. We're hunting darkness today, folks. End. Of."

I slide in tight to Sloan's side and watch the smooth stone resting in his palm. "Okay, little dude. Any time now. Go. Activate. Transmute!"

We wait, but nothing happens.

"This is sadly anticlimactic," Calum says.

"That's what she said," Dillan scoffs.

Calum grins. "If it was a *she*, yeah, she likely did."

The chuckling keeps us entertained for a moment but then things sober, and we're back to watching rocks.

"Maybe it's like an Etch-a-Sketch, and you have to shake it to wake it," Dillan says.

I reach over, close my palm over Sloan's and give it a shake. When that does nothing, I poke it with my finger. "Come on, little dude, wake up."

Da looks at me and frowns. "Do ye think the wee rock is sleepin', *mo chroi?*"

"Maybe."

That sparks a round of male amusement.

"Well, go ahead and share your ideas, fellas. At least I'm putting it out there."

Dart comes over and looks at what we're doing. He's anxious for our adventure to get started and doesn't understand the holdup.

Yeah, join the club.

"Wait." Calum points at the front of Sloan's pants. "Either one of the other stones has activated, or you've got some weird shit going on with your junk."

"Is your cock part glow-stick, Irish?" Dillan asks.

I lean to get a better look and chuckle at the glow emanating through the fabric of Sloan's pants. "No. That's new. I would've noticed that."

Da reaches back into the bag and picks out another rock. This one is throwing off a white light and glowing too. "We have a winner."

When he holds it out for us to see, I get it. "Samuel said they each will find and track one entity. I guess we don't pick the stone. The stone picks."

Sloan reaches into his pocket and pulls out the other three. "Point to the red-headed lass."

"Ye might want to put the others into yer jacket, mate," Eric says. "No need to risk magical radiation around yer mickey."

I don't suppose there would be any magical side effects, but I'm happy when Sloan takes Eric's advice.

With two glowing stones, the excitement of the moment rachets up.

"Ready to disembark," Dillan says.

"How do we follow the beacon to track?" I ask.

Sloan swings his extended hand slowly, gauging how things work. "It seems to be similar to a game of Hot and Cold... assuming when the stone warms, that's the way we're supposed to go."

Da swings his stone through the air and takes a few steps. "Agreed. It's been a great many years since I played the game with the kids, but I remember the gist."

I giggle and hold out my hand. "Can I be in charge of the stone? I used to crush that game."

Dillan and Calum bark a laugh.

"What?"

Calum smacks Dillan in the chest and shakes his head. "Nothing."

Dillan snorts. "Calum's pants are on fire. Sorry, Fi, but you sucked at the game. You only crushed it because we constantly changed what you were looking for to let you win."

"You did not."

Calum flashes me a guilty smile. "We did. We had to. You got so sad when you couldn't find the object we sent you searching for. Nobody wanted to see you cry."

I frown. "Well, I don't care. I *do* crush this game. Now is my chance to prove it."

I scoop the stone out of Sloan's hand and tromp off with my baby dragon, Manx, and my team in tow.

As we approach the river, I swing my hand left to right. When I have my direction, I stride off. "Yep. You're right, hotness. It is like Hot and Cold."

Sloan jogs along beside me and Calum and Jarrod catch up.

"Jarrod?" Sloan says. "Would ye mind askin' Darcy and Davin if they've found an effective illusion spell to help keep dragonborn unseen?"

Jarrod pulls out his phone and makes a call.

"Darcy and Davin?" I whisper to Sloan. "Are they the twins?"

Sloan chuckles and looks down at me. "Are ye all right, *a ghra*? Did the dark entity affect yer memory?"

"No. I'm fine. I never knew their names."

Sloan blinks at me. "Ye've talked to them a dozen times over nearly a year. Ye've fought with them, and ye introduced them to the Dragon Queen as caregivers."

I chuckle. "I know, right? I always knew them as the Perry twins and meant to ask, but then time passed, and it seemed too late to ask. Then it just got awkward."

"So, ye referred to them as the Perry twins?"

"Every time."

Sloan shakes his head, chuckling. "Yer ridiculous, Cumhaill."

I let him have that one and focus on the stone guiding us along the shoreline of the River Boyne. Now all I have to do is *remember* their names. Darcy and Davin. I should write that down.

We find out soon enough that the compass on the spelled stones doesn't take us on the route for the easiest travel. It's an "as the crow flies" navigation, which, if we didn't have Sloan with us to *poof* us over the river or down muddy slopes or across vast spans of green fields, would have added tons of time of backtracking.

As it turns out, we arrive at a remote gas station up a country road about an hour later.

In the distance, a man in overalls is next to the pumps. He's filling a silver car while a blonde woman sits in the driver's seat of her swanky BMW, looking impatient to get outta Dodge.

I swing my palm toward the building, and the stone cools down. When I point it back toward the pumps, it grows hot to the touch.

"Which one of them is it?" I ask.

"I'm going with Gas Station Guy," Calum says.

"Why?"

"Because he's here and has been here the past hour. The woman drove here and stopped for gas. If we were tracking her, the stone's trajectory would've had us bouncing all over the place tracking her."

"Sound logic," Sloan says. "The woman is settlin' up fer the petrol now. When she pulls away, we'll move in on the attendant."

Calum and Jarrod seem good with that.

I pat Dart's back and look at him and Manx. "You boys stay here. Let us check things out."

Manx sits on his haunches. "Let us know if ye need a distraction. I've been takin' pointers from Emmet, and Dart is a distraction all on his own. If ye need us, we're here and ready to wreak havoc."

"Thanks, buddy. I'll let you know." It's bittersweet to think of Emmet teaching the companions how to stir up trouble. The Emmetness of it is perfection, but it spears me with worry again.

Where is he and what's he doing?

Okay, I have a good idea of what he's doing, but that doesn't make me any less worried.

"He'll be all right." Sloan places a gentle hand at the small of my back. "He's smart and resourceful, and even with Dionysus's impulses, he still has the Cumhaill code guiding him at his core."

"I hope you're right."

"I am. Ye'll see."

We strike off toward the gas pumps as the silver sportscar pulls away. We're not thirty feet closer to closing the distance when the stone starts going cool.

"Uh-oh, hold on a second."

I swing the aim of my hands toward the car driving off, and the stone heats up again. "Crappers. It might've been the attendant before, but it's the woman now, and she's getting away."

Sloan frowns. "Dart! We need ye to stop that car."

Dart's grin is dazzling as he starts on a run and launches into the air. He super-sizes on the fly, his wings unfolding to propel him toward the shiny silver speck moving toward the horizon.

"One question, hotness? How did you see him stopping that car when you set him in motion?"

Sloan frowns at me. "Landin' in front of it, so we can portal there. I'll have to adjust her memories, but—"

I giggle. "Oh, that's funny."

"Why? Do ye not think that's what will happen?"

As if in answer to the question, Dart lets out a cry of glee and dives. Pulling his wings back, he propels himself toward the ground.

"Och, fuckin' hell."

"Yep. You gotta be careful what you say to kids. Clear expectations are the key."

The screech of metal meeting a mythical beast is loud even from this distance. Sloan mutters something under his breath, grabs my wrist, and *poofs* us to the scene of the accident.

Debris skitters and scatters past our boots as metal and glass rain down from the wreck. The radiator hisses its discontent as oil and antifreeze drain onto the ground.

I marvel at my boy sitting pretty on the crushed and mangled front hood of an eighty-five thousand dollar sports car. "He's so proud. Look at that face."

Sloan swipes the tracking stone out of my hand, shoves back the airbag, and reaches in to press the spelled stone against the dazed woman's forehead.

She goes limp the moment it contacts her skin.

"Feckin' hell." He tosses me the stone, which has ceased to glow and tries the door handle. When that gets him nowhere, he reaches through the broken window to unlock the car. "*Arragh*, what a feckin' mess. How do we explain this to the woman once she wakes up?"

I'm fighting to keep from laughing.

It's not often Sloan makes a gaffe like this. It's refreshing not to be the one responsible for the chaos.

"How about we say she was in a bizarre accident in the middle of the Irish countryside? We found her and got her help. All true."

He eases her out of the car and carries her to the grassy shoulder of the road.

The energy of his healing abilities soon surges forward, and I leave him to his patient. She doesn't look that broken. Cuts and likely whiplash and maybe damage from the seatbelt or airbag.

Maybe I'm cynical after all my injuries, but I'm not too worried. He'll fix her up.

While he's doing that, I coax Dart off the hood. "You stopped the car like Sloan asked you to. That was great listening, buddy."

Dart steps free of the debris and shrinks to his adolescent size. The way he prances over to me is *waaay* too cute.

"Tell him how good he did."

Sloan casts me a dirty look. "He demolished the car and could've killed the woman."

I shake my head. "That was poor communication on your part. Don't give us the stink-eye."

He grunts as he scoops the woman off the asphalt and hikes

her higher into his arms. "I'll drop her at Tad's cabin and be right back. Try to figure out what we can do to salvage this."

"Will do. The good news is…two down. Yay, Mackenzie Frenzy. I'll check with the McNifficents and see how they're doing."

Twenty minutes later, the Mackenzie Frenzy search party is plodding across the country setting with another glowing stone in hand, and a fire lit under our asses.

"Fi. There is no winning. They're on their second tainted soul. We're on our second tainted soul. That's it. It's not a contest."

I cast a sideways glance at Sloan, then Calum and I bust a gut.

"Have you learned nothing since last summer, Irish?" Calum asks. "When there's a challenge in front of one Cumhaill, we're all for one and one for all. When there's more than one challenge and a chance for us to outdo one another—it's game on."

I laugh at his expression of confusion. "Competition isn't a bad thing, hotness. If you think Dillan and Da aren't pushing hard now working to show us up, you're cracked."

Sloan looks at Jarrod and holds up his hands. "It's them, right? They have this family brand of lunacy goin' on and think it's normal."

Jarrod shakes his head. "Sorry, mate. Yer the one talkin' crazy. Between me, Ginny, and the twins, we take any chance we can get to outdo one another."

"It's all good fun," I reassure Sloan. "A win only means razzing rights and a bit of harmless teasing."

Calum points toward the sign of the first town we've seen and we course-correct straight for it. That's fortunate. The land near Newgrange is remote farmland. There's the odd road and farmhouse, but compared to Toronto, we're the only ones out here.

That works for us in this situation.

While tracking evil fugitives from fae purgatory in the company of a dragon—isolation is a good thing.

"How about that illusion spell, Jarrod?" Sloan asks. "Cloaking our dragon would be good, right about now."

Jarrod calls up a screen on his phone. After finding what he's looking for, he looks from Dart to me. "Would ye rather do it yerself, Fi? Would it make him more comfortable?"

"Comfortable? It won't hurt him, will it?"

"Och, no. I meant comfortable havin' someone he trusts spell him."

I reach for the proffered phone and scroll through the spell. "It's completely in Irish."

"Uh…yeah. Most of us do our spells in Irish."

I scratch my head and return the phone. "I'll leave it to you or Sloan then. I wouldn't feel comfortable in case I mess up on pronouncing something and cause more harm than good."

"That's cool." Jarrod checks with Sloan.

"No. Yer fine, Jarrod. Carry on."

Jarrod presses a hand on Dartamont's snout and reads off the spell his younger brothers sent us to mask his presence. When my blue boy fades away, part of me panics, and I want to pull the plug on the whole thing.

"He's fine." Sloan takes my hand, and the power of his true sight ring brings my boy back to me.

I breathe a huge sigh of relief. "Thanks, hotness."

"I've got ye."

Back in business, Calum leads the way along the outskirts of town. "We're getting close. The stone's pretty warm now."

We follow the spelled stone, and I read the sign welcoming us to Duleek Civil Parish, County Meath.

"I'd rather not cause a major scene in town." I frown at the locals coming and going along Main Street. "Maybe we can get in and out without too much—"

A shrill cry shatters the serenity of the little town. Digging in, we race up the street, and I have a sinking feeling we know the cause of the commotion.

When we find a woman on the ground, Jarrod bends to help her up. "Are ye all right, then? What's amiss?"

"It's my man, Gerry." She brushes her hair out of her face and accepts her bag. "He's the sweetest man, dead-on, but his eyes just now...Jaysus, Mary, and Joseph, that was *not* my Gerry."

I frown. "Don't worry, ma'am. We know what's wrong and he'll be back to normal by tonight."

"What's wrong with him?"

Calum and I take off and leave Sloan and Jarrod to handle the explaining.

The beauty of the Irish people—and Scottish too—is that even though their civilizations have grown and modernized, they still hold a healthy fear of the faeries.

It may not be something they talk about outright, but if Sloan tweaks her superstition, she likely won't ask any more questions.

"There." Calum points at a beige building with gray block stone. "He's in the library with—"

"—Colonel Mustard?"

Calum laughs. "Let's hope there are no candlesticks handy. Come on."

The two of us race across the road. "Manx. You have the back door, buddy. Dart, stay with Manx."

I'm not even sure my boy is with me, but I assume when I ran, he came too.

Calum's in the lead as the two of us rush in the front door and —*bam*—practically crash right into a librarian.

She's not the matronly stereotype librarian with the silver bun and glasses with the chain that goes around her neck, but she's killing the look of stern disapproval. "Stall the ball. Ye know this is a library, aye?"

Calum slides the glowing stone into his jacket pocket and drops his gaze. "Yes, ma'am. Sorry."

Her lips purse tight and pinch to a fine line. "Tourists, then, are ye? Well, if yer lookin' to get on the Internet, the computers are taken at the moment."

Calum nods. "Thank you. We'll look around until we find what we need."

"I'll take ye back and show ye where."

"That's all right." I point at the ginger-haired girl with braids waiting at the desk. "Go ahead and help the girl. We'll be fine. And we'll slow down."

Before she can answer, I slide around her, making my escape.

The moment we're in the library proper, Calum retrieves the stone and points. "Okay, we're in business. Upstairs and near the back."

CHAPTER TWENTY-TWO

We find Gerry, aka the sweetest man, aka the dark soul's hostage in the upper stacks, completely wigged out. He's scanning left and right, looking like he wants to escape but likely not realizing the thing he's trying to escape from is inside him.

"Hey, Gerry." I approach from the front, my hands up to draw his attention as Calum weaves through the aisles, looking for a way to come at him from another angle. "My name's Fiona."

The glare he pegs me with is more predator than prey, and it makes my shield burst to life. Does the darkness in him recognize me from the tomb?

When his eyes make a *snick* sound and flip to solid black, the hair on my neck stands on end.

"Cool trick. Your girlfriend's right. That's freaky."

"Maeve?" The guy's voice is twisted and tormented.

"Yeah, Maeve. She's worried about you."

My peripheral vision catches Calum's approach out of the corner of my eye. I shift my footing a bit to turn Gerry's back to him more.

"I know what you're feeling right now. The anger. The betrayal. The frustration of everyone in your life turning on you.

I know you want to lash out, but I also know part of you doesn't want to hurt anyone."

"Wrong." He rolls his muscled shoulders and flexes his fingers. "I need to hurt someone and didn't want to hurt Maeve. Now that you're here…it's perfect. You're the bitch from the tomb. The one trying to put us back."

"That's me. I'm not trying to put you back…I *will* put you back."

He shakes his head, and his eyes flicker back to brown. "You need to leave. I'm sorry. I can't fight him."

"It's okay, Gerry. I promise, I'm going to get rid of the darkness, and you'll be you again in a few hours."

Snick. His eyes flick back to full black. "You'll be dead in a few hours, and I'll be gone."

I chuckle. "I wouldn't bet on it."

Calum is hard on his six now. To get any closer, he has to step out in the open and expose his presence. I ease closer, making my position more threatening to keep Gerry's attention.

"Tough as Bark." When I activate my body armor, his gaze narrows and his frame goes rigid. "That's right. You and I are throwing down. There can be only one."

I think I have him locked down when the train jumps the rails. I don't know if he hears something or simply senses Calum coming in on him, but he turns at exactly the wrong moment.

Gerry lets out a primal growl and evades Calum's approach. After avoiding being touched by the stone, he kicks Calum, sending him flying.

I launch forward on the attack, very aware that I can't hurt him. Gerry—the sweetest guy—is innocent.

Jumping the sweep of his foot, I barely have my boots back on the carpet before I'm ducking a meaty fist. I'm not sure if Gerry is a fighter or if the dark soul possessing him imported these abilities.

Either way, he's quick and skilled.

He throws a right cross, dances away from my blow, and flies back at me with a roundhouse kick to my side. I don't have time to evade, so I take the hit.

The contact is solid, and even with my armor up, it's one helluva blow.

I stagger, struggling to stay on my feet. Man, if I'm the badass lady druid the universe needs me to be, I should at least be able to avoid ass-planting in front of the enemy. Amirite?

Calum's crawling up the aisle on his hands and knees, and I understand why.

"Find it quick."

"Yep."

While Calum looks for the lost tracking stone, I reengage.

"Don't let the darkness touch ye, *a ghra!*"

I hear Sloan's warning too late.

Gerry tackles me, and I fly backward in his grasp. I hit the carpeted floor with a *thud* and brace my arms against his shoulder to keep him as far away from me as possible.

Sickening darkness invades, and I fight not to hurl. Releasing my fae vision, I see the dark taint for what it is. The vile entity that has me in its clutches has its front claws extended, and his long canines bared to clamp around anything he can get close enough to chomp.

His snarl vibrates in my chest as I fight his hold.

Darkness pushes at me. I'm not sure if it's trying to skip hosts and take me down or if it's fighting me.

I swallow and try not to gag.

His skin gives off a distinct musk of decay, and it settles on the back of my tongue. It's similar to the stink of dark magic that clings to the necromancer assholes.

There's a scramble by the bookshelves, then Gerry goes limp and collapses on top of me.

Jarrod swings into view above and grins down at me. "What's the craic, Cumhaill?"

I groan. "I'm trapped under a possessed psycho trying to fang me, so no craic at the moment. You?"

"Oh, great craic." He chuckles as he and Calum pull Dark Gerry off me. "Here you go, Irish. Another catch for ye."

Sloan bypasses the handoff for a moment and comes straight to me. "Are ye all right, *a ghra*? Do ye feel hurt or angry as ye did last night?"

I take stock and shake my head. "I don't think so. I don't know why I'd be able to sense it and fight this time when I had no idea last night, but I feel fine."

Sloan nods. "Yer cleansing last night was quite powerful magic. Samuel mentioned ye might be resistant to dark possession goin' forward."

"You have darkness possession antibodies now," Calum says. "One less thing to worry about."

Sloan rolls his eyes. "With yer sister, the list of things to worry about is still two miles long."

"True story."

Sloan takes possession of Gerry and straightens. "I'll be back in a moment. Clean up here, and I'll meet ye out back to collect Dart and Manx."

I reach up on my toes and kiss his cheek. "Go, Mackenzie Frenzy. Hurry. See if we win."

After restoring the library to its original state, the gang returns to the riverbank at Newgrange. We have three remaining stones and wait out the next couple of hours, hoping to get a hit on Mingin. I'm pretty sure the four we have at Tad's cabin plus the dark soul banished from me is the extent of the smoky wisp escapees.

The problem is, we're missing the headliner.

I check in with Nikon and Garnet, but there's no sign that

Mingin has crossed the pond and is gearing up for a lovers reunion.

"Okay, so, how do we find Mingin if our spelled stones aren't telling us anything useful?"

Sloan frowns at the gray stones sitting on the black velvet bag. "What if someone is masking Mingin's darkness to keep us from tracking him?"

Da frowns. "Samuel's spell was advanced. I can feel the potential energy still workin' its magic. It would take a great deal of power to block it."

"Maybe that's how we find him," I say. "Like when Toronto PD did a big crackdown on grow-ops before they were legal."

Da looks at me and smirks. "Yer suggesting that instead of focusin' on Mingin, we track high-outputs of magical energy and switch our hunt to find the person casting the blocking spell."

"Yeah. Like when you used the power meters and the helicopter with infrared to figure out where the heat outputs were in the city."

Da nods. "I like that plan. The only problem is we don't have a helicopter, and even if we did, with portaling available, Mingin might not even be in Ireland anymore. He could be anywhere in the world by now."

I frown. "Yeah, there's that."

"Honestly," Dillan says. "If I were on the lam, I'd put as much space between the people who want to drag me back to that tomb as possible and me."

I sigh. "Yeah, well, that's not comforting. Okay, so I guess we stand in a field and wait."

After another hour or so, we regroup in Riordan McNiff's summer cabin and prepare for nightfall. While Samuel, Sloan, and my father tend to the four captured victims, I do the nosy thing and take a self-guided tour.

The master bedroom and two guest bedrooms are upstairs with a balcony that opens over a great room with a tall, glass wall. On the main floor, there's an open-concept kitchen/living room, an office, and a library.

"Okay, wow." I step into the library, and the bulk of books lining the walls reminds me more of the bookshop than a home library. "What kind of reading occupies the attention of a man like Riordan McNiff?"

I met Tad's father once. It was at the Imbolc dinner a few months ago when he challenged me to a shot-for-shot standoff. He thought the little Canadian girl would be an easy target to bully.

He learned differently.

"Can I get ye somethin', Fi?" Tad catches me snooping.

I jump and offer him an apologetic smile. "Sorry. Your dad's an enigma for me. I thought I'd look around and get a better sense of him."

"Careful what you wish for."

I hear the joke in the guy's words but under the jest simmers the strain of their relationship. "Have you ever been close with him?"

Tad shrugs and leans his shoulder against the doorframe, settling in. "He was away a lot when I was little. Before Mam died, he had her to keep me busy. When she passed, I don't think I fit into his plans. They conceived me because he needed an heir, and Mam wanted someone to love who would love her in return."

"Do you want me to beat the snot out of him? 'Cause I totally will."

He chuckles. "I have no doubt you would. Thanks for that."

"No worries." I step deeper into the library and read the spines. "Wow. This is quite a collection."

"Riordan McNiff prides himself on being well-informed and educated. Goddess forbid someone knows more than him and shows him up."

"Oops."

He grins. "Watchin' ye drink him under the table in front of everyone is one of the highlights of my life, Fi. Don't ever feel bad about it." It's sad to hear the venom in his tone.

I know our family dynamic is special, but it's become more evident recently that it's also quite rare.

Deciding to offer Tad a change of subject, I spout off a random thought. "Nothing furnishes a room quite like books."

"Says the girl who works in a bookstore."

"Surround yourself with what you love, right?"

"I wouldn't know." He steps into the room and runs his finger along the spines.

After almost a year of working with Myra, I recognize some of the titles but more importantly, I recognize how rare and valuable some of these tomes are.

"Yer boyfriend and I never had much use fer one another growin' up. We crossed paths at Order events but weren't friends. I envisioned myself a free-thinkin' maverick, and he was always such a straight-laced, stick up the ass, lapdog."

"Careful."

He shakes his head. "No, my point is that seeing him evolve since last summer has enlightened me. He walked away from the structure of his parents' hold, the money, and the expectation. I admire the hell out of that. Ye've been really good fer him."

I like to think I inspired him, but that gives me too much credit. Besides, Sloan didn't walk away from his family's money. The money is his. People simply don't know that. "Sloan's relocation to Toronto and his growth in finding his path are his doing. He decided what he wanted, and now he's making it happen."

Tad pulls a book, reads the cover, and sets it back into place. "Maybe there's hope fer me too."

I hold out my knuckles for a bump. When he meets my fist with his, I meet his gaze. "Whatever you need. Anytime. Anywhere. We're behind you."

The corner of his mouth quirks up, and he nods. "Thanks, Fi. I may take you up on that."

At eight o'clock, Tad checks that Newgrange is vacant and gives us the green light. He and Sloan transport us and, with the help of Jarrod and Eric, they also transport the four people possessed by darkness. Samuel and Nikon meet us inside soon after.

"I'll be right back." Sloan bends to kiss my cheek before *poofing* off.

"Where's Irish off to?" Nikon asks.

"He's picking up Quon Shen and Ahren. Wallace says they're ready to resume their place as banishers of evil and they're eager to get back to it."

"Noice," Calum says. "I'm glad they're better."

I'm about to say me too when they arrive, so I tell them. "You look much better than the last time I saw you, boys."

Quon Shen grins. "You mean when evil choked us out."

"Yeah, then." I give each of them a hug. "The important thing is that you're whole and you're here for the grand finale."

"True enough," Ahren says. "Thank you for saving us, Fi. Your father-in-law said if you hadn't cleansed the taint when you did, we wouldn't have survived."

"I'm glad it worked and that Samuel was there to know what to do. It was truly a team effort."

Quon Shen smiles at the gathering and the four on the ground. "The party got bigger while we were gone."

"It did," Samuel says. "It seems Fi always has an entourage of some sort."

I'm getting used to Samuel's gruffness, but I understand his frustration. "Can everybody duck into the alcoves so we have the main chamber to work?"

When they do, Samuel speaks the spell that calls our circle into being. When the closed pentacle glows orange against the sandy floor of the tomb we're ready to begin. "Quon Shen and Ahren, arrange the innocents for the banishing."

Jarrod and Calum bring over Dark Gerry and hand him off. "Can you see the weakness in the seam, Fi?" Jarrod squints at the air above the pentagram.

"No. Not on this plane, but when I use my shaman powers and astral project as my spirit-self, I can."

Jarrod's eyebrow arches. "That's wild."

I laugh. "For me too."

"Are you going to do that now?"

"No. The banishment happens from the physical plane."

Samuel frowns.

"Yeah, yeah. I'm holding you up. Consider this a teaching moment. It's new for some of us."

That extinguishes his ire for the moment, and he double checks the positioning of everything.

"I felt the surge of Samuel's power." Boann appears in the chamber. "Is it time?"

"It is, goddess," Samuel says. "If you would take the position of fire, that would complete our circle."

Boann dips her chin and steps into place. "To rid my lands of this taint—it will be my pleasure."

CHAPTER TWENTY-THREE

It's after nine-thirty when our day of tracking and banishment ends, and we head back to Granda's to relax and go over everything we've learned. Sloan *poofs* us onto the back lawn to get the animals settled, and the moment we're home, Dart stretches his wings and yawns. "Yeah, buddy. It was a long day, wasn't it?"

"So, you got everyone squared away and back where they belong?" Granda asks.

Gran and Granda are stretched out by the fire pit with a blanket over their laps and smiles on their faces.

They both look more like themselves than they have the whole time we've been here, and it's a balm to my weary state.

"All the innocent folks are darkness-free. The only issue remaining is the whereabouts of Mingin," Da says.

I pull out the stone and show them. "The last three stones aren't tracking anyone, but we'll keep an eye on them just in case. If darkness draws near, we'll know it, and we'll deal with it."

"I have no doubt ye will," Granda says.

Gran scrubs her fingers against Manx's fluffy cheeks and

points under the treehouse. "I have a wee surprise fer the boys if ye have a minute to take a look before ye turn in."

Turn in? I wish.

Even though everyone is meeting us upstairs, I nod and give her the time she's asking for. Gran doesn't ask for much and gives everything in return. "Of course. What have you been up to?"

I follow her gesture and smile at the stone structure under our guesthouse. "Gran...what did you do?"

She pats Dart's side and grins. "I can't have my boys sittin' and sleepin' in the cold drizzle, now can I?"

I release Bruin so he can join the fun and the three boys explore what looks like a private cave.

"Oh, you used the luminescent moss on the ceiling like in the bathroom."

"I did, aye. It's not full-bright, but it's enough to make yer way after nightfall."

Like the corner dedicated to the companion animals in the mancave of our home, this cave offers a spot for everyone to sleep or hang out in their designated area.

"Look, Dart. Gran made you a nice dugout in the earth for you to sleep. Go curl up. See if it's comfy."

Dart drops into the shallow pit, tromps in a circle once, and plops down. After wrapping his tail around his body so it coils in front of him, he grins and lets out a long purr.

"He loves it."

Manx climbs onto the jungle gym of branches above and leaps down to the ones below. "This is lovely, Lara. So thoughtful."

"My pleasure, sweet boy. I know ye like yer comforts, so there's a cushioned platform in the back there for ye."

He climbs back up and disappears over the edge of a raised platform. "Och, it's heavenly."

"I'm glad ye like it, luv. My hope is that if there's room fer everyone to spread out and feel at home, ye might all stay a little longer when ye visit."

Bruin curls up in a rounded stone hollow against the back corner. He fills the small alcove with his massive, grizzly body. I know how much he likes the feeling of being in a secure den, so the tight fit is perfect for him.

"Och, and ye padded my sleepin' mat. Much appreciated, Gran. I'm not as young as I used to be and nature can be hard on my elbows."

Gran nods. "I'm glad ye all approve."

"You shouldn't have gone to all the trouble, Gran," I say. "It's amazing, but you don't need to bribe us to stay. We're happy to come, and we're happy to stay, even when we're a little crowded."

Calum chuckles beside me and lays a heavy arm across my shoulders. "We grew up with six kids, Mam, and Da in one house with one full bathroom. Crowded is our wheelhouse."

Gran reaches up to adjust the wandering tendrils of the luminescent plants on the roof. "It was nothin' more than a little stone and soil work and a couple of crafting projects I put together from swatches of old fabric. I didn't put myself out. It was an absolute labor of love."

"Well, thank you," I say, hugging her. "They love it. Don't you, boys?

"Yes, Gran."

"Aye, Lara, we do."

Dart nods and lets out another long purr.

"Now then," Gran says. "I won't keep ye from yer meetin' of the minds above. I know yer tired, and Lugh has things to tell ye that he's been workin' on all day. I put a large pot of stew on yer stove. I wasn't sure when ye'd be back, so I thought stew would be best."

I sink against her and laugh. "No, Gran. *You* are the best...but stew is a close second."

Up in the treehouse, I head straight to the kitchen, pull a bunch of bowls down from the cupboard, and set them on the counter. "What do we know about Mingin and him escaping from the Neitherlands, Granda?"

"Not a lot, but what I did find wasn't good."

"You gotta work on your delivery, Granda," Dillan says. "As pep talks go, that sucked."

Granda grunts. "From what I found, the longer an entity spends in the Neitherlands, the greater the toxic energy it possesses."

I dish out bowls of stew and start lining them up. "Mingin was in there for what—six or seven centuries? That can't be good."

"No. I don't suppose."

"He wasn't all that great when he went to purgatory. I'm sure," Dillan says.

Samuel accepts some late-night sustenance and frowns. "No. From what I've learned about him, he was a dark and ruthless man."

"Yet Melanippe still fell for him," I say.

"She seemed so solid too," Ahren says.

"Until her crazy leaked out," Quon Shen adds. "Crazy and immortal is a bad combination."

"It is, but it could be worse."

"How so?" Jarrod asks.

"There could still be six tainted fugitives loose."

Calum pauses with his fork in the air. "What I still don't understand is how Melanippe ended up as part of the Barghest crew. Was she with them all along?"

I snap the tab of a Guinness, expertly pour it into a glass, and sip. "What was the benefit of them teaming up? Droghun doesn't do anything for nothing. If he has his fingers in this, there's a payoff for the necromancers."

"More dark power," Dillan suggests. "That's what everyone wants lately: the witches, the warlocks, the necromancers. It always comes back to the darker sects scrambling for more power."

"But why?" Calum asks. "There are always people who want more power, but what suddenly gave all the sects such a hard-on to put everything on the line for the big payouts?"

"You gotta risk it to get the biscuit," I say.

Eric and Jarrod both laugh at me.

"What? That's not a saying here?"

"No," Jarrod says. "But I think that's the right question. Ye mentioned somethin' similar at the Order's Imbolc dinner. Ye wondered why everyone seemed to be in such a stir fer more power."

Exactly. "So, what's the answer? What's approaching that they know about and we don't?"

"The Culling." Dionysus appears, naked and lounging on the couch by the wall.

Everyone jumps and spins.

"Whoa, dude," Calum shouts while patting his chest. "Where the hell did you come from?"

"Originally or just now?"

"Do ye not have clothes, sir?" Da frowns. "Every time I see ye, yer airin' yer bits. I support free expression, but maybe not when we're discussin' murder and dark possession as a group."

Calum grabs a tea towel and tosses it over. "Back to your comment. What's the Culling?"

Dionysus sits up and drapes the red and white checkered swatch of cloth over his lap. "Better?"

"Better than nothing." I make a mental note to burn that dish-towel. "Not as good as clothing."

He chuckles and stands. As he rises, he flashes on ripped jeans and a long-sleeved jersey. The entire room seems thankful. "I suppose the fertility part of this vacation has come to an end. Fine. You win, my prudish friends. The party is over."

"The Keenin'," Da says with a bit more edge.

I pop the tab of another Guinness, pour it into a glass, and hand it to Dionysus. He dips his chin and holds it up to toast the group. "The Culling happens once every millennium and is a resetting of the preternatural scales. Good, evil. Light, dark. They are always at odds, you know?"

Da frowns. "Yes, we are aware."

"Right, well, over time, the balance distorts, and we must redefine boundaries."

"Redefine?" Da says. "How?"

"Natural selection, the strongest survive, only the good die young, that sort of thing. The Culling is a no-holds-barred test of the sects that stands as the baseline for the next millennium."

I blink. "No holds barred? What does that look like?"

"For five days, once a millennium, the empowered sects around the world fight their fights and try to right the wrongs they see in society. It's like a giant, tip the scales in your favor and get the upper hand free-for-all."

"It's the fucking *Purge*," Dillan says.

"Only it's longer and with powers," Calum adds.

I scrub a hand through my hair, my head starting to pound. "When does this Culling take place?"

"During the Winter Solstice. More specifically, during the five days surrounding the Winter Solstice when sunlight illuminates the passage of Newgrange and fills the chamber with light. Those are the five days of the Culling."

Sloan gathers my hand in his and squeezes. "So, yer sayin', you think Barghest turning to necromancy, and the witches betrayin' Mother Nature to ally with the Unseelie Prince, and the warlocks attemptin' to summon a greater demon were attempts to start gainin' power for this empowered free-for-all?"

"I've seen it before. Since the countdown to the Culling is upon you, that would be my guess."

"Sweet goddess almighty," Granda mutters. "Let's keep it between us, fer now, and look into it further. Right now, let's focus on the immediate problem—Barghest and yer escaped Hunter-god, Mingin."

Da tips back his beer and swallows. "All right. Run it down with me, boys. Barghest wants or needs some kind of connection with the dark souls of the Neitherlands. They want more dark energy, which means more death and more dark power for them to grow stronger."

Calum nods. "At some point, they cross paths with Melanippe and find out she plans to release her long-lost love, so they join forces. When do you think that was?"

"I think that was a new alliance," Samuel says. "From what she said to me this afternoon, she'd set her plans centuries ago, and I ruined them by enlisting Ahren, Quon Shen, and Fiona. She planned on splitting the seam and welcoming Mingin and his friends."

"Then I'm glad we mucked up her plans," Ahren says.

"The fae universe did that by putting us in play."

Noice. "Here's to the Fates." I raise my can and toast those three beautiful ladies.

Sloan borrows my beer and takes a drink. "I tend to agree with Samuel on it being a new alliance. We fought with her at the raid in Tipperary. If she favored the Barghest in any way, I didn't see it. She was ruthless and skilled at cutting them down."

"If she was on team Barghest then, why not tip them off we were about to raid and recover the elders?" I ask.

Da nods. "Let's assume she didn't know about the Barghest until we raided them to retrieve the elders."

"Who the necromancers kidnapped to stop the equinox ceremony and make the druids lose face in front of Ostara as well as the fae," Dillan adds. "They wanted to diminish our hold as guardians of the natural world and reduce the fertility and growth of the lands."

"They wanted to weaken our base of power early in the game," Calum says.

"Then we found the elders and figured out how to not only complete the ceremony but give it a gigantic fertility boost." I tip my beer toward Dionysus.

"You're welcome." He bows.

"So then, Melanippe contacts them and invites them to join her quest. Maybe they thought they could free the darkness by tearing open the seam and get more power that way."

"But we bungled her plan and captured her," Quon Shen adds.

"Then Samuel repaired the seam and blocked them out." The pieces are falling into place for me now. "So, it's a case of the enemy of my enemy is my friend."

Da nods. "I think so."

"So, are we thinking Barghest knows where Mingin is? If they were allied with Melanippe to free him, maybe they'd hide and protect him until she gets back."

Sloan tilts his head from side to side. "Droghun and the necromancers have a strong dark connection and enough power to block Samuel's tracking spell. That's one possible answer."

Samuel frowns. "Or another answer is that he's simply not here. Like Niall mentioned earlier, he could be halfway around the world by now."

"Or, if he knows where Melanippe is, halfway to Toronto by now." I set the dirty dishes in the sink and try to rein in everything we've learned. "Okay, so what's our move?"

My phone rings and Garnet's Lion King ring tone stops the conversation. "Hold on." Accepting the call, I hold it up to my ear. "Hey, Garnet, what's up?"

"You know your misplaced dark fugitive?"

"Yes? Have you found him?"

"Well, there is a ghostly thundercloud shrouding the Acropolis. I think your banished soul is here to pick up his girlfriend for their big date."

"Shit on a stick. Okay, we're coming right now."

In a scramble, Nikon and Sloan transport the group back to Toronto, and we form outside the elevators on the tenth floor of our Acropolis. "Welcome to the Batcave, everyone."

Calum pulls out his pendant first and sets his hand on the scanner. When we meet the security protocols, we rush inside.

"Garnet? You here?"

The furious roar of lions follows a thundering *crash* in the back.

My shield flares to life and I push off into a run. Bolting through the door to the safehouse apartment, I round the corner for the holding areas.

Holy hell.

Forward momentum makes it impossible to stop on a dime. I put on the brakes and backpedal as people crash into me from behind, and we become a chain-reaction collision on an icy highway.

My boots squeak against the polished floor, and I try to figure out what happened in the two minutes since I spoke to Garnet.

He and Anyx are battling a dozen men in black, and my gaze locks with the man leading them into battle.

"Bruin, have at it. Help Garnet." I release my bear and recognize the leader in this madness. "Droghun."

"Where the fuck is the roof of my building?" Nikon shouts, grabbing a length of iron rebar.

I shelter my eyes from my hair whipping me in the face and cast a glance at the night sky above as I shift out of the open and duck for cover.

"Fuckety-fuck, would you look at that thing." Dillan's emerald green eyes are blown wide as he lands on his back beside me behind a section of fallen ceiling and points at the possessed storm cloud funneling into Melanippe. "He's massive. Will he even fit in her?"

I have no time to wonder.

The wind is incredible. Dark energy bites at my face and screams in my ears as Mingin's cyclone of dark power attacks. *"Tough as Bark."*

That takes care of the hair issue.

"How do we get her down from there?" Calum asks. He calls his bow and is shooting arrows at the Black Dog forces. The wind is ripping the projectiles out of the air and spitting them wherever it wants.

"You're getting nowhere, bro."

"Yeah, I thought so too."

"What's with her face?" Dillan shouts.

Melanippe is hovering off the floor, back arched and arms outstretched. She's been swept into the air by her dark daddy, and despite the chaos, wears a triumphant smile as if being possessed by her dead lover's evil is what she's wanted all along.

Cray-cray.

Like Miranda says, "It takes all kinds of kinds."

Nikon and Dionysus join Garnet and Anyx in the battle against the necromancers, but more importantly, we need to keep the Mingin cloud at bay.

"How do we battle a storm cloud?" Dillan asks.

"Cloud seeding?" Calum offers.

Tad snorts. "What do we seed a fugitive cloud of darkness with to destroy it?"

"Sunshine and rainbows?"

"The only thing that worked against him in the tomb was *Purify*," I say, "but he's a helluva lot bigger now than when I fought him in the tomb."

"What's our move, people?" Tad asks. "He's possessin' her fast."

I rush as close as I can get and call Birga. "Push them back, boys. We need space."

Droghun sneers and storms forward. "I'll take care of the druid bitch. She's mine to make suffer."

I brace for the impact of a head-on attack from Droghun and widen my stance. A moment before he's close enough to engage, he vanishes.

Straightening, I search around my surroundings, thinking he might be *poofing* in behind me or something. "Where did he go?"

"Antarctica." Dionysus is locked in a melee fight with two opponents and still able to smile and chat. "He needed to cool off. You are neither his to make suffer nor a bitch. You're lovely and the Jane to my Tarzan."

"Aw, dude. That's sweet."

"Yo, Fi? Back to the clusterfuck at hand, please."

I turn on my heels and get back into it. Dillan's right. It's time we deal with this. "Druids, we're going in for a mass cleansing. The spell is *Purify*."

Da, Dillan, Calum, Sloan, Tad, Eric, and Jarrod push forward and disengage from battle until the eight of us are standing shoulder to shoulder, hands raised.

"*Purify!*"

I send as much cleansing energy forward as I can, and though it slows Mingin's possession, it certainly doesn't stop it.

"It's not going to be enough," Da says. "If he finishes the transference, he'll only get stronger."

"Plus, she's immortal," I remind them. "We won't be able to take her down."

Samuel has his hands up, and his lips are moving in a steady stream of casting.

Still, nothing seems to be working.

"Be right back," Sloan says.

I don't have time to ask him where he's going before he's gone. A moment later he *poofs* back with a steel chakram and a book. "Nikon, do ye know how to throw one of these?"

"Uh…yeah. It's been ages, but I do."

"All right, hold it while I read the spell. Calum, join us. I'll spell yer arrows too."

They follow the instructions and as much as I want to see what they're working on, I continue to focus on cleansing Melanippe of the toxic soul possessing her.

"Give it everythin' ye've got in three, two, one—"

We go all-in on Sloan's mark.

I throw as much power as I can summon into purifying Melanippe of evil. My hands are shaking, my cells vibrating with the demands of magic.

The druids throw everything we have at Mingin.

Arrows fly. The chakram hits Melanippe solidly in the sternum. Bolts of Samuel's magic hit the Mingin cloud, lighting up the night sky with pyrotechnic flare.

"It's not enough," I shout.

"Anything you can think of, boys," Sloan shouts. "Leave it on the field."

"Fire in the hole!" Dionysus is locked in a stance, holding a long metal barrel pointed at Melanippe. With a gleeful grin, he pulls the trigger. The *hiss* of the weapon discharging launches a rocket-propelled grenade directly at the Amazon.

"Get down!" I turn and dive to the floor as the incendiary device detonates and the world around us explodes.

Debris rains down on my back, and I cover my head.

I close my eyes. The ringing in my ears seems to go on forever. When the raining shrapnel ends, I push up to my hands and knees to check that everyone is all right.

Ahren and Anyx are sloppy and struggling with the last two Black Dogs, so I scramble over to help. Before I get there, the assholes jump off the roof. I selfishly hope they're plummeting to their death when I look over the edge and see them vanish through a portal rift.

Garnet lets out another furious roar as he pushes up, panting on all fours. Anyx shifts back and sits back against a chunk of the ceiling.

The vortex of evil is gone, and all that's left is our team groaning and pushing up to our feet.

"What happened?" Jarrod raises a hand to the gash in his shoulder and ass-plants back down. "Did we win?"

I have no idea.

Sloan meets my gaze, and I nod. "I'm fine. Da? Calum? Samuel? Anybody seriously hurt?"

Everyone sounds off that they're fine and my adrenaline starts to level off.

"What the fuck was that?" Eric asks.

I chuckle. "Sloan said anything we could think of. Dionysus thought an RPG was the way to go."

Cue the wide-eyed looks of amazement.

"Seriously, badass," Dillan says, chuckling.

Dionysus brightens. "Really? You don't think it was overkill?"

Calum pushes up to his feet and returns his bow and quiver to his tattooed forearms. "We weren't winning before you blew her up, so I'd say extreme force was a good call."

Da is up now, brushing himself off. "A little more warning would be good next time."

I laugh. "He did yell, 'Fire in the hole.'"

"Aye, he did at that."

"Do we think that killed her?" Jarrod asks. "I get that she's immortal, but a direct hit from an RPG is pretty major. That could've killed her, couldn't it?"

"I wish," Dionysus says. "No. Unfortunately, she'll be back."

I don't even care. "That was epic, my friend, and the good news is that she didn't absorb the inkblot."

He dips his chin and takes a slight bow. "You will have the

opportunity to take another run at your dark fugitive and send him back."

"That is good news," Sloan says. "We know he'll be searching fer Melanippe, so maybe we can track him and trap him that way."

"Do we have any idea where she'll regenerate?" I look at Dionysus and Nikon.

Nikon frowns. "No. We don't. She's from Scythia, but that doesn't mean that's where she'll turn up. If she does, we don't know how long it'll take for her to resurrect or even if it will be in this time."

Dionysus steps forward and frowns. "If she is *the* Melanippe of Scythia, her parents are Otrera and Ares. That's a powerful bloodline. My advice is to find and banish Mingin before Melanippe comes back into play."

"That's great in theory but difficult to put into practice. Damn it! I hate that they got away."

Da frowns. "Ye don't always get yer man on the first try, *mo chroi.* There are times it's best to regroup and figure out what yer dealin' with."

"He's right." Sloan wraps his arm around my hip and hugs me to his side. "Thanks to Dionysus, we were able to keep Melanippe and Mingin from joinin' forces. That's a huge win in itself."

"Yeah, battling Minganippe would've been way worse," Dillan says.

Da arches a brow and chuckles. "They are each lethal strengths, but yer right, Minganippe would be worse."

I let out a long sigh and look at the damage done to our beautiful new building. "Nikon, you can literally claim 'act of god' with insurance on this one."

CHAPTER TWENTY-FOUR

The next two days are a scramble to manage the chaos. Nikon snaps Sloan and me back to Ireland with Jarrod, Eric, and Tad. We give them two of the tracking stones to monitor for any sign that Mingin has returned. We'll do the same with the last stone in Toronto.

Before we return to Toronto, I escort Dart back to the lair, and I spend a few hours with the dragons. While I'm there, I talk to the Dragon Queen about Dart coming to stay with me on a trial basis. We agree once he's powerful enough to cloak his presence, we'll try it out.

There's still no word from Emmet, but with so much to clean up after the attack on the Acropolis and our Batcave, I try to keep busy and not obsess.

Part of me is on edge, expecting that at any moment I'll hear about some dark atrocity we could've prevented if Mingin hadn't slipped through our fingers.

Samuel, Ahren, and Quon Shen are on that, though. They left right away for Ukraine and are scouring the area that would've been ancient Scythia, searching for her place of origin. They've vowed to track her down and figure out a better way to track Mingin's dark signature.

Then there's Droghun and Barghest.

If they're looking for ways to get powered up before the Culling, when will they ambush me or someone I love to try to take us off the board?

When nothing happens immediately, I realize that as usual, Da is right about all things bad guy. We need to regroup and figure out how to challenge Mingin's darkness and Melanippe's shaman skills and immortality.

We need time to strategize for the coming of a five-day empowered Purge in December.

We need to find my brother and undo whatever damage a five-day fornication fest has done to his life.

Standing at the fridge, I stare at the piece of paper I put there when we first got back.

Ní neart go cur le chéile.

There's strength in unity.

I took a banana bread next door to chat with the old woman in the rocking chair when we first got back. The man who answered the door said he didn't know what I was talking about. He rented the place from a realty office and is in town on a three-month contract.

He has no idea who was in there before him.

I used the computers at the Batcave to double-check his story, and it all checks out.

So, if the old lady is fae or an empowered messenger of some sort, she seems to be gone for now.

"Are ye ready, *a ghra*? Dora's all set."

I blink out of my distraction and hand him the sodas. "Yeah. Sorry, I zoned out there for a second."

"Not a problem."

Following him down into the man cave, we find Dora set up in the dealer's seat at the poker table. She's looking mystical and magical in her cyan blue wig and glittery gold eye makeup.

"Thanks for helping us." I offer her a Coke and take the seat opposite her. "We've tried to scry for him ourselves, but either we're no good at it, or he's way beyond our range."

"Or he doesn't want to be found," Dionysus adds.

I stick my tongue out at him, and he laughs. "Ignore him. He doesn't know Emmet like I do."

Dora accepts the can, cracks the tab open, and sips before setting it in the drink slot in her part of the table. "Happy to help, girlfriend. I love Emmet, and I agree, five days without a word is worrying."

"Ha!" Dionysus laughs at the bar. "I once fell in with a pod of nomadic water nymphs exploring the Amalfi Coast and didn't lift my head for three months. Emmet has a lot of me in him. He's fine."

He uncorks a bottle of red and pours himself a fishbowl of wine. It's not a real fishbowl, but it's one of those massive glass goblets that restaurants set out to collect cards or offer candies at the door.

No one would mistake it for a glass—except the God of Wine and Intoxication.

"I honestly hope he is fine," I say. "In which case, we'll check in and know for sure. I don't think he would intentionally not contact us or fail to come home or miss work if everything was tickety-boo."

"They've been having this argument fer days," Sloan says. "Since we've had no luck scryin', we thought Tarot might give us some insight."

"I'm sure it will," Dora says.

Dionysus frowns and comes to sit next to me. "Why assume he's lost or suffering? He tapped into *my* powers and vices. That's nothing but the good stuff in life. I honestly don't understand why you're so worried."

I squeeze his hand. "I know you don't, sweetie...but I *am* worried. Let's just find him and bring him home."

Dora pulls her well-worn deck from a black velvet bag with a tree of life symbol embroidered in hot pink silk. "Do you remember how this goes?"

"While you shuffle, I focus on what I need to know, then we pull the spread and see what the cards say."

"Like a pro, girlfriend."

While Dora shuffles her deck, I focus on the backs of the cards and try to connect. I study the triple goddess moon symbol glowing against the galaxy pattern of constellations. I lock my mind on Emmet, where he is, and how to find him.

Dora finishes shuffling, lays the cards face down, and fans them in front of me in a skillful and smooth arc. "We'll do a five-card spread. Point the cards that hold energy for you, in any order, and I'll draw them from the deck and set them into position."

I know better than to touch her cards.

Some Tarot masters allow others to touch their cards. Dora does not. It's her process, and I'm not about to argue. She's never led me astray.

Leaning forward, I stare at the deck and the card I'm meant to pick practically vibrates on a frequency that sings to me. I point at the first card, then rinse and repeat from my second through to the fifth.

When I finish, Dora flips each one and lays them out on the felt of the table.

"All right, let's see what we have. The first card of this partic-ular spread signifies the past and what brought us to this point. Then we have present and future. The fourth card signifies obstacles. The fifth and final card is the outcome card."

I nod, excited and nervous to see what turns up.

"The card for past is the Fool."

"No surprise there," Dillan says.

"The Fool is at the beginning of his journey. He's open and daring and walking on the edge of the cliff of life. He lives either unaware or uncaring of the risks and traps of societal norms. This card signifies someone living outside the box. The fool is open to new prospects."

"Well, that's certainly Emmet," Kevin says.

It is. He may be a fool, but he's our fool, and we adore that part of him.

Dora turns the second card and smiles. "The present card is the Knight of Swords. If I had to sum up this card in two words, it would be 'no fear.' When the Knight of Swords appears in a reading, expect excitement, movement, and adventure. It signifies courage, swift change, and forward progress."

"That sounds awesome," Calum says. "Emmet's killing it in this reading."

Dora moves to the third card and flips it over for us to see. "The future card is The Empress."

"Of course it is."

"The Empress is pregnant in this card, but before you lose your mind, that is not to be taken literally. It can be the birth of new ideas or opportunities or a reinvention of self."

"Oh, thank you, baby Yoda," I gasp, pounding my fluttering heart.

"The five-petaled flower in her hand creates a natural pentagram. She wears a rich green gown that stands as a link to the powers of life, growth, and nature. When this card appears, it's a message from the Mother Goddess to respect the power of nature and to embrace creativity, sexuality, and fertility."

"Hallelujah," Dionysus shouts, raising his hands in benediction.

Dillan snorts. "Isn't them embracing their sexuality and fertility what brings us here in the first place?"

Aiden grins. "I bet they have checked those boxes."

Dora flips the card and points at the image on the fourth card. "Nine of Wands. Can we guess who's coming in at the point of obstacles and fears?"

Dillan chuckles and points. "You mean who that determined-looking woman with wine-red hair, wearing a heraldic dragon embroidered on the center of her tunic is? That's a little on the nose, don't you think?"

Dora grins. "The cards don't lie."

I roll my eyes. "So, obviously that's me. What does that mean? Why am I an obstacle?"

"Well, look at her. She's standing with a quarterstaff ready to defend her turf. Do you maybe think that's the universe's way to bring your attention to the fact that you're on guard to ward off trouble in Emmet's life?"

"Of course I am."

"But is the trouble you're concerned about truly a danger to him, or might it be Ciara or him forming an attachment to her?"

"I'm honestly not thrilled my brother is having a passionate liaison with Sloan's ex-lover, but I think I'm justified. I'm worried about my brother, not defending my turf."

Cue a round of coughing and snorting by my brothers, Kevin, and Nikon.

"You assholes shut up. Dora, last card, please."

She does as I ask and turns the last card. "Justice. You might recognize Themis here, sitting in her temple. She holds a double-edged sword in one hand and the scales in her right. The sword symbolizes that balance must be preserved, even by force. The scales also represent balance."

"I remember."

Dionysus leans in and smiles. "It's not a bad likeness of her. She'd approve."

Dora taps the card with a long, polished nail. "When Justice appears in a reading, it can either be prompting you to ask what is out of balance or signaling a restoration of balance. It indicates that harmony is coming, that situations will work out, and that you must trust and leave the future to the gods."

"So, what? You're saying we *shouldn't* try to find Emmet to stop whatever is happening?"

Dora waves that away. "My job isn't to tell you what to do, girlfriend. It's to show you the way of things so you have an informed path moving forward."

"All right. So, let's say I want to find him anyway. Despite him having no fear and living an adventure, where would I go if I want to bring him home?"

Dora arches a manicured and penciled brow and gestures at her scrying tools. "Let's see if I have more luck than you did, shall we?"

Unfolding a map of the world, Dora lays it out and spells it to straighten perfectly flat. Then she points at me. "You have a keepsake gemstone that is perfectly round, yes?"

I reach into the pocket of my pants and pull out my navy, bronze, and teal fae rabbit poop.

"Place it on the map and focus on your brother. Concentrate on where he is."

I close my eyes and do as she said. "Where are you, Emmet?"

"It's working," Kevin says.

I open my eyes and watch the psychedelic poop roll around the map. Then it heads south.

"Be in Vegas," Dillan waves it over with his hand. "I want to go to Vegas."

"It's not Vegas," Nikon says. "It's going the opposite way, dumbass."

Calum grips my shoulders and leans over me to see. "It might be...oh, we're heading into the South Pacific."

Dillan chuckles. "See, tropical with an open bar."

The little turd stops rolling, and it's sitting over solid blue. I frown. "He's on a raft in the South Pacific?"

"A yacht, maybe," Aiden says.

"No wonder the cards say he's happy," Kevin says. "He's cruising the South Pacific, sexing it up and living without any inhibitions."

Dionysus raises his hands. "That's what I've been trying to say. My life is fucktabulous. Him having even a portion of that is a celebration."

I nod. "Okay, I agree. It's looking like you're right, and I'm worrying for nothing. Let's figure out where he is and find out for sure."

Sloan has his tablet in hand, and Google Earth open. "I don't think he's on a raft in the ocean. There's a cluster of islands in that area of the rim, which is called the Pacific Ring of Fire."

"And it burns, burns, burns. The ring of fire…" Clan Cumhaill breaks into a boisterous ode to Johnny Cash.

Dora chuckles, and we make it to the end of the chorus and put everyone out of their misery.

"Thanks, fer that," Sloan says.

"For serenading you or for stopping?"

"The second one."

I laugh and get back to looking at the map. "Okay, who's coming with?"

"To witness Emmet and Ciara going crazy jungle love on an island in the South Pacific? Hells yes, I'm going," Dillan says.

Calum grins. "Wouldn't miss it."

Kevin waggles his brows. "The two of them *au natural* in paradise? Count me in."

Sloan has the good sense to say nothing.

I see the answer in Dionysus's grin.

"All right. Should I have asked who's *not* coming?"

Aiden laughs and raises his hand. "As much fun as I think it would be, I'm sure Dillan will record Emmet's embarrassment. Kinu has a migraine. I have to pick up the monkeys from a play date with Imari and start dinner for the fam jam."

"Good man," Dora says. "I love your brother, but I've lived through enough hedonism in my life to take a pass."

"Enough hedonism?" Dionysus scoffs. "Can those two words even be said in the same sentence?"

"Apparently yes." I lean in to see the zoomed-in map of the area we're looking at. "Set my Ostara poop on the zoomed-in map."

Sloan shifts his gaze to Dora. "Do ye mind if we get a more accurate location to target?"

"Not at all, Irish." She passes her hand over the screen, and we're back in business. When my gemstone picks the island, I look at Nikon. "Does that work for your transport location? Can you get us to the archipelago of Vanuatu?"

Nikon checks out maps and destinations with a few tourist websites and nods. "Yep. Not an issue. All aboard who's coming aboard."

The six of us link up and snap out.

CHAPTER TWENTY-FIVE

Nikon flashes Calum, Kevin, Dillan, Sloan, Dionysus, and I to the tropical island of Tanna, which is one of eighty islands in the archipelago of Vanuatu. Geographically, it's across from the top of Australia and directly above New Zealand.

"It says here that sixty-five of the islands in this archipelago are inhabited. Crazy. I've never heard of any of them. That blows my mind."

"The world is a big place, Red," Nikon says. "Any time you guys want to explore it, I'm happy to play tour guide."

"I love that idea, Greek." Calum grins at Kevin. "We might take you up on that."

"Please do."

Dionysus lifts his face to the wind like a dog on a scent and points. "This way. I sense my signature."

"Awesomesauce. Go, Dionysus!" I fall in line behind the Greek god, relieved that we're close and soon, Emmet and Ciara will be back where they belong.

"This island is something out of an episode of *Survivor*," Calum says.

Sloan still has his tablet open and is scrolling through info sheets. "Even more than ye realize."

"What does that mean?"

"It says here that Tanna Island was inhabited as far back as 2000 BCE and has a rich history in cannibalism and murder."

I glance over my shoulder and peg him with a look. "Not anymore, right?"

"Not so much, no. Exposure to first-world standards during World War II changed things. It initiated a heavily followed cargo cult by the natives on the island."

Dillan scoffs. "So they shifted from cannibalism and murder to being a cult? Oh...that's much better."

"What is a cargo cult? Are we talking the Kool-Aid drinking kind of cult or the human sacrifice kind?"

He scrolls further and frowns. "By definition, a cargo cult is any religious movement that exhibits belief in the imminence of a new age of blessing. They believe this blessing or 'cargo' is sent from supernatural sources beyond the island's reach."

Dillan chuckles. "So, they think if they pray, the gods will send them cargo shipments? That's whacked."

"It's thought the belief began when tribal locals witnessed the delivery of supplies to colonial officials during the war."

"They confused military shipments as divine gifts?"

"Seems so. They believe tribal divinities, culture heroes, and ancestors will return with the cargo, or goods they need as they need them."

"Seriously?" I shake my head. "Dillan's right. That *is* whacked."

"On the upside, it seems they no longer practice cannibalism and torturing of disobedient wives."

Calum snorts. "That's very progressive."

I don't love any of this. "Is the cult following only part of the island population? All of it? Or what?"

"It says the cult remains strong on Tanna today, especially at

Sulphur Bay in the southeast and Green Point in the southwest of the island."

I lift my head and search the skies. "Where are we?"

Calum checks the compass on his watch and frowns. "Southeast."

"Of course we are."

Sloan chuckles and slides the tablet into his backpack. "The point to take from this is that largely the island is steeped in old-world tribal beliefs."

"If we get into a jam, Nikon can snap in and bring them some cargo, and we'll be gods," Dillan says.

Nikon laughs. "Um...yeah. I can. Do we know what kind of cargo they want?"

"Cargo pants. Cargo shorts. Cargo jet."

Nikon waves that away. "I'll improvise."

I smack a bug biting my cheek and frown. "Are we there yet?"

Dionysus shakes his head and points at the conical mountain directly in front of us. "No. My homing signal tells me Emmet's on that volcano."

"Of course he is. I know I'll regret asking this but is there any chance that volcano is dormant?"

"No," Sloan says. "I didn't mention it, but Tanna's claim to fame is that it's the home to Mount Yasur, one of the top ten most active volcanos on the planet."

"Better and better," I grouse. "Now tell me I was overreacting by worrying."

Dionysus nods. "I admit, this isn't an island I would've chosen to spend my vacation on."

Dillan curses and squishes something biting his arm. "Bugs, volcanos, and cannibalistic natives don't sell the place, do they?"

We tromp through the heavy brush for another five minutes before the rhythmic tattoo of drums starts in the distance. I love drums, but for some reason, this rhythm makes my shield wake and tingle against my skin.

"Bruin? Can you check out what's happening up the volcano and try to locate Emmet? My shield is firing up, and I have a bad feeling."

On it.

I release my bear and push forward. "Step up the pace, boys. The universe is telling me something, and surprise…it's not good."

We tromp and climb and sweat for another five minutes, then Kevin points up the rocky slope of Mount Yasur. "There. There's movement in that cave opening."

"Good eye, Kev. That's Emmet!"

"The natives are moving in on him," Calum says. "Look, they're swarming up the slope with torches."

My heart is hammering in my chest, and I stick my hand out. "Screw walking. It's time to portal. Get us into that cave fast."

Sloan grabs my arm and Dillan's while Kev and Calum reach for Nikon.

Dionysus remains unbothered by any of this and simply looks amused.

We materialize inside the cave and Ciara screeches. "Feckin' hell. Do ye know how to knock?" Scrambling off a pallet of hides, she pulls one of them up to wrap around herself like a towel. "Some of us are naked here."

"We see that." Dionysus grins. "Enjoying the freedoms of unhinged desire, are you?"

Emmet grins. "Thankfully, we worked through the unhinged part. Welcome to our cave of wonders. Great timing, by the way."

"You're really fucking naked, brother mine," Dillan says. "How about you sheath that bad boy so we can get out of here?"

Emmet shrugs. "Oh, that I could, D. The natives took our clothes."

Nikon laughs. "The tribal people of this island set you up in a volcano love nest and took your clothes?"

"Crazy as it sounds, they love us here."

Ciara chuffs and pulls her hair forward and over the swells of her breasts. "They didn't at first, but once Emmet jumped in the volcano for them they—"

"You *what?*"

Emmet laughs and waves a middle finger at Dillan, who is, of course, capturing the moment on video. "The tribe sacrifices someone every year to appease the volcano. I volunteered, jumped in, and *poofed* back here to Ciara. After that, they loved us. They think I'm a god."

"Och, yer definitely a god." Ciara looks him up and down.

I rake my fingers through my hair and try to find the words. "No. He's a moron. You jumped into an active volcano?"

Emmet laughs. "I was buzzing with Dionysus's power at the time." He looks over to the god and lifts his fist for a bump. "Thanks, by the way. Best. Sex. Evah. Like, seriously off the hook."

Dionysus waggles his brow. "You are welcome. I'm delighted to see you two appreciate my gifts."

Ciara's cheeks flush bright pink. "I can safely say we made excellent use of yer gifts."

Eww. "Wicked TMI, you two. Dionysus, can you please clothe them? Better yet, let's get out of here."

Bruin breezes in and materializes on the vacant pallet of hides. "Red. The natives are restless."

I chuckle. "Seriously? Did you actually say that?"

Bruin's deep baritone laughter fills the space. "I did…but it's also true."

"Yeah," Emmet says. "They want me to swan dive into the volcano again, but Dionysus's mojo is gone. I wasn't sure how I would get out of it. They took our clothes and smashed our phones when we got here. Like I said, good timing."

I feel vindicated in my worry but don't care about that right now. "All right. Everyone, hands in."

"You go," Dionysus says, stepping up to the edge of the cave mouth. "I think I'll stay for a bit and take a swan dive for them. There's a law among gods. Try never to leave your followers disappointed."

Whatevs. "You do you, dude. We'll see you at home when you get back."

Dionysus strips off his shirt, tosses it, and starts popping his way down his button fly. What a surprise, Dionysus is getting nakey.

"That's our cue, boys. Home, please."

After getting everyone home and catching everyone up on all the events of the past week, Sloan and I spend an hour in the grove hot spring lounging in the decadence of magic and warmth. When my muscles are mush, and I've finally released the anxiety of the past week, he *poofs* us up into our ensuite bath to get ready for bed.

Pulling a towel off the heated rack, I groan as I dry myself off. "See, this. All I need to be blissfully happy is some naked time with my guy, a heated towel, and the prospect of spending the next twelve hours hidden away in the confines of King Henry's walls."

Sloan dries his legs and feet and wraps his towel around his hips.

I take in the sight and amend my statement. *Annnd a view of Sloan's abs and sexy hip v muscles.*

"I know that look," Sloan says around his toothbrush. "My answer is yes."

Pulling the elastic from my hair, I brush out my tangles, and when he finishes with the electric base of our toothbrush, I change the bristles and move to my teeth. "Do you think we're too domesticated to lose ourselves in each other for five days like that?"

Sloan grins. "Domesticated? Is that what we are?"

I point at the two of us in the mirror and the tooth brushing and him hanging the damp towels.

"Yeah, we are." I finish, spit, and rinse.

Sloan waits for me to finish and turns off the bathroom light before leading me toward the bed. "I like domesticated...but if yer askin' if I could whisk ye away and do nothin' but make wild volcano jumpin' jungle love with ye for five days straight, the answer is yes. In fact, I think now and then we should unplug from the chaos of life and do just that."

"I like how you think, Mackenzie. Where and when?"

He grins, pulls back the sheets, and slides in. "I'll work on a few getaway options and get back to ye. Yer birthday is comin' up. Maybe we run away and shut out the world."

"Oh, I'm looking forward to it...except, the twins are due right around then. If they aren't born yet, I don't want to miss it."

"Agreed. A birthday getaway after the babes arrive."

I snuggle in close. We're lying on our sides, chests pressed together, and our skin is still warm from the hot springs soak. He draws two fingers gently over the rise of my shoulder and down toward my elbow. "What have ye got tomorrow? Do we have plans?

"Nothing unless Samuel and the guys get a lead on Melanippe. Which, in all honesty, I don't think will happen...not tomorrow anyway."

In the muted moonlight from the window, his eyes practically glow silver. "Then let's not get out of bed until we have to. In the morning, we'll post a message on the family channel and excuse ourselves from life. The world might not give us five days, but we'll take what we can get."

"It's a plan." I claim his mouth and sweep the seam of his lips to gain entry. He tastes like peppermint toothpaste, and I ease back for a second. "I like domesticated too, hotness—at least domesticated with you."

"Tá mo chroí istigh ionat." He rolls me onto my back.

I tilt my chin and give him access to my neck. My heart is picking up at a steady pace, and I breathe my first deep breath in a week. "I love you too, hotness."

Thank you for reading – *A Shaman's Power.*

While the story is fresh in your mind, and as a favor to Michael and me, click <u>HERE</u> and tell other readers what you thought.

A star rating and/or even one sentence can mean so much to readers deciding whether or not to try out a book or new author.

And if you loved it, continue with the Chronicles of an Urban Druid and claim your copy of book seven:

A Fated Bond

IRISH DICTIONARY

comhghairdeachas—congratulations

dead-on—a solid, upstanding person

Jackeen—what a rural Irish person calls someone from Dublin

Ni he la na gaoithe la na scolb.—The windy day is not the time for thatching.

Tá mo chroí istigh ionat—I love you (Your heart is dear to mine)

ní neart go cur le chéile—There is strength in unity

NEXT IN SERIES

The story continues with *A Fated Bond*, coming July 18, 2021 to Amazon and Kindle Unlimited.

Pre-order now to have it delivered to your Kindle on as soon as it publishes!

AUTHOR NOTES - AUBURN TEMPEST

WRITTEN MAY 20, 2021

I was thinking about what to say in my author notes when a fan email came in about my focus on animals in the books. I realized maybe I hadn't explained my passion for wildlife.

I was born a farm girl outside of Toronto and lived in the country until my life-threatening allergies forced my dad to sell and move us to town. We all missed the farm, but he got a job building what was to be the Metro Toronto Zoo.

That changed everything—I was raised a zoo kid.

Growing up, dinner table talk was what Mayas the orangutan did or Bingo the bongo or Rosie the pigmy hippo. During the summer holidays, my brother and I would get up and go with him. (My sister didn't get up until noon) We'd wander the zoo while he worked. It was—and still is my happy place.

Then we got jobs there. We were kids, so that meant working in the McDonald's on-site, but it was zoo adventures every day. I met my first boyfriend/husband working there when I was 15. Love-at-first-sight is real. (That was 35 years ago.)

Then I worked with World Wildlife, Northwood Animal Ranch, and then hubby and I moved the kids to the rainforest of Panama to start a wildlife sanctuary for animals displaced by copper mining. Unfortunately, that was in 2008 and when the world economy suddenly crapped out, our funding did too.

But I'm a firm believer in life turning out as it's meant. That year in the rainforest was the first time I was ever truly still. No lessons. No events. No phone calls. Just the four of us enjoying the beauty of nature. It's where I found my storytelling muse and started writing.

And look where that brought me—here to you.

Blessed be,
Auburn Tempest

AUTHOR NOTES - MICHAEL ANDERLE

WRITTEN MAY 20, 2021

Thank you for both reading this story and these author notes in the back!

CHILI UPDATE

For those who follow my author notes in other stories, you know I've been trying to mimic (as close as I can) my mom's chili. My mother passed away in 2019, and while I did speak to her about her chili efforts in the past, I was not so focused on making something that was just like hers.

Until I started missing her and wishing I could pick up the phone and call her.

Making a recipe that I can make over and over that mimics her chili is an exercise (I think) in trying to stay connected to her wherever she happens to be.

Even if she is only in my memory.

One of the premier ingredients I know she used was whole peeled tomatoes. For the longest time, I just went straight tomato sauce or paste and called it good.

I really don't like eating tomatoes. I figured out that using diced/peeled was a huge mistake a month and a half ago.

I won't make THAT mistake again. I was picking out small chunks of tomato in every one of my bowls. *It was horrible.*

For this latest batch of chili, I used a can of Hunts whole peeled and did NOT touch them after I poured the can into the chili. My theory is the tomatoes soften the spices a bit and provide a mellow flavor, and by not touching them, they would be easier to get out of the chili. Once I emptied the can, I added a small can of tomato paste as well.

It was either that or smush the tomatoes, and I *really* don't like picking them out. I think I mentioned that once or twice.

I can tell you that it *kinda* worked. Probably 70% at a minimum and maybe closer to 90% if I had cooked the chili longer. My wife HATES the smell of chili, so I didn't want to fumigate the house and possibly cause her to keel over.

I'm not a beans guy (already spoke about this), but I am a rice guy. I'm also a spaghetti guy, but that requires a thicker chili than I made. My mom used potatoes, so I guess I'm a potatoes guy as well.

And crackers. Lots and lots of crackers.

I'd give this pot about a B... Not a B+ or B- but a solid B.

For the record, picking the chunks of tomato out of the pot was VERY easy. I will do this again.

BOOK 09

THANK YOU to everyone who reviewed the latest book in this series and encouraged the extension to twelve books!

Now I'm just working on devious plans to see if I can lay the groundwork for anything past twelve. Give me ideas in the reviews, please. I'm not above asking for help!

Ad Aeternitatem,

Michael Anderle

ABOUT AUBURN TEMPEST

Auburn Tempest is a multi-genre novelist giving life to Urban Fantasy, Paranormal, and Sci-Fi adventures. Under the pen name, JL Madore, she writes in the same genres but in full romance, sexy-steamy novels. Whether Romance or not, she loves to twist Alpha heroes and kick-ass heroines into chaotic, hilarious, fast-paced, magical situations and make them really work for their happy endings.

Auburn Tempest lives in the Greater Toronto Area, Canada with her dear, wonderful hubby of 30 years and a menagerie of family, friends, and animals.

BOOKS BY AUBURN TEMPEST

Exemplar Hall – Co-written with Ruby Night

Prequel – Death of a Magi Knight

Book 1 – Drafted by the Magi

Book 2 – Jesse and the Magi Vault

Book 3 – The Makings of a Magi

If you enjoy my writing and read sexy/steamy romance, my pen name for the books I write in Paranormal and Fantasy Romance is JL Madore. You can find me on Amazon HERE.

CONNECT WITH THE AUTHORS

Connect with Auburn

Amazon, Facebook, Newsletter

Web page – www.jlmadore.com

Email – AuburnTempestWrites@gmail.com

Connect with Michael Anderle and sign up for his email list here:

Website: http://lmbpn.com

Email List: http://lmbpn.com/email/

Social Media:

https://www.facebook.com/LMBPNPublishing

https://twitter.com/MichaelAnderle

https://www.instagram.com/lmbpn_publishing/

https://www.bookbub.com/authors/michael-anderle

OTHER LMBPN PUBLISHING BOOKS